– Book 2 –
Shadowed Space

SHADOW RISING

Lucinda Pebre
A K Duboff

Published by Dawnrunner Press
Cover Copyright © 2020 A.K. DuBoff

ISBN-10: 1954344090
ISBN-13: 978-1954344099

0 9 8 7 6 5 4 3 2

Produced in the United States of America

TABLE OF CONTENTS

Key Terms, Cast, & Locations........i
Chapter 1.. 1
Chapter 2..14
Chapter 3..25
Chapter 4.. 37
Chapter 5.. 46
Chapter 6..56
Chapter 7.. 67
Chapter 8.. 76
Chapter 9.. 86
Chapter 10 93
Chapter 11...102
Chapter 12...112
Chapter 13 118
Chapter 14 124
Chapter 15...137
Chapter 16 152
Chapter 17 166
Chapter 18 179
Chapter 19 185
Chapter 20...197
Chapter 21...207
Chapter 22...218
Chapter 23... 235
Chapter 24...244
Chapter 25...249
Chapter 26...258
Chapter 27...270

ADDITIONAL READING...........................280
AUTHORS' NOTES...................................281
ABOUT THE AUTHORS........................285

THE CADICLE UNIVERSE

Tarans are the predominant race in the Cadicle Universe; humans are a Taran sub-race. Most of the Taran sphere falls within the purview of the Taran Empire, governed from the planet Tararia by a council of High Dynasties. Earth is one of several rogue colonies on the outskirts of the Empire, separated so long ago that they have forgotten their Taran ancestry.

The Tararian Guard is the primary military force for the Taran Empire. Its counterpart, the Tararian Selective Service, includes a specialty branch with Agents gifted in telekinetic and telepathic abilities. The TSS is headquartered in Earth's moon, and its iconic Agents are known in Earth lore as the mysterious 'men in black'.

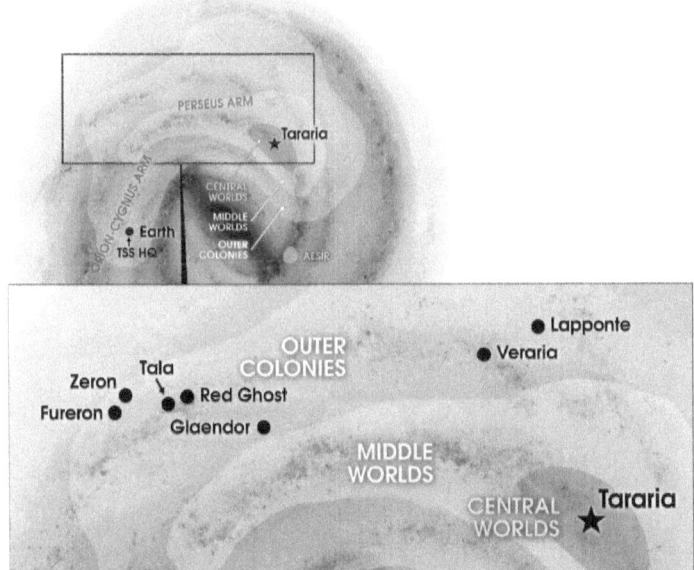

KEY TERMS, CAST, & LOCATIONS

KEY TERMS

Taran – The race of all people in the Taran Empire; synonymous with human

Tararian Guard – The primary military force for the Taran Empire

Tararian Selective Service (TSS) – A quasi-military organization with Agents specializing in telekinesis; a complement to the Tararian Guard

Jump – Faster-than-light travel through subspace

Beacon Network – The navigation method for subspace jumps, maintained by SiNavTech

High Dynasties – The seven ruling families of the Taran Empire, collectively a governing council

Lower Dynasties – Influential families throughout the Taran worlds, second only in power to the High Dynasties

CAST

TSS Agents
Kali Wietris – Newly graduated Agent, born to the Wietris Lower Dynasty

Andy Renteria – Experienced field Agent; Kali's former internship proctor and advisor

The Bruisers Band

Mika Hendri – Owner, captain, and lead engineer of the *Sepiantia*; Tregaren's son

Owen Bruiser – Lead singer and guitarist

Vaira Destitutty – Drummer

Honk Da Moog – Keyboard/Sax player

Caryanne Westby – Lead Guitar

Luca W. Aitchtooh – Former bass guitarist (deceased)

Additional Key Characters

Tregaren – Ex-Priest who independently pursued illegal genetic experiments (deceased)

LOCATIONS

Tararia – The capital planet of the Taran Empire

Glaendor – Tourist-catering world in the Outer Colonies

TSS Headquarters – Located in Earth's moon

CHAPTER 1

HERJA SURVEYED THE *Alacrity* through the viewport. At more than three hundred meters long, someone had gone to a lot of trouble to make her look like a standard cargo ship, with a boxy shape and rough paint job. Without a doubt, she was heavily armed, and—if the rumors were true—complete with an independent jump drive.

The *Alacrity* was on a steady course, away from Glaendor, and Herja didn't think that anybody on board had noticed the *Hyperion*'s pursuit yet. Once they were detected, Herja would have to rely on the captain's need to keep their black-market jump drive a secret. If activated, the *Alacrity* would disappear and be untraceable through the SiNavTech beacon network. Herja's own independent jump drive made her just as maneuverable, but it didn't do her any good if she couldn't track her target.

An incoming request came over the comm. It was from the *Alacrity*.

Herja's stomach flipped at being spotted so much earlier than she'd planned. But, if the captain wanted to talk, they were still in the game.

She smiled. "Gosta, be ready to move."

The big man sighed in response, as if she was causing him pain for the fun of it.

She shook her head as she activated the comm link and turned her attention to the viewscreen. A seated man in his early forties, with close-cropped dark hair and angular features, stared back with half a smile on his stubbled face. "You've picked the wrong target. We never cooperate with pirates." He smirked, anticipating her reaction to his next words. "This ship belongs to Marco Steyn of the Steyn Corporation."

Before responding, Herja checked that their transmitting signal remained disguised. "Who?" She gave him a serene smile.

"You've got to be kidding!" he snarled.

Herja didn't mention that they were targeting the ship *because* it was owned by Steyn. "You should cut your engine and prepare to be boarded. Do not attempt to alert any other ship. If you cooperate, your lives will be spared."

"No, it's *you* that needs to prepare to be blown into atoms."

Herja abruptly ended the transmission. "I foking hate pirates, and Steyn is the biggest crook of all." Gosta raised one eyebrow, which she managed to ignore for a whole two seconds. "We're not pirating. We are appropriating assets."

"Whatever you say, Captain."

"And, you'd better believe it." She opened a comm link to the shuttle bay. "Kinder, you ready?"

"Yes, Captain."

"Hold tight." She muted the comm and straightened.

Kinder was too young, but weren't they all? It wouldn't be long before he was leading a boarding party. Despite it being a standard attack—not that any attack was routine—Herja couldn't help recognizing the risks her crew took each and every time they raided a ship.

An alert sounded, and Gosta reported, "Their weapon's system just activated."

Herja wasn't surprised. "Evasive maneuvers," she spoke calmly. "Why do they never just foking surrender?"

Gosta scowled at her from the other side of the console,

and she knew without asking that he would have handled things differently.

She scowled back, firmly stamping down her impulse to explain. *It's my responsibility, nobody else's.*

With her full attention on the situation, she switched over to manual inputs to maintain maximum control in the skirmish that was sure to come.

As usual when things got hot, Gosta sounded bored, "Their weapons are fully charged, and…"

Herja tuned him out as she felt for the missiles heading their way, ignoring the display. She took the *Hyperion* into a series of gentle, random rolls, dodging enemy fire as volley after volley launched from the *Alacrity*. It was a fine line between taking a hit or two to get in close enough to use the Catch-All, and maintaining safety. She spun the *Hyperion* to focus fire at the midsection of the *Alacrity.*

"Prepare to Catch," Herja ordered. "Lock on target, but do not go active."

"Aye, Captain," Gosta said. He would have had a firm lock on the ship from the moment the sensors had picked up the *Alacrity.* "Catch-All locked in."

They were almost within range. Herja felt her heart thump as everything that could go wrong surged through her head.

"Activate!" she said as soon as the system confirmed they were in range.

Gosta authorized the well-aimed beam set up by the computer. The enemy ship attempted to execute a jump to avoid what they probably thought was a weapons blast; they would have made it two seconds earlier. Instead, the shield flickered as the Catch-All overtook the target ship's systems and disabled everything except for life support. The *Alacrity*'s automated defenses would eventually overcome the remote hack, but not before *Hyperion*'s crew had boarded and secured the vessel.

The *Alacrity* was at her mercy. Herja could blow the ship out of space now, if she hadn't wanted to take its cargo intact. Not to mention, there was also the danger that such a blast would expose them to the security patrols around the nearby planet.

Herja checked the live feed from the sensors, trying to determine if there were any other vessels in their immediate vicinity, then scowled in irritation. It was impossible to be sure. There had been a lot of covert TSS activity in the sector recently, and they were still too close to Glaendor for her to turn down her internal threat level.

We need those resources, she reminded herself as she glanced at the holographic display.

"Open a channel," Herja ordered. She waited for the nod from Gosta before speaking. "You have one minute to surrender before I blow *your* ship into atoms." There was a long pause—long enough that Herja wondered if the Catch-All had inadvertently rendered the *Alacrity* unable to respond.

The same captain's head and shoulders filled the screen. Only, this time, he looked like he wanted to strangle her with his bare hands.

"Hold your position," Herja told him. *Like they have a choice.* "And, Captain," she continued despite his glare, "be ready to greet us. All weapons will be stowed in lockers and any onboard security systems will be disabled."

"We are a cargo ship, not military," the captain snapped, his face going red with fury.

"A Steyn Corporation cargo ship. I know—you said." She sighed. "Cooperate, and you will be spared. Resist, and I will destroy your ship." She switched channels to her crew, who'd been waiting in two shuttles, ready for as soon as she gave the go ahead. "Kinder, you have permission to launch. Good luck."

The display updated in real-time as the shuttles arced away from the *Hyperion*, heading toward the crippled ship. Herja tensed as they entered weapons range, knowing that a single plasma beam could pick off a small shuttle before anybody knew they were under attack.

She activated the comm channel for engineering, trying to distract herself. "Hold position until we have searched the ship, then we will resume our journey to Glaendor."

"Aye, Captain."

The console bleeped with an incoming transmission. "We boarded the *Alacrity*. There was no resistance." Kinder sounded calm and steady; he may be young, but he had the makings of a decent team leader.

"Good."

It was a shame that they couldn't take the ship as a prize, but Herja couldn't see how they could get it somewhere to sell that wouldn't ask questions. Plus, what would she do with the crew? Though she'd planned to let them live, first they had to believe they were going to die; it was necessary in order to keep everyone in her crew safe. While it would be easier and more profitable to sell them into slavery, that was a line she wasn't willing to cross—a line that would make her a true pirate.

"There's a problem," Kinder said over the comm.

"Problem, what problem?"

"Their cargo is farming equipment."

"Are you sure that—"

"I'm sure."

Herja would have laughed if it wasn't so tragic. Farming equipment could top the list for the most dreadful haul— hard to sell and useless to her people. *Well, fok! What do we do now?*

— — —

Treva was neck and neck with Nash as they raced through the covered walkway on the outskirts of Glaendor City. With his breath loud in his ears, Treva strained to gain the lead from the older boy. Nash's longer legs wouldn't save him from the humiliation of losing to the 'little one' this time.

With the metal floor clattering underfoot, their

laughter bounced off the riveted walls before the sound escaped upward toward the protective dome enclosing the city. Turning a bend, the walls to either side were covered in dark patches—gang tags. They had crossed the invisible threshold into Starhills.

Every other week, there were reports on the local news of someone who'd gone missing in the area. Treva wondered why people didn't stay away. And yet, here he was.

All their pick-ups were on the outskirts of Starhills. Today there was only one, but it was further in than usual, and Nash had been late.

Treva glanced around, senses alert for danger. It was deserted, with most sensible people already tucked up in their allocated quarters for the night. The boys' gleeful shouts faded, but they maintained their speed.

No way is Nash going to win again. Even as he thought it, pain stabbed the area beneath Treva's left ribs, causing him to gasp and slow down. He struggled on, knowing that there was no chance of beating Nash with a stitch but unwilling to give up.

Predictably, Nash pulled ahead, powering on without slowing or looking back. It was too dangerous to split up, but Treva just jogged on, clutching his side.

In the fading light, he made out Nash's silhouette jumping headfirst into a large disposal unit next to a transport stop. Limping over, Treva's gasps of pain turned to giggles, which intensified the pain until he doubled over, sucking in air. When Nash's legs started to thrash and kick, shaking the whole tube, Treva couldn't catch his breath. He should be keeping watch to warn Nash of anyone coming, but he couldn't help himself.

Nash emerged, smelling strongly of rotting vegetables but triumphantly brandishing a small bag. His fair hair, a stark contrast to Treva's own dark curls, was plastered to his head. "That's the last." He scowled. "And if you don't stop laughing, I'll make you do all the retrievals in future."

Treva's chuckles eased off. Nash wasn't kidding about making him stick his head into the dirty black tubes to retrieve the packages taped to the inside. "But you do it with such style."

Ignoring Nash's glare, Treva checked his battered handheld. It was difficult to make out the time through the cracked screen, and he had to tilt it toward a bright spot on the walkway until the numbers came into view. He forgot about his side-stitch and Nash's threat. "Shite, we've eight minutes to get back to the Blue Pixie."

Nash sighed as if it was Treva's fault. "Try to make those little legs work if you don't want me to leave you in the dust."

As they ran back the way they'd come, Treva wondered why he'd bothered to come along. Though, there hadn't been a choice; not really. He didn't like to admit, even to himself, that he was already too deeply involved to bail.

In his mind, he could see Ava's beautiful scowl and hear her snap in her heavy accent. "This is no game, and I've no time for stupid or lazy," she'd say.

Treva pressed a hand to the painful area under his ribs as Nash gained a sizable lead. The pressure didn't help him run any faster, but he couldn't bring himself to release the spot.

"Stitch," he shouted by way of an explanation for his slow pace when the older boy glanced back to check on him. A transport shuttle passed overhead, and Treva wistfully watched it disappear; the deliveries would be so much easier if they didn't have to run everywhere. "Couldn't we—"

Ahead, Nash stopped to wait for Treva to catch up, his scowl adding ten years to his face. Treva felt the air vibrate with the other teenager's irritation. "You know that we have to avoid being logged anywhere. Besides, what excuse would we give for being so close to Starhills? We don't live there, thank fok."

We might be visiting friends," Treva suggested when he

reached the spot where Nash was waiting.

Nash shook his head. "Don't be stupid. Nobody visits. Most of the kids don't go to school. They're too busy robbing, so where would you have made friends? They don't have nothing to do with outsiders."

Treva shrugged. Nash was right again, but he wouldn't say so. "As if people are going to be staring at us like we're celebrities or something," Treva muttered under his breath, still annoyed that they were reduced to going everywhere on foot.

All the same, Nash made a valid point. It was obvious that whatever was in the packages was illegal, and it was much easier to maintain secrecy if they stayed off the grid.

The older boy set off at a fast walk. "Come on. The cameras haven't been working down this way."

How can he be sure they aren't fixed? Treva couldn't ask since Nash was already too far ahead; besides, he probably wouldn't answer.

They crossed back into Glaendor City, and Treva felt that he could breathe more easily. They weren't far from his tiny home. He was lucky enough to live in a district within the city proper and not in one of the outer neighborhoods. Like Treva, other locals tended to live in the zones ringing the ritzy center of town, where rich tourists liked to try their best to buy happiness. Occasionally, one of the wealthy off-worlders would wander outside the areas where flashing credits would prompt good service rather than turning them into an easy mark. Reading the invisible borders between neighborhoods was one of the lessons any kid needed to learn fast, and it always amazed Treva how some adults could be so oblivious.

Their path took them to another covered walkway tunneling through the ground level of several mixed-use buildings. Fortunately, they only encountered a few people.

Nash stopped short. "Shite."

Treva followed his gaze to see Mr. Patrache, his

neighbor, scowling as he marched toward them. *Stars, it's just my luck we had to bump into him.* Treva looked behind; they could find another route, but they were already late and couldn't afford further delays.

Nash sped up as if relishing a confrontation.

Treva could see from Mr. Patrache's determined expression that there was going to be trouble. *Why does he have to be so nosey?*

Treva caught up with Nash, unsure whether to back him up or stop him doing something stupid. The two of them against one grumpy old man wasn't fair.

Mr. Patrache shouted, "Treva, what are you playing at?"

Treva looked at the ground, unable to meet Mr. Patrache's gaze. For a second, he hated the old man for making him look weak, but the feeling didn't last; his stomach rolled over, realizing that there was little he could do to stop things from escalating.

Deep down, I'm just as bad as Nash.

The older boy halted in the middle of the walkway, eyes narrowed. "None of your foking business."

The old man was bad-tempered, but he wasn't a bad person. In the twelve years he had known Mr. Patrache, he'd helped out Treva's mother hundreds of times. The trouble was, he thought it entitled him to act like Treva's father.

Desperate, Treva grabbed Nash's arm. "We're late. No time for this."

Nash planted his feet, pulling free with ease. In his mind, Treva pictured a flash of the knife that Nash carried in his pocket, with Mr. Patrache crumpling to the ground.

I have to stop it.

"Your mother would be upset to see you hanging around with people like him." Mr. Patrache nodded in Nash's direction.

True; if his mother had known, she would have been worried. Another part of him shouted that she was the one who'd left, taking with her any right to tell him what to do.

Nash loomed over Mr. Patrache. "Get lost, old man."

Mr. Patrache stayed focused on Treva while a tremor ran up his arms. "I won't be intimidated by shite like him."

Doesn't he see the danger?

"Tell him how it is," Nash snapped at Treva as his hands curled into fists.

Treva couldn't find the words that would save them all, so he gripped Nash's arm again and tugged. "Come on," he pleaded.

Nash shook him off, stepping into Mr. Patrache's face, his expression hard and fists clenched. "Get out of our way. Treva doesn't need you poking your nose into his business."

The old man wasn't going to back down, and Treva suddenly knew that he *was* afraid but was trying to protect him.

Increasingly desperate, Treva searched for a way out. "Nash, people are watching."

It was only after he'd said it that he realized it was true. A woman a block away nudged her companion and pointed at them. They *were* drawing attention, and rule number one was to operate unnoticed.

Nash must have realized it too, because he shook out his arms and moved backward. "Stay away from us."

Mr. Patrache started to respond but Nash was already going. Treva pressed his lips together, hoping to escape quickly and yet, he remained frozen in place by manners or guilt. He wasn't sure which.

"Treva, listen—"

Treva started to back away. He intended to run after Nash, but Mr. Patrache's surprisingly strong hand landed on his forearm.

"I know you won't listen, but he's dangerous, and... I owe it to your mother to look out for you. If you need anything, come find me."

Nash dangerous! Treva wanted to laugh it off, but he couldn't after what had just happened.

Mr. Patrache's bright determined eyes glinted in the walkway's light. "Promise me." The old man's grip tightened until it was painful.

Treva found himself saying, "Promise," just to make him let go.

Nash can be moody and a know-it-all, but he's not dangerous. It was no good. He couldn't even convince himself.

Before Mr. Patrache could say or do anything else, Treva broke free, running as if his life depended on it. He caught up to Nash, only because the older boy had waited for him again, and he didn't look happy about it. Treva's heart was beating harder than it should and his stitch had been forgotten.

Nash didn't say a word on the way to the Blue Pixie, and there was a tension that hadn't been there before the confrontation. Treva kept quiet and tried to keep up, not wanting to stoke Nash's temper further.

The Blue Pixie was a good two hundred meters off the main walkway, along a footpath that always seemed to collect garbage. It was just inside the city, which gave it a legitimacy that it wouldn't have inside the residential district.

Nash glanced at the time on his handheld. "Sixteen minutes late; not the end of the world."

Treva let out a relieved breath when he saw that the club was still shrouded in darkness. He had been told not to be seen going in, once the club was open for business, since he was underage and Ava didn't want to risk her license.

Lights positioned on the walls outside glowed orange but gave off little illumination. They would light up the area once the club opened.

A pair of hard-eyed bouncers glanced their way as they scooted past. Although he never said anything, Treva suspected that Nash spent more time at the club than he did with his family. Now that he thought about it, Treva didn't know anything about Nash's home life.

Friends should know things like that about each other.
He shut the thought down, not sure that he could take
anymore this evening.

The usual bartender was absent and a friendly young
woman was frantically stocking the shelves with heart-
shaped bottles. If Treva had been on his own, she might
have asked for identification, but one glance at Nash and
she returned to her work.

Has it really only been five weeks since I first came here?

Treva bumped into a table, almost upsetting a blue
bowl with a red fish swimming circles at its center. Nash
glared and Treva shrugged apologetically.

*I have to be more careful. I need the money now more
than ever and they barely seem to tolerate me as it is.* He
rubbed his face. It had just been a bad day, that was all.

Nash slipped between the tables and chairs as if he
could see in the dark and made his way down a narrow
corridor to a well-concealed door halfway down, where he
knocked loudly.

There was a pause, and then the door swung open to
reveal an elegant blonde woman in a pantsuit, which did
nothing to hide her long legs. Ava's ice-green eyes studied
the two teenagers before she opened the door wider.

Treva stayed behind Nash as they went inside. The
clean, fresh scent of Ava's perfume permeated the
claustrophobic space. As soon as the door closed, he felt
trapped. The only light came from a holodisplay over a
desk, and he could just make out the shape of an internal
door to the left and an identical one to the right.

Nash relaxed and grinned, becoming more like the boy
Treva had admired at their initial meeting. Six weeks ago,
outside school, Nash had approached him, and Treva had
thought he'd mistaken him for someone else. But no,
despite the age difference, the boys had quickly become
friends. Shortly after, Treva had started to help collect the
packages.

Ava sat behind the desk, staring at them. "Well?"

Nash started talking, "Just made it, even with Treva's old friend showing up to cause trouble."

Treva was about to argue that it wasn't his fault when Ava's attention snapped to him, causing him to shrivel up inside. She didn't like him, but he had no idea why.

Treva swallowed. "He's not a friend, just a neighbor."

"I don't care who he is. Don't talk to him."

Treva nodded, relieved when Ava turned her attention to the small package Nash dumped on the desk.

Ava did something on the touch-surface desk before she focused on the viewscreen, effectively dismissing them.

Nash glanced down at his handheld. From his smile, they had been paid.

Treva looked forlornly at his own device, disappointed that he couldn't see the screen in the low light. He stayed quiet, feeling stupid for not knowing how much they'd get. It hadn't occurred to him to ask earlier and now he didn't want to draw attention to his ignorance.

Nash leaned against the desk in the sort of insolent manner Treva admired but could never imagine emulating. Based on the spark in his eyes, he must have received a lot of credit.

The boys looked up as the back door swung open. Marco Steyn strode into the room.

Nash straightened and the grin disappeared. He gave a respectful bow of the head while sliding his handheld into his pocket.

Ava stood with a smile.

Marco nodded to Ava and Nash, but his smile focused on Treva. "I was hoping to catch you here." His intense, brown eyes and dark complexion reminded Treva so much of his own; it'd always been obvious the traits hadn't come from his mother's side.

Treva was glad for the low lighting because it hid his burning face. "Hello, Father."

CHAPTER 2

KALI LOOKED OUT at the solemn crowd and took a deep breath. She'd faced harder challenges, although battle strategies and TSS tactical training weren't helpful at the moment.

The bass-guitar hung awkwardly around her neck and banged against her chest whenever she moved. To make matters worse, the skirt she'd borrowed from Caryanne kept riding up, and it was already too short. She didn't need to humiliate herself by flashing her underwear, not when her playing would embarrass her all on its own. She had refused the heeled shoes, despite Vaira telling her they would make her legs look longer. *So would stilts, but I can't walk on those, either.*

Kali was trying to work out whether it was good or bad that the stage was only a step up from the floor when from behind, Mika said, "You'll be fine."

She gave him a scathing look. "You've heard my playing."

"Well, yes, but did you hear the local music? It's terrible."

As far as she could tell, the local music consisted of pitched buzzing, which did not bode well for the Bruisers. Their sound was an acquired taste on the most liberal of planets.

"Is that supposed to make me feel better?" Kali suddenly wanted to laugh at the absurdity of the situation. A month ago, all she'd wanted was to pass her internship, and now... *I'm an Agent, not a musician.*

"Besides," Mika continued, "this is little more than a village hall. Wait until you're playing a huge venue to get nervous."

Now, she did laugh. "Your motivational talk needs some work."

Caryanne swept past, her expression calm and distant—*living in the moment.* Kali had tried that and succeeded—for all of two seconds before she was back to worrying about the investigation.

Her shoulders ached from tension rather than the weight of the instrument, and she was wishing she could get it over with when Owen stormed on stage. He looked like a bizarre mixture of military and rebel. Green eyes flashing, he managed to convey a determination to deliver the best performance he could, regardless of the audience.

Kali thought that she might need the toilet, but it was far too late. Belatedly, she recognized the music accompanying Owen. She should be part of it and yet hadn't played a single note. Her brain caught the melody and she joined in, tripping along a touch behind the driving beat, hoping that nobody would notice her delayed start.

She looked down at the strings, seeing where she placed her hands helped. While she was focused, an unanticipated shove propelled her into the middle of the stage. She almost bowled Honk from his feet; he managed to keep playing but cast her a stern glare. She glanced back over her shoulder and saw Mika flinch. *I'm going to kill him later.*

From there on, she didn't have a moment to think, let alone worry about what she sounded like. The set was so tight, there weren't any breaks between songs. At least Caryanne and Honk were having fun. They looked and sounded like they were trying to 'out-show' each other, while for Kali, it was a nightmare that took far too long to finish. It wasn't until the brief breather before the encore that Kali realized the audience hadn't had a proper chance to react to the music, whether it be praise or dissatisfaction.

The band finally fell silent, and there was nothing for a long, drawn out moment. Then, the place erupted with claps, cheers, and whistles.

Kali could almost see the attraction of playing in a band as she staggered off-stage, head buzzing with noise and adrenaline. Though it was her first live show and she'd played terribly, pleasing the audience was the best result she could have hoped for. *I'm sure it helps that we're playing obscure music from Earth; no one knows how it's supposed to sound!*

The others disappeared into the back while Mika began packing away their equipment.

Finally, she could get back to her real job. She'd been looking forward to following through on a potential lead—which was really just a gut feeling. But, she was learning to trust her instincts.

She passed the guitar over her head, placing it carefully on a stand before heading toward Centre Bar across the street. The locals were bound to hang out there after the gig.

Kali had discovered the hard way that most of the bars on Tala only welcomed locals, and unless she was willing to cross illegal telepathic boundaries, which she was not, she wouldn't discover anything useful. Hotels were concentrated near to The Centre, making it likely that Tregaren had stayed somewhere close; besides, there were signs that someone like him had visited Centre Bar. She'd started scanning the surface of people's minds after detecting gaps that had to have been caused by interference.

"Kali, wait up," Mika shouted. The tension in his face

prevented her from telling him she was in a hurry.

Instead, she stopped and gave an exaggerated grimace. "I know. I was awful."

"It's not that." He looked tired.

She couldn't remember the last time he'd smiled and for some reason that made her sad. *I wonder how he's sleeping.*

"Are you any closer to finding anything out?" Of course, he had to ask the most frustrating question of all. She opened her mouth to answer, but he interrupted, "I need to do something. It feels like we're wasting time on this backwater planet. Why aren't we checking out any of the other places that Tregaren visited?"

There was a desperation in his tone that she hadn't noticed before, and she wasn't sure how to respond. "We'll get a break soon."

His eyes narrowed. "I can't believe I agreed to let you have a neural link to the *Sepiantia* for this. You are not trying hard enough."

She studied him, trying to work out if she'd misunderstood. From the determination in his eyes, he'd meant it. Pushing her instinctive anger to one side, she thought about how frustrating it must be for him. Stars, it wasn't as if she found it easy to sift through the meager trail that Tregaren had left, but at least she was doing something to find the missing women.

There was little connecting missing women from the border worlds to Tregaren, but Kali was convinced that he had been involved in illegal genetic experimentation. She knew which planets he had visited, thanks to the records on his ship. Kali had spent long hours cross-referencing his route with the Bruisers' tour schedule prior to when she joined them, and there was evidence of a trail. He had probably picked up the women that Mika identified. Tala was one of only two planets he'd visited frequently, and she didn't know why.

Kali was determined to track down all possible leads

from the psychopath's files. She hoped to find the missing women alive and it was her duty as a TSS Agent to get them to safety if possible. Mika was just as committed, but she suspected that his motivation was rooted in guilt over being Tregaren's son. Kali appreciated that he wanted to set things right, but she didn't like him insinuating that she wasn't doing everything she could to complete her mission.

"Mika, I have to go and do my job." Her nails dug into her palms as her hands reflexively tightened into fists. "I'll let you know as soon as we can move on."

She hurried off but couldn't resist a glance over her shoulder to see him watch her walk away. His face was flushed and his stance unapologetic. She had an irrational but perfectly understandable desire to shake him.

Andy would tell me to look at the situation from another angle. It was weird how just the thought of the older Agent and mentor made her more reflective. What she really needed was to talk to the man himself.

Instead of the bar, Kali went to the room she shared with Vaira and locked the door. She put a call through to TSS Headquarters and couldn't help smiling when Agent Andy Renteria's face appeared on the viewscreen. He hadn't been her supervisor for long before she graduated to Agent, but they'd been through a tough time together. It felt good to know that he still had her back.

"How are you doing?" he asked with an intensity that told her that he was asking about her post-traumatic stress symptoms.

She chose to ignore the question. "I don't just call when I have a problem, you know." She was only half-joking.

He smiled, letting her off the hook for now. "So, you're just completing your mandatory check-in?"

Kali considered if it was a trick question since she only had to make contact every three days or if there was a pressing reason. It wouldn't have escaped his attention that only two days had passed since they'd last spoke.

She thought for a few seconds, trying to decide whether

to come clean. "Yes, but I also wanted to talk to you about Mika."

"Go on, I'm listening."

"We haven't got very far with the investigation, and he seems to think that it's my fault." Andy let the silence drag, but she wasn't about to fall for that old trick.

Eventually, he sighed. "Is it?"

"I'm trying." She paused. "In fact, I'm going to talk to the locals after we finish speaking to find out if any of them had any contact with Tregaren. There are indications of telepathic control, which could have been the ex-Priest, but I admit that I'm acting on gut instinct in the absence of anything else to go on. It makes it difficult to defend my decisions."

"Perhaps you should explore one of the other planets he visited regularly—"

Kali spoke over him, "But he stopped for short periods, often for a matter of hours and always after the Bruisers had played days before. Whereas, he visited Tala three times and on one occasion stayed for ten days. He must have been doing something here, and we still don't know what."

"Kali, don't take this the wrong way, but it can be dangerous to pursue one angle at the exclusion of everything else. Have you thought that there might be some truth in what Mika says?"

"There has to be a thorough investigation if we are going to find those women. At the moment, I can't see why he would visit Tala." She didn't like the way his eyes remained soft. They were conveying empathy, like a foking counselor. "I'm fine," she added.

"It's just that I haven't seen you bite your nails in some time, and—"

She dropped her hand from her mouth. "Andy, I'm fine. If I could learn to play that foking instrument, I would be happy."

"No nightmares or flashbacks?"

She hesitated, unable to tell a direct lie. Besides, it was too late; the hesitation had given her away. Andy radiated understanding even through the small viewscreen, which just served to annoy her even more.

"No flashbacks and the nightmares are the normal sort." He raised his eyebrows, and she realized what she'd said. "You know what I mean."

He nodded, but she wasn't convinced that he understood because that softness had not gone away. "Just think about what I said."

Anything to get off the topic. She inclined her head. "Okay, I'll let you know if anything changes."

"Take care, Kali."

She signed off with a feeling that the conversation hadn't gone the way she'd wanted. It was Mika she was worried about, not herself.

Kali had chosen Tala as a starting point for her investigation, and Mika had agreed. After all, he knew Tregaren the best. She might need to remind him of that fact, but while they were in this awful place, it was important that she do a thorough job. Tregaren had visited for a reason, and it wasn't to experience the culture.

The information guide hadn't conveyed just how primitive the infrastructure was. Stars, most buildings were made from wood and clay, and they were playing in a building called 'The Centre'. How unimaginative was that? The capital was described as "progressive due to its exposure to off-worlders." Whoever had written the travel guide either had never been there or was comparing it to the jungle that pressed in on all sides.

People rode around on the backs of humped animals, for fok's sake. The beasts might have looked as if they'd been designed for people to nestle in soft fur without the fear of falling off, but still the place was so dilapidated that calling it a city was ambitious.

If she could find one person who admitted to knowing Tregaren, she'd have somewhere to start. She just needed a break, that was all. She ignored the little voice at the back of her head saying that it was the safe option. *Mika's being unreasonable.*

Kali wandered out of the room she shared with Vaira above the entertainment venue. It's simple, tasteful furnishings were a pleasant change after the bizarre finishes found throughout the *Sepiantia*.

Kali scratched at her bare arms as she stepped into the open air of the main street. Small, biting insects were something else Tala had in abundance. Mika told her they were harmless, but if he'd gotten his information from the same source that described the city as 'progressive', it couldn't be trusted.

Kali walked across the road to Centre Bar. She'd gotten used to the smell of damp wood in the event venue but here, it was stronger and accompanied by the stench of old sweat. Someone had to have seen Tregaren; it was just a matter of time until she got lucky.

There were no seats available, so she leaned against the rotting bar along with a handful of other men and women. Someone smiled at her, all teeth and shining eyes in the dim light. The person moved closer and Kali saw that it was a woman with a pronounced limp.

Her voice was heavily accented when she spoke, "Your music is strange but I could grow to like it." She looked Kali up and down in a way that made it clear she was talking about more than the music.

Kali wanted to retreat, but she had a job to do. "Would you like a drink?" The man behind the bar was already pouring something into two small glasses. Kali smiled before taking a sip of the strong, bitter alcohol; she tried not to grimace.

If she was going to find out anything about Tregaren, she needed the locals. She refused to listen to the voice at the back of her head, telling her that she was wasting her time.

The woman leaned back on the bar, thrusting out a

large chest. "We don't get many bands coming to the city."

"We go everywhere." Kali ran her finger over the patterned glass. "How do you know what a place is like until you visit?"

"We like our music."

Kali decided to change the subject since the last thing she wanted to talk about was the gig. "Are you from the city?"

The woman laughed. "If I'd been born in the jungle, that's where I'd stay. City folk don't mix with the Dahala. We have very different ways." She shifted her body toward Kali. "Do you want sex?"

Kali spluttered cold liquid onto her arm before swallowing the rest. "No... I mean... I'm only visiting. I'm not looking for... anything."

"Relax, I'm selling sex, not offering marriage."

Kali flushed; she should have guessed. "No." Getting herself under control, she spoke more firmly, "No, thank you."

Kali shouldn't have been surprised. She'd seen barefoot children and thin beggars outside and wondered how badly the planet was governed.

She had been warned about conditions on some of the planets in the Outer Colonies of the Taran Empire, but it was hard seeing them for herself. The TSS didn't have the resources to address all of the problems at once, and it was definitely not part of her current mission to get involved. All she could do was put in a report.

It had proved impossible to speak to anybody with any authority on Tala. If only she could tell them who she was, it might be different. Then again, she might have disappeared without a trace.

The woman was about to move off. "Be careful. It's dangerous out there."

Wondering, whether she was offering a genuine warning or if it was a threat, Kali scanned the surface of her mind and caught a feeling. Like a lingering smell,

Tregaren's presence was there. If Kali hadn't had him invade her mind so completely, she might not have detected it.

Suppressing a shudder, Kali said, "Let me buy you another drink to make up for the misunderstanding."

The woman, who had not disclosed her name, pursed her lips, but after scanning the crowd, nodded. She popped some plant bark into her mouth and started to chew. From the way her body softened, Kali guessed it was some sort of muscle relaxant.

While Kali did not condone the use of unnecessary chemicals, she thought this might be the ideal time to ask some questions. So, she took a chance. "I expect that there are some advantages to living in the Outer Colonies." When the woman cocked her head to one side and indicated that she was listening, Kali added, "No Priesthood out here, even before their fall."

There was no response. The woman smiled, but her expression was vacant, suggesting that the drug was having an effect.

Kali decided to be more direct. "Did you see the news about the ex-Priest who was kidnapping women from different planets? I hope he didn't come through here."

The woman laughed. "People go missing from here all the time, but there ain't no ex-Priests involved." She laughed again as though something was hilarious. "Don't you know we take a vow of secrecy?"

Kali was tempted to read her mind to find out what she was talking about. If she hadn't known any better, she would suspect that Andy had sent her as a test to check that Kali wouldn't abuse her power by doing just that.

The woman rambled on about her life, becoming increasingly incoherent. Even though she couldn't ethically read minds, Kali realized that it didn't matter because Tregaren had done a thorough job of eliminating his presence.

Kali needed to think. *What would Tregaren want with a*

prostitute? She was sure that it wasn't for what she was selling.

She made her excuses and left.

Outside, the sun was setting, casting a maroon light over the low buildings and giving people an eerie tint to their features. As Kali strode toward The Centre, she really wished the passersby wouldn't smile, because their teeth looked as if they had just torn into a fleshy animal.

The whole exercise felt hopeless, and she wondered about rethinking her strategy. Making progress with the mission was one consideration; the other involved maintaining her cover, and to do that, she had to keep the band happy. *I guess I better practice that foking bass-guitar.*

CHAPTER 3

MARCO WATCHED HIS son from across the crowded dance floor, still amazed by how much he'd grown in the years since his mother had stolen him away. Though Treva was small for fifteen, he had a good head on his shoulders and was eager to please. Once they'd had a chance to build a relationship, he had no doubt the boy would make a suitable heir for his part of the family business.

Ava slinked up behind Marco. He felt her heat just before her small hands reached around his chest.

"Don't do that. Not where Treva might see," he snapped.

"He's hardly likely to notice with fifty people on the dance floor between us," she said, taking a step back anyway. "Besides, I'm always careful."

"Yeah well, this thing between us has to stop until he's settled. I thought that I'd made that clear."

"Of all the times you could have found him..." Ava shook her head. "It's just, now that we finally have a way to control the weapon, shouldn't you focus—"

"Nothing is more important to me, now or ever, than my son."

She muttered something that he didn't catch, before smiling brightly and saying, "Whatever you want. As always."

He wasn't fooled by her easy cooperation. She had too much invested in their relationship to give up so easily, which was his fault. He should have stopped things as soon as he'd found Treva. He had to make her understand that he would not allow anything to interfere with getting his son back, no matter the delicate stage of their larger plans. Besides, he was just responsible for transportation logistics; the rest of the duties regarding their new weapon fell to others.

Moreover, they weren't a couple, no matter how desperately Ava wanted it to be true. Marco had always made it clear that he didn't want anything more from her than sex. The trouble was that she was extremely attractive and smart, not to mention integral to his business. It would be unfortunate if he had to let her go permanently.

Marco caught glimpses of Treva through a mass of people dancing to a fast beat. The boy stood with Nash, looking anxious and meek compared to the older teenager. His mother had clearly sheltered him, but Marco could begin toughening him up in short order. "He seems lost without her."

Ava let out an irritated huff. "Don't tell me you regret getting rid of her."

He turned sharply, and she looked away, saying, "I didn't mean anything. Only that you were so sure that you wanted Anissa out of Treva's life. Surely, that can't have changed so soon?"

Marco's chest constricted as always at the mention of Anissa, Treva's mother. "She took my son away when he was a few months old and it took me too many years to find him. Obviously, I couldn't risk her taking off again, not when she had already told Treva to stay away from me. I had no choice."

Marco didn't know why he was explaining himself. It was clear what Ava wanted. That was why their relationship had to end.

Perhaps sensing his mood and worried about saying the wrong thing, Ava kept quiet. Although, knowing her, she would be trying to manipulate him. That might work with others, but it wouldn't affect him.

"He's too young to be on his own. Tonight, I'm going to ask him to come stay with me, but I'm worried that he'll say no."

She gasped, but quickly recovered. "Isn't it a bit soon? She only disappeared a few weeks ago. He's bound to be suspicious."

"You don't think I should tell him everything? Treva never had anything good to say about her."

"Are you crazy?" Ava was staring at him as if he'd lost his mind. "Have you thought about how disruptive it will be? A teenager will make a mess of the apartment and interfere with your business—"

"I want him to live with me. It's all I've wanted for the last fifteen years. That's not what I asked—do I tell him that I'm the reason his mother disappeared?"

Her eyes went wider, "No." He caught an urgency to her tone that made him believe her. "Every teenager gets frustrated with their parents. It doesn't mean they want them to disappear for real." Her mouth flattened as if stopping herself from saying more.

Perhaps, she didn't want to point out how clueless he was as a father, which would be funny if he wasn't so anxious. It wasn't as if Ava had any experience with children, either, but she was the only one he could talk to about the situation.

"I want Treva to know he's important to me and nothing is going to get in the way. That's why we cannot continue meeting up like we have."

She glanced away, refusing to meet his gaze. When she looked back, her smile was too bright. The contrast made him suspicious. "Of course. Family first."

Marco returned her smile, choosing to accept her agreement. "I will take your advice and progress slowly, but I cannot leave Treva without a significant adult in his life. He will be too vulnerable. It's taken a few weeks to make sure nobody is going to interfere so that he has to rely on me."

Ava frowned. "I thought someone was looking out for him?"

"Sandra," he couldn't help spitting the name out. "A friend of Treva's mother. She's full of poison. When he comes to live with me, that final tie will be broken."

"You're already an important part of his life. And now, look at you, considering his feelings and thinking about what will make him happy." Ava spoke without any trace of bitterness.

"I know." He smiled. "What boy that age can properly take care of themselves on a day-to-day basis, anyway?"

Ava muttered something under her breath. Marco could guess what she was upset about, but Treva was the only one that mattered.

He took a sip of the smooth whiskey he'd been savoring for the last twenty minutes. "Okay, I think that I *will* ask him to come and live with me tonight."

"If that's what you want to do." Ava's smile was strained, but at least she didn't argue or try to talk him out of it. "Just don't tell him you're the reason that his mother is no longer around."

"I will speak to him tonight before he runs off to his former home. It won't take long for him to settle in with me. I have lots of room and he can learn the business. I've already thought of a way to push him into taking the next step."

This time, he heard her muttered words. "He hasn't a clue."

"Perhaps not, but I plan to ease him in gradually. He isn't a child anymore."

Ava, wisely, did not respond. Marco looked up to find his son watching him. He waved, pleased when Treva, although clearly self-conscious, lifted his hand in response.

It was all going to work out for the best.

— — —

Treva didn't believe that anyone really liked the bitter-tasting liquid that he forced himself to drink, but he was grateful they'd allowed him and Nash to remain in the club past opening. Nash acted like it was normal, but there had been no disguising his excitement when Marco had suggested they stay longer.

The thing was, Treva distinctly remembered Ava warning him about being careful who saw him enter the club; he was to disappear if patrons were present. Marco had dismissed those concerns without speaking to anybody or asking for permission. It made Treva think that his father had more to do with the Blue Pixie than he'd thought, as it had become clear that he had a lot of influence.

The dancefloor looked like fun, but there was no way in a million years he'd make a fool of himself by dancing. It was good to watch though.

Nash had disappeared a few minutes ago and Treva wasn't sure whether to go look for him or wait in the exact spot he'd last seen him. Despite his father's assurances, Treva was nervous that if he went anywhere, he'd be thrown out.

A waiter headed in his direction. Treva prepared to argue for his right to stay: he was waiting for his friend, Marco had said that it was okay, and Marco was his father.

The waiter didn't smile. "Mr. Steyn wondered if you would like to join him."

"Mr. Steyn? Oh, right."

Let the ground swallow me up. Treva scanned the crowd for Nash. He couldn't refuse, but neither could he abandon his friend.

The waiter must have seen his dilemma. Before moving away, he said, "Your associate left a few minutes ago."

Treva frowned. *I can't believe that Nash would ditch me.* He would never have left Nash alone in the Blue Pixie amongst a couple of hundred strangers.

Perhaps Nash had met someone, but the women were much older than the two of them; and even if that was true, it was still rotten behavior. Treva would work out what to do about it later.

Since Treva had been conscious the whole time of exactly where Marco was standing, he started to make his way over. Before he could get there, he saw Ava weaving her way through the crowd in his direction. She had just been talking to Marco. Something about her measured movements frightened Treva, but it was too late to change his course.

Her hips swayed gently and she had a bright smile that captivated people, but only because they didn't know the ruthless side that Treva had glimpsed beneath her alluring exterior. She was looking right at him. He averted his gaze, knowing that it wouldn't save him.

As they reached each other, her blue-green silken scarf floated to the ground. Treva instinctively scooped it off the floor.

Her fingers gently brushed his as she took it from his outstretched hand. "Do you ever wonder about seemingly unrelated events?" She didn't give him a chance to respond. "There are no coincidences."

What does she mean? Treva's mouth refused to work. Before he could force out a response, she was gone.

When he turned back to his original path, he found Marco approaching.

"What did she want?"

"Nothing," Treva replied. "I just picked up her scarf." It was the truth, but it felt like a lie.

Treva wasn't sure why he didn't tell Marco what Ava had said about there being no coincidences; it just felt like there would be trouble if he did. He had a sneaking suspicion that it was a reference to his mother's disappearance. He had to admit, it was strange that she had vanished so soon after he'd reconnected with Marco, whom he hadn't seen since he was a baby.

No, he can't have had anything to do with that. He's my father.

It was sad their reunion had been spoiled by his mother's lies, even though she knew how much finding his father meant to him. She must have been jealous, after having Treva to herself for so long. That would explain why she had never talked about Marco before he turned up. If Marco really was a criminal and dangerous—why hadn't she said anything earlier?

Treva realized he'd been standing silently, unable to think of what to say. His father was studying him while people flowed around them.

A waiter hurried over through the crowd. "Can I get you anything, Mr. Steyn?"

Marco spoke to Treva, "Have you eaten?"

He shook his head and then changed his mind. He didn't want his father thinking that he wanted stuff from him. "I had something earlier."

"Burger and fries okay?"

His mouth watered. "Yes, sure." 'Earlier' had been a *lot* earlier.

"Have it sent to the back room," Marco told the man.

The waiter bobbed his head and hurried away. The respectful way people spoke to Marco made Treva proud. He knew that his mother would disagree and say that a criminal couldn't raise a child, but nothing would get in the way of this new relationship with his father.

Marco stared intently at someone or something on the other side of the club. Treva followed his father's gaze and spotted a woman. She was scary—an opinion reinforced by the wide berth others gave her and her companion.

The woman stood tall with a wide stance, laughing as if there was nobody else in the room. A mass of fiery red hair was pulled away from her face to fall down her back. She was slightly taller than Treva but smaller than his father, with sharp features that stood out from the locals with their delicate, soft faces.

While most people appeared to avoid her, Treva wasn't at all surprised when Marco headed in her direction. Just walking next to his father, Treva felt more confident. People got out of Marco's way as if everyone knew who he was.

As they got nearer, the corded muscles on his father's neck stood out, and Treva sensed a tension in him that hadn't been there before. Treva fell back a couple of paces, hoping not to be noticed. Suddenly, he wasn't so sure that he wanted to be somewhere reserved for grown-ups.

The woman was in deep conversation with a rough-looking man. His nose was too big and his hair was far too long. Inked tattoos of serpents disappeared into the shirtsleeves of both arms.

How cool! Treva's eyes went to them—once, twice, three times. Whenever he looked away, they appeared to move, but that hardly seemed possible.

When they reached them, the woman was laughing at something. Treva didn't think it could be anything her companion had said because he was glaring at them, his frown so deep that it might be permanent.

Marco cleared his voice. Treva wondered if he was the only one who could see how furious he was. It felt like it would be dangerous to ignore his father's anger.

Finally, the woman turned to him and cocked her head to one side. "Ah, Mr. Steyn. Is there anything we can do for you?"

"Leave my foking ships alone."

What ships? Treva shuffled back. Despite everything, he hadn't expected such a venomous response from his father.

They were standing in the busiest part of the club, and yet the space around them broadened as the crowd edged away. Treva had to suppress a traitorous thought that his mother might have been right about his father's dark dealings.

The woman didn't seem alarmed by the menace in Marco's voice and actually chuckled. Nobody close would have thought it a happy sound, which made it worse. It was intended to provoke, and Treva did not think his father needed inflaming further.

Marco's jaw tightened. "You have nerve to come into my place after attacking my ships."

Treva tried to hide his confusion. *How many ships does he have?* He was torn between not wanting to miss anything while being prepared to run if things escalated.

The woman's companion said in a warning tone, "Herja." He had a thick accent, marking him as being from another border world.

"Don't worry, Gosta. I'm not looking for trouble." It was the first time the woman's expression matched her words. She looked at Marco. "What makes you think that I attacked your ships?" When Marco didn't answer, her attention returned to Gosta. "Once a lady gets a reputation, apparently she's haunted for life."

"Do you think I'm stupid? Two of my ships were robbed on their final approach to Glaendor, then you show up here in the bar a day later. No other pirates would even dare enter the system."

"Pirates?" Treva didn't realize he'd spoken aloud until the woman's eyes flicked to him.

"Who's the boy?"

Marco stiffened and glanced at Treva. His eyes were panicked for a second until he took a deep breath. "Stay away from my ships." With that Marco put a hand on Treva's shoulder and steered him toward the same back room where he'd begun the evening.

It was hard to suppress all the questions that came to mind, but Treva managed it—mainly because silence seemed the wisest option. His father was in a rush to get away, and his fingers dug into Treva's shoulder. He wouldn't be surprised if he had bruises there tomorrow.

Treva hurried into the small room, shaking off his father's grip. After the liveliness of the club, he found it awkward to be alone with the man he'd wondered about his entire life. He didn't know what to say. They had yet to have a serious conversation, except about his mother's version of things, but now Treva wished he'd kept her statements to himself.

There was thick silence while Treva studied his shoes. The white fabric was spattered with grime from during his run with Nash.

Marco cleared his throat, and Treva realized that his father was also at a loss for words. Somehow, that made him feel a little better. He looked up to see Marco manipulating information on the holodisplay.

Marco pushed away from the desk. "I wanted to talk to you tonight, before that..." He waved his hand in the direction of the bar.

Treva wished he could say something to lighten the mood, but he couldn't think of anything. The recent confrontation with pirates was fresh in his mind. *Was her name Herja? I can't believe I was that close to a real, live pirate! Nobody at school would believe me.*

When it looked like his father wasn't going to say anything else, Treva forced a laugh. "Just say it. How bad can it be?" Belatedly, he remembered his mother's warning: never challenge the universe to make things worse, because it invariably will.

"I'm trying to think of a way to ask you something, but I don't want you to think that I'm taking advantage ..." Marco leaned against the desk. "Stars, this is hard, and I'm messing it up."

"Whatever it is, I want to know." Treva needed to hear it now. *He's making me nervous.*

"I wanted to ask, and it's okay if you say no, but do you...?" There was a long pause and then he said in a rush, "Would you consider coming to live with me?"

It took a few seconds for the question to sink in. Even

then, Treva had to make sure that he hadn't misunderstood and wasn't only hearing what he wanted to hear. Whenever he'd thought about who his father might be, he'd dared not hope that the man would want a relationship with him.

Treva wanted to say 'yes'. He wasn't sure why he hadn't agreed already. *What's stopping me?*

The trouble was that while Treva might have disagreed with his mother about whether or not his father belonged in his life, he had never doubted her commitment to him. Even when they argued, he'd known that she loved him. Accepting Marco's offer would be going against everything she'd wanted.

Marco shifted uncomfortably. "It's just that now, with your mother gone, you need someone to take care of you. I'm not trying to replace her or anything, and she might come back soon, so it doesn't have to be a permanent arrangement. But I would really like it if you would consider it."

What if his father expected him to be someone he wasn't? *Stars, he has ships that I knew nothing about!*

All the same, Treva needed a guardian. He wasn't prepared to fully care for himself yet, and no one else had stepped up to the plate. Did he have any choice other than to accept? Not really. Treva's modest stash of credits might run out even if he continued doing the jobs with Nash. Admittedly, he had no idea how long he could stretch the credit because he'd never had to think about bills or buying food before. *I'm not ready to be an adult.*

When it came down to it, Treva couldn't imagine a future without his mother. Deep down, he knew she wouldn't have chosen to leave him, no matter how angry she may have been about him showing interest in his father. Treva moving in with Marco would be her worst nightmare.

For the past three weeks, Treva had been telling himself that she would return soon, but now he was starting to wonder. Something could have happened to her, and she might *not* return. What would he do then? A small, traitorous voice pointed out that her disappearance might have worked in his father's favor. If so, Treva had been the one to give him a reason for wanting her gone. *Was Ava right, that it's not a coincidence at all?* Guilt churned at the back of Treva's mind.

His father was saying something about an apartment and a private room. It filtered through Treva's confused thoughts. He was excited, even as it felt wrong to set aside all of his mother's warnings and trust this man.

Treva knew he had to answer. "Sorry. I mean, I was just thinking..."

"I understand. It's a big decision that could affect your future." His father claimed to recognize how Treva felt, but he didn't stop to let Treva think. "I have everything you need, and if you want to finish school, we can stay or go anywhere."

If he *wanted* to finish school? Like there was a choice. This was too good to be true.

"What you're offering sounds wonderful. I've always wanted..." He suddenly felt like if he hesitated, the opportunity would be snatched away. "It's a lot to think about, but I mean, yes, I would love to live with you."

His father grinned. "That's great! We're going to have a wonderful time."

A knock interrupted whatever he was about to add. The door swung open and the waiter from earlier strolled in with a tray laden with burgers and fries. No vegetables; just the way Treva liked it, even though it wasn't good for him.

His father motioned for Treva to sit. "Make yourself comfortable. We have much to discuss."

CHAPTER 4

KALI LOOKED AROUND at all the serious faces and wondered what she'd walked into. Bad enough that they were in a storage room, which was in reality a dank cellar. There was everything from food to building materials. It was not the best environment for a band practice.

Kali felt like she was interrupting something, and from the way everyone was staring, they'd probably been discussing her. Honk was the only one who was too busy polishing his saxophone to pay any attention.

"I'm not late, am I?" she asked, looking for somewhere to put down her instrument case.

"I can see what you're thinking," Vaira replied, "but we have to rehearse whenever and wherever we can when we're touring. And, frankly, you need the practice."

Kali ignored the dig because it was true. It'd been almost a week of them playing nightly gigs, and she'd hardly improved. "Okay."

Owen blew into his microphone. "Let's get on with it." It still felt like the band members were skirting some vital piece of information that only Kali wasn't privy to. Before she could press the issue, Owen started to tap his foot, prompting Vaira to start a beat on the bass drum. It wasn't until Caryanne joined in that Kali could identify the song.

She set her case on a box and got out the bass-guitar. Once she had fought to get the awkward strap over her head and had the instrument slung across her stomach, she waited a few beats to join in. As usual, she fell behind.

They hadn't even reached the part where the vocals came in when Vaira stopped playing and stared at Kali. "There's no point unless you're going to make an effort."

Kali flushed. She *was* trying. It wasn't her fault that she wasn't a natural musician. With more time, she would pick it up. Now, she was *sure* they'd been talking about her, and Vaira wasn't alone in her opinion.

Embarrassed, Kali felt a familiar surge of anger that they weren't giving her a fair chance. "What do you want me to do?"

"It would be nice if you could practice more," Vaira answered immediately. "It's been a week, and all you've done is hang out in the bar or go sightseeing."

Oh, if only they knew what I've endured for this investigation. "I'm sorry, performing doesn't come naturally to me." How could she explain that she'd never really listened to music before she'd had to play gigs, without insulting what they did? She'd never wanted to play an instrument, but if she said that, they would have even less patience with her. Being in the band was her cover, not her actual assignment.

Owen closed his eyes as he took a long drink from a bottle. As he tilted his head, she caught sight of lighter roots where the hair dye had grown out. When he opened his eyes, they were unfocused.

Has he always drunk that amount? It never affected him as much as it did now.

He noticed her looking and grinned. "We know this isn't your main priority, but you chose to take on the job, and if you aren't going to do it properly, we need to find someone else."

Except, they all knew that nobody else could replace Kali in the band so long as she continued to travel with them. How would they explain the dangers when they couldn't tell anyone what they were really doing? It wouldn't be fair to endanger new people. The current band members were already aware of the risks, after their experience with Tregaren; they'd lost one of their own, and it had made them committed to seeing the mission through.

Kali decided that her musical ineptitude would only wind the band up further at this point. She should go and concentrate on the investigation. That way, she could at least make some progress, which would please Mika.

"I'll practice later tonight on my own time so I don't mess up your session. I promise, I *am* committed." She took the guitar off much more carefully than she needed to and left. As she walked upstairs, she could hear the murmur of voices behind, but she didn't care.

If they couldn't be more tolerant and understand that she was learning, they would just have to play without her. She knew she was being unreasonable even as she thought it, but she would be more rational later. For now, she needed to pretend that it wasn't an issue because there was such a thing as too many problems.

Kali was on her way through The Centre to get to the bar across the road when she heard Mika shout her name. She sighed. The last thing she wanted was another argument, but she couldn't ignore him.

"Where are you going?" he asked.

"I'm going back to the bar." It was critical for her to find the missing women and prove her capabilities as an Agent. It hadn't escaped her notice that her decision might result in another miserable evening sipping the foul beer without discovering anything worthwhile.

Mika stopped in the corridor behind her. "Is there any progress?"

She paused, knowing that Mika was sensitive about mind control after experiencing it for a prolonged period of time. "Tregaren has definitely been messing with some of the locals but other than that, you know what I know. I'm not keeping anything from you."

"Okay." He looked at the floor and she thought he wanted to apologize. She was about to go when he started talking, "It's just that I was expecting to have gotten somewhere by now."

So, not an apology, just more of the same. Well, Kali had had enough. "I'm doing my best. What more do you want?"

His breath was audible as he inhaled. "I know you're trying, but you're focusing energy in the wrong direction." He continued to meet her eyes with hands held out, palms raised, but she couldn't mistake the barely contained anger. "Kali, I need to do something. We need to make some progress before the women die of old age." He shook his head, making an effort to pull back words she could see forming in his mind. "Sorry."

There it was, an apology at last, even if it was pathetic. "I'm glad you are sorry, because I can only work with the information I have—"

He glared at her, speaking slowly, "This is a dead end."

"I'm the one who is trained to investigate and—"

"*I'm* the one with the foking ship."

This wasn't getting them anywhere. "I thought that we were in this together."

"We are, but we're wasting too much time while you try to find out what Tregaren was doing here. There are other planets where he went more frequently."

Suddenly, Kali was too tired to argue. "Let me see if there's anything I can find out tonight. If not, we'll consider other options. Okay?"

For a second, she thought he was going to argue some more, but then he seemed to realize that it was the best he was going to get. They wouldn't be able to leave without making preparations, anyway.

He nodded and turned away. "Okay, I'll go and alert the others that we might be leaving soon."

Kali remained rooted to the spot for a long moment, wondering why she felt as if she'd just lost something vital.

Mika might be right. Andy had asked her to think about it, and the more she did, the more she struggled to justify staying on Tala when there were other places to investigate. But she still felt there was something here.

Unable to find a solution, Kali headed to the bar with little hope of discovering anything new.

The few patrons were sitting in the booths that lined the walls, making it difficult to approach them. Kali sighed. It looked like it might be a complete waste of time. But, she was here now, so she bought some of the foul-tasting alcohol and took a seat at the bar where she was more likely to engage someone in conversation.

Kali let her mind wander over the argument with Mika. He was becoming increasingly impatient with any delay. It wasn't just about finding his mother, although that had to be part of it. She wondered if he wanted some sort of redemption for what Tregaren had made him do. It couldn't be easy, knowing that he'd caused that amount of suffering even if he was being coerced and controlled at the time.

After another two mouthfuls of the sour drink, she'd worked out that it wasn't her argument with Mika or even her failure to master the bass-guitar that was bothering her. What really worried her was putting the others in danger. They'd consented, but it was her duty as an Agent to be responsible for their safety.

A familiar man entered the building—Adam. *Oh, no. The last thing I need after this evening is another round with that lecherous bastard.*

The cargo pilot's light-reddish hair and broad shoulders made him stand out as a visitor, which was why she'd spoken to him in the first place. It had been a waste of time because he'd been very drunk, and she hadn't understood much of what he'd said.

The man picked her out easily amongst the handful of people at the bar. He looked sober enough now, and she wondered what he remembered from the other night. He headed over and took the vacant seat next to her without asking for permission.

Since she'd already made eye contact, there didn't seem much point in trying to ignore him. "I thought you would be gone by now."

"Off in a few hours." His eyes lingered on her face and he smiled. "Sorry about the other night. I'd had a little too much of the local brew."

So, he does remember.

He waved the barkeeper over and started to order for both of them. When Kali tried to stop him, he said, "Accept it as an apology."

She was tempted to make her excuses and leave. He did seem different now that he was sober, but the last thing she wanted was to land herself in a situation where she had to use her telekinetic abilities to stay safe. Then again, he was more likely to have useful information than anyone else in the bar.

He ordered their drinks and on taking a sip, closed his eyes as if wanting to savor the taste. "Would you believe that I was looking for you?"

Kali shifted uncomfortably, wondering if she had made a mistake. Unsure how to respond to what appeared to be a pickup line, she cleared her throat, ready with an excuse to leave.

"Don't look at me like that. I didn't mean it that way." He was staring at her, with laughing eyes. "Nothing dodgy, I promise. When I woke with a sore head, knowing we're off to that desolate rock—Red Ghost—I knew that before we left, I needed to apologize."

Red Ghost! At the back of her mind, Kali remembered that Red Ghost was one of Tregaren's regular destinations. From what she could recall, it was deserted and he'd no reason to visit, except it would be a good place to hide something or someone. It was the only place she'd been forced to disregard when planning stops for her investigation. All ships needed a visa to enter Red Ghost's airspace, which meant they'd have no chance of getting one without pulling her TSS credentials, but that would defeat the purpose of being undercover.

Adam had just presented her with a brilliant opportunity. While her investigative antenna was alert and willing, she was conscious that it would be incredibly risky; the visa requirement meant that even if they got access, getting backup would be more difficult than normal if they ran into trouble. Still, it was too good of an opening to gain access to the suspicious planet for her to pass up.

Before she could second-guess herself, she gave Adam a telepathic nudge. As she did so, she caught an image of him sticking his tongue in her mouth. Shuddering inside, Kali smiled, planting a suggestion firmly in his mind.

Adam straightened. "Hey, I've just had an idea." Eye's bright with excitement, he said, "There's nothing to do there, and nowhere to go, so why don't you bring the band and play a few gigs? We'd welcome you with open arms."

Kali raised an eyebrow. *That's what I'm afraid of.*

"I can guarantee it would be worth your while," Adam was saying.

"I thought the planet was closed to visitors," she replied.

"Don't worry, I can get you a visa."

Kali nodded thoughtfully. "Thank you for thinking of us. Who would I contact to make arrangements?"

The man grinned displaying too-perfect teeth. "Here."

Kali's handheld bleeped as he shared his contact details. "Okay." She pushed her drink away. "I'm not promising anything, but I'll speak to the others."

"No skin off my nose. Just trying to do you all a good turn."

Kali thanked him and left. She couldn't stomach any more of the beer and wanted time to think before she discussed the development with the others.

Outside, the light was fading fast. She'd better hurry if she didn't want to get caught in the street after dark. She was armed, but the locals rarely used weapons. Fortunately, The Centre was only across a narrow road. Kali wasn't especially eager to return to the basic accommodation, with its thin mattresses and drafty wooden floors. She'd told herself the uncomfortable bed was why she hadn't been sleeping well, but she knew it was the mission that was keeping her awake. For better or worse, at least they'd be moving on soon.

Ahead, a figure emerged out of the grey.

Kali tensed and then relaxed. "Mika?"

"There you are." He waited for her to reach him. "I'm sorry about earlier. It's just frustrating when there's nothing I can do."

"Yes, well, I'm sorry, too. But I do have some news."

She was about to explain when there was a sudden movement in her peripheral vision. She turned to see two figures. They were just visible in the area behind The Centre where a narrow walkway linked the building to a housing complex. It acted as a shortcut for any local who wanted to spend their credits on alcohol and live music.

She couldn't make out any detail and wasn't sure what it was about the figures that bothered her. One of them let out a muffled cry.

Kali ran toward them, half aware of Mika's footsteps pounding a few paces behind.

The cry had sounded like a woman. A shape became clearer until Kali could make out a man holding a limp body.

The man's head snapped up at the sound of their footfalls. A pair of bright eyes flashed and he darted away, dropping the body, which hit the dirt with a sickening thud.

Kali stopped a step away, torn by wanting to check on the woman and chase him down. *Screw it.* She reached out with telekinesis and grabbed his legs. He fell forward, smacking his face hard on the ground.

Whoops! She hadn't meant to knock him out.

Mika was at her shoulder and she felt the buzz of his

abilities. She could guess what he was about to do because she'd been tempted, herself, to learn what the altercation was about.

"Mika, don't. You can't raid his mind. I'll be forced to report it." She spoke directly mind-to-mind, not wanting there to be any chance of being overheard.

Her priority was to make sure that the woman was okay. She bent down, feeling for a pulse at her neck. Relief flooded through her when she found the woman's skin was warm and she had a strong heartbeat. Still, she might need medical attention.

When Kali looked up, she couldn't see Mika. No doubt, he'd gone to find out what the perpetrator knew, despite her warning. "Shite."

CHAPTER 5

MIKA HAD WATCHED Kali check on the victim before he'd grabbed the attacker and carried him to another nearby alley. The young woman who'd been assaulted was exactly like those Mika had found for Tregaren, right down to her bright aura indicating she was Gifted. It couldn't be a coincidence that she'd been attacked here, in Tregaren's former hunting grounds. However, it was worrying to think that such activities had continued after Tregaren's death. *Who was he working with?*

Mika couldn't forget what he'd done to those women. Others excused it because of the mind control involved, but he'd also made bad choices. It was easier to tell Kali that he wanted to find his mother rather than try to explain that he needed to make amends. He'd spent too long avoiding the consequences of his crimes, and although he did miss his mother and would do anything to have her back, he hadn't been responsible for her kidnapping.

If he could make things right, he could learn to live with what he'd done to Tregaren's other targets. If not, he didn't know what would happen to him. How was he going to fix things if those women—some of them he didn't even remember—were impregnated with clones, or worse, died in the attempt?

When Kali set her mind to something, nothing stood in her way. It was one of the things he admired most about her. So, given that they'd been on this backwater world for more than a week and had nothing to show for it, either she was stalling, or she wasn't applying herself. He'd sensed her concern for the band's safety, but that wasn't reason enough to hold back.

He returned his thoughts to his present predicament. The attacker was still lying in the dust, where Mika had deposited him a short distance into the alleyway. It was rapidly becoming dark, but Mika could see that the man wasn't much older than his victim. It might have been a lover's quarrel that had gotten out of hand, but Mika didn't think so. Kali was right that Tregaren had visited this planet for a reason—and finding a young woman with abilities being attacked was too similar to ignore.

Mika had heard Kali threaten to report him to the TSS if he tore through the attacker's mind, and he knew he should take her command seriously. Before the TSS had released him, they'd been clear that because he was not formally trained in the use of advanced abilities, he was not to use telekinesis or perform direct telepathic readings under any circumstances. They'd even made him sign something, agreeing that he wouldn't. At the time, he'd just been happy not to be locked up for the rest of his life, but now, this was more important than TSS rules. Besides, he didn't care what happened to him; he deserved to be punished for what he'd done.

He could secure the young man until Kali could interrogate him, but he was worried that the local authorities might intervene before then. Since Kali was an undercover TSS Agent, she couldn't rely on credentials to take custody of the suspect. If it came down to Mika and Kali's word against the man's, he could very well end up released.

Even if Mika did manage to get Kali alone with the man, he wasn't confident that she'd do what was necessary to get information. The TSS was very particular about its code of conduct for telepathy, prohibiting invasive mind-probing in all but extreme cases. Almost certainly, this man's situation didn't qualify. *How much is enough evidence of a crime to make them listen?*

Mika's interference could cause harm, but his priority was to find out what was in the man's head. Even though he hadn't gone through TSS training, he had been trained by Tregaren in how to extract information from people. He winced, remembering Tregaren's disregard for his subjects' well-being.

Am I like him? Mika didn't think so. This wasn't about personal gain. *I'll scan his surface thoughts and take it from there.*

"*Mika?*" It was too dark to see Kali, but her telepathic thoughts reached him instantaneously.

"*I'm okay,*" he replied.

"*Where are you? The victim is coming around, but I can't leave her.*"

Victim. Mika wanted to laugh at how much Kali sounded like an Agent. She'd somehow deluded herself into believing that she could blend in with the rest of them, but Mika had seen enough to know that she was TSS through and through.

"*I won't be a minute.*"

Kali wasn't stupid; she must have guessed what he intended to do, and she would stop him if she could. That was why he had to be fast. It didn't help that he hated telepathic contact after being controlled by Tregaren for so long. He made exceptions for Kali; he liked their shared connection when she spoke into his mind.

Mika crouched and brushed the surface of the man's thoughts, noticing immediately that he was regaining consciousness. He could smell stale sweat and something sweet.

Mika sensed the man's confusion about why his head and face ached. He was disoriented, unable to work out what had happened.

"You hit the ground pretty hard." There was little reaction to Mika's telepathic prompt.

Mika caught his name—Rolle. With no time for subtlety, Mika dove in; images immediately surrounded him. None of them made any sense until he looked closer. He quickly discarded the petty jealousies. Rolle didn't like that his abilities had never developed beyond spotting bright auras. That was what Tregaren had him do, which was enough to prompt Mika to dive deeper.

Rolle tried to resist. Thankfully, it was more the natural instinct for self-preservation kicking in rather than a conscious defense. If he'd fought too hard, Mika would cause more damage to his mind. Pushing against the man's resistance, he disregarded the mass of uselessness—a wobbly doorframe that Rolle needed to fix, riding for free, claustrophobic bars and strong alcohol. Fortunately, Mika's familiarity with Tregaren drew him to the memories he wanted, else he might have been lost for days. Picking them out quickly, Mika went deeper.

"Mika." Kali's voice was urgent. She could probably sense what he was doing. It didn't matter, since he had every intention of sharing whatever he found.

Fok it. Mika went in as far as he could.

Tregaren's red eyes blazed from his shadowy form. It was surprising that Rolle had had direct contact with the ex-Priest. Rolle watched a man kneel in front of Tregaren and tell a story. Rolle knew that Tregaren was an ex-Priest, come to free them from the fear of people with Gifts.

Mika didn't have time to hear the tale since it wasn't what he was searching for, but he recognized that it was significant. Tregaren would never have interacted with such primitive people if it hadn't been for something important. Mika moved on before Kali could interrupt, and he found what he wanted. He'd been right. Rolle had been watching potential targets for days. This victim was one of three.

There was too much irrelevant detail to see everything, and it was taking too long. Mika rubbed at the dust clogging his nose and tried to ignore Kali's impatience.

"What happens to them?" he sent in the hope of provoking something useful.

Mika felt Rolle's mind jerk as he surfaced into full consciousness. *Good, I'll be able to direct his thoughts easily now.* He looked into the man's eyes. *"What happened to the other two?"*

The man glanced to the side, assessing his surroundings. *"I've gotta get out of here."*

Mika heard that loud and clear.

Rolle rolled onto all fours, but Mika had no intention of letting him run. He would paralyze him if he had to.

Mika tightened the mental vise around him. *"What happened to them?"* he repeated with more force, focusing all of his attention on extracting an answer.

An image of a transport ship flitted through the man's mind. Rolle *knew* it was going to Red Ghost.

Kali grabbed Mika's upper arm hard enough to bruise, and he lost his mental lock on Rolle.

"Ouch."

She hissed in his ear, "Move it. Now."

"Okay, okay. I have what we need, anyway." It was just as well, because when he looked back, the young man had run off.

After one final squeeze, Kali released his arm.

Mika tried not to rub the sore spot. "You didn't have to do that. He was guilty."

"Doesn't matter. We have policies."

Mika shrugged. What could he say when he didn't regret it?

They jogged back to the young woman, who was now propped against a wall. Mika knew better than to say anything about what he'd discovered just yet.

"You should have secured him here." Kali's mental tone was tight with anger.

He flinched at her unexpected telepathic contact so soon after being in Rolle's head. *"Why? What were you going to do with him? The local authorities probably won't be bothered, and it's not as if you can order them to do anything."* He rubbed his arm where it still stung.

"That kind of mental invasion is illegal for a reason."

"Let's talk about it after we've helped the girl."

"Oh, now, you want to help her! How lovely."

Mika couldn't help smiling—she was being so like Kali—but he was glad she couldn't see his amusement. Besides, he had something to be genuinely happy about; he knew where they needed to go to find the missing women. Then, he remembered why they had ruled Red Ghost out. They would have to think of something.

The woman was clutching Kali's jacket around her shoulders. Mika extended his hand to help her to stand. While she was reluctant to hold onto him at first, she changed her mind when she almost fell back down.

"I guess you don't want to know what I found out, then." Mika couldn't resist teasing Kali, even though she would make him pay later.

Kali muttered a curse under her breath. "Let's get Carla somewhere safe."

Mika didn't think their attacker would return, but Kali was right; they needed to make sure they were away from this spot.

Carla was steadier on her feet now. "Thank you. I just want to go home."

They moved into the street where small orbs were attached randomly to the sides of buildings. Each one let out enough light so that they could make out the direction of the street and see the buildings.

The street was empty, so there hadn't been any witnesses. Yet, Mika had a sense that Rolle didn't operate alone. Whatever was going on with these kidnappings was much larger than Mika had ever suspected when he'd been one of the hunters.

Kali took Carla's free arm. "Do you want to report—"

On a purely selfish level, Mika thought that it would be better if she didn't report the attack, but it was so like Kali to try to do whatever was best for Carla. She rarely thought of the cost to herself.

Carla clasped the coat more tightly. "No, they won't do anything. It happens all the time."

"Surely, the authorities will try to find him."

"Not on Tala." Carla gave a hopeless shrug. "I'm nobody. They won't care."

"Let us walk you home, at least," Kali offered.

She smiled tentatively. "Thank you. I don't know what he did to me."

"Telepathic attack?" Kali looked at Mika.

"We're back on speaking terms?"

Kali narrowed her eyes, but before she could blast him, he said, *"No, he wasn't trained."*

"What do you remember?" Kali asked Carla.

"It was like an electric shock, and then I must have passed out."

"A pulse weapon?"

Mika shrugged and gave Carla a reassuring smile when she looked at him for an explanation. That was the trouble with telepathic communication; it was too easy to respond with the body as well as the mind.

They stopped at the edge of an area surrounded by boxy residential structures. Mika wondered how many people were expected to live in the tiny spaces.

Carla was walking unaided now. "I'm okay. That's our place." She pointed to one of the identical buildings. "It might be best if you don't come with me. My family can be overprotective and will want to ask you a gazillion questions."

Was she implying that her family might think *they* had something to do with the attempted kidnapping? Best not to find out. Kali must have thought the same thing because she didn't argue.

Carla returned Kali's jacket before walking away. As soon as she'd gone, an alarming shuffling noise came out of the dark. Mika met Kali's eyes.

"Slowly," she instructed telepathically.

"It sounds large."

"Perhaps there's more than one."

"What a comforting thought."

Side by side, they slowly retraced their steps. Mika couldn't hear anything beyond his own breathing and his racing heart. Once they were sure nothing was going to lunge out of the darkness and snatch them up, they ran and didn't slow down until they got back to their hotel lobby.

"What the stars was that?" Mika asked.

"It must have come out of the jungle. There are all those warning signs about not being out after dark."

Mika looked over at Kali as they crossed the threshold of The Centre. She wasn't even breathing heavily.

She waited until they were in one of the cramped rooms to say, *"Your illegal mind-reading better have been worthwhile."*

"Hey, it wasn't me who started it." When she frowned, he added, "By using telekinesis."

"I didn't have a choice. That woman's life was in danger. And I work for the TSS; you don't."

Mika grinned. "Don't forget that I saw everything— how you brought him down when he was well out of reach. Just...bang!"

Kali started to argue but then clamped her mouth shut. She flopped onto the edge of the bed, putting her head in her hands. "I think I need a break."

Mika immediately felt guilty. He didn't care that she had hurt Rolle, but she obviously did. Rolle had assaulted at least three women, and two of those were missing. If having him eat the dirt blew their cover, then so be it.

Mika sat across from her, on the other bed. "It was worth it. He was as guilty as they come." He tried to keep his excitement contained, but some leaked out. He switched back to telepathy, recognizing the sensitivity of the information, and liking the closeness of the mental connection to Kali. *"There were two other women before Carla. He sent them off-world."*

Kali sat up. *"Does he know where they were taken?"*

"Red Ghost. It's one of the planets Tregaren visited regularly when he was alive. We discounted it as a starting place because we needed a visa."

Kali looked away.

Mika frowned. "What is it?"

"Nothing."

"Kali, why are you acting strangely? I know that it will be difficult to get there, but we have to try."

She stood, almost banging her knees on the footboard. "I just need to think."

"You should be excited to have a solid lead, but instead, you 'need to think'." She hadn't reacted like he'd expected, not even close. "Why are you so reluctant to progress with the investigation? Do you want to find the women or not?" He couldn't think of any reason for her reluctance.

"Be honest with yourself before judging me," she snapped.

Mika didn't respond, too shocked by the accusation.

Kali sighed, softening. "Sorry, hey... I have some idea of what you're going through because I've been there." He wasn't sure what she meant. "Not in exactly the same way, but trauma and grief don't ever completely go away."

Mika frowned. "You think I should feel bad for killing my father? He would have killed all of you."

"That's not what I said."

"It's what you meant. Why can't you accept that isn't how I feel?"

"It isn't about him," Kali replied. "It's about you and what he took from you for years—your autonomy. It was the worst sort of abuse. He forced you to betray yourself."

Mika tried to shake something loose from his head. Kali was doing a fantastic job of distracting him. For now, he would let her believe that she knew what was going on in his head. *I need to convince Kali to go to Red Ghost. Maybe I'll finally get the answers I've been looking for.*

CHAPTER 6

MARCO STARED OUT across the lake. So far, everything was working out like he wanted, but he wasn't going to get complacent. He knew from experience that it was precisely at these moments when things usually went disastrously wrong.

It hadn't been as difficult as he'd expected to settle into life with a teenager, although he suspected that Treva was still on his best behavior. Marco supposed that he was guilty of that, too. He'd put few expectations on Treva, but if they were going to move forward, that had to change.

Treva hadn't gone to school since he'd moved in almost a week ago—which was fine, but that didn't mean he was allowed to waste his life. Marco hadn't needed a formal education to get to his position, and neither did Treva. The real world contained a wealth of teaching opportunities. Marco intended to use those experiences to build Treva's confidence in himself.

"Zoro, ask Treva to join me."

A soft bleep acknowledged that the automated assistant had heard his command. It took a few seconds for the female voice to reply through the hidden speaker in the ceiling. "He is on his way."

It took longer than it should for Treva to appear in the doorway, causing Marco to suppress a little irritation. *Remember, he is a teenager.*

Treva wore lose sweatpants and a purple t-shirt that was wrinkled like he'd slept in it. His dark hair covered his ears and looked as if he hadn't brushed it since moving in. Something was going to have to change. Marco was already working with his own father by the time he was Treva's age, providing whatever support was needed. But it was too early to tell Treva about any of that. Marco needed to proceed slowly.

He understood that Treva had lived most of his life without the luxuries that Marco took for granted. That included nice clothes and regular haircuts, but things were different now.

"Come in and sit down." Marco kept his voice soft, refusing to show his exasperation. "How are you settling in?"

Treva came into the room tentatively and perched on the edge of the chair nearest the door. "I'm alright."

Marco waited for more. When it was clear there wasn't any, he said, "You must be bored with nothing to do all day." Treva shook his head and opened his mouth, but Marco continued, wanting to move things along. "It would be really good if you could get involved in the family business. I was trying to think of the best way for you to start, and—"

"What is it you do, exactly?"

Marco should have anticipated the question but hadn't. Now, he considered how much to disclose. It would be easier if Anissa hadn't already told Treva her version of what he did for a living. Marco didn't want to frighten Treva off by confirming his mother's fears, but he didn't want to lie either. "At its simplest, it's a transport company. People pay us to move goods around the neighboring star systems."

Treva swallowed, clearly wanting to ask something

specific but not quite daring. When Marco waited, he just shuffled.

"What's bothering you, Treva? Just ask." He needed to know even if he had to lie. Ignoring an issue would only allow it to grow.

Treva took a deep breath. "Do you have anything to do with the packages we deliver to the Blue Pixie?"

Ah, he's reluctant to confess that he's involved in illegal activity. Marco relaxed. "Not that I'm aware of."

It was a lie, but if he told the whole truth, Treva would certainly connect the packages to the ships, and it was too soon to tell him everything. Marco satisfied himself that he could always claim he hadn't known, if it came up at a later date. *Lies only matter if you get caught.*

Marco cleared his throat, determined to move on quickly. "Nash told me about that old neighbor of yours," Marco began.

"You know Nash?"

Marco cursed himself. *Stupid mistake.* How could he explain how he knew Nash without revealing that Nash worked for him? "I spoke to him that night at the Blue Pixie. It's important that I get to know your friends."

Treva shuffled into the chair. "Okay."

"Anyway, as I was saying, he told me about your old neighbor, and I think you should pay him a visit."

"It's okay. I don't like him that much."

Marco shook his head. "Not a friendly visit. More of a visit that makes it very clear he should stay away from you." Treva was staring with wide eyes, but Marco plowed on, "It's important that people understand you are my son and nobody messes with you. This isn't something I can do for you. I wish I could."

"Mr. Patrache is harmless," Treva blurted out. "Besides, I don't think he'll bother us again. Not after how Nash spoke to him. And I don't—"

"That wasn't what Nash said." Marco held up a hand when Treva would have protested. "This is something I'm asking you to do as a first step into the business. You understand that I can't have people from your past interfering in your life now, and this will send out a firm message. Do you understand?"

Treva looked as though he was about to argue some more. Then, he nodded and stood. "Is that everything?"

Marco smiled, relieved to have the conversation over with. He realized just how much he'd been dreading it. Thankfully, it had gone well.

"Yes, why don't you give Nash a call and invite him over? I have to go to a business meeting in the city…"

Marco sighed. Treva had already gone back to his room.

— — —

It was hot in the apartment. Treva had instructed the control system to increase the temperature, and his father was too worried about making him feel at home to override the command. The thermostat adjustment had been an impulsive move, but Treva knew better than to fight his subconscious when it was up to its tricks.

He was having a hard time believing what Marco wanted him to do. *Threaten an old man! Why?*

Treva tried to think about things from Marco's point of view. Perhaps it was like an initiation to prove that he was loyal. It could be a way of ensuring that Treva cut ties with all the people he'd known—to make him isolated. That way, he'd have to rely on Marco for everything. Although he'd still have Nash. They hadn't been friends for long, and Nash hadn't told him that he'd spoken to Marco, but he would. Treva was sure.

Besides, his mother might show up soon. Treva had told himself that she must be okay—that she had gone away to frighten him into doing what she wanted. There had always been a niggling voice at the back of his head that insisted she'd never do that. A voice that constantly reminded him that she had never lied to him. That same voice said that whatever reason Marco had for wanting Treva to threaten the old man, it was wrong.

Treva couldn't imagine visiting Mr. Patrache to frighten him. He could only picture knocking on the door, being invited inside, and then sitting at the tiny table and drinking juice. Mr. Patrache would be pleased to see him. At what point was Treva supposed to threaten him? *Fathers don't ask their kids to terrorize someone.*

Treva scowled at his luxury bedroom. He was getting to know his dad; it should be great. He had everything that he'd ever wanted and instead, he felt more lost and directionless than before.

Treva groaned inwardly. He knew in his heart that he couldn't threaten Mr. Patrache, but if he didn't, would he have to give up everything he'd gained? *What can I do?*

Treva wandered through his bedroom, which was the size of the entire downstairs living space in the place he'd lived with his mother. A breeze ruffled the sheer curtains and he flopped on top of the silk comforter and stared at a wall-mounted viewscreen, which was perfectly positioned so that it could be seen from anywhere in the room.

Initially, his few possessions had looked sad in the empty drawers and cupboards. Now, he had new clothes and games and even a top-of-the-line handheld that he suspected had enough power to run a small planet. His mother could never have afforded anything half as sophisticated.

In fact, Marco had agreed to pretty much all of Treva's requests and hadn't asked anything of him in return. Well, at least, not until today when it appeared that there were conditions to his generosity.

His father hadn't even missed a beat when Treva said that school was a waste of time. Marco had agreed, saying that he had grander plans for Treva than the opportunities school could offer. If Treva was honest, the relaxed attitude toward school bothered him, although he wasn't sure why.

Treva was afraid it was too late for second thoughts. By moving into the apartment, he'd committed himself. Now, he was worried that his father wouldn't let him go back to school or have friends from his past. Worse, what would happen to Mr. Patrache if he refused to talk to him?

I'm overthinking things, as usual. Treva sighed. *Best go do something fun to take my mind off everything.*

Treva tried to focus on all the good things that had happened to him. Smiling, he anticipated how envious Nash was going to be of his new living quarters with its high ceilings, giant windows, and views across the lake. Light and clean, it was nothing like the tiny rooms where he'd lived for his entire life. He felt guilty because he couldn't imagine returning to his previous home. *Only a week, but it feels like a lifetime ago.*

Treva decided to call Nash. "Hey." He couldn't contain the grin that spread across his face when his friend appeared on the screen.

Nash's face was clear against a dark background. "Hi. Whatcha doing?"

"Just hanging out in my new palace." Treva suddenly felt self-conscious; he didn't want Nash to think he was bragging. "Do you want to come check it out?"

"Marco's? It's nice enough."

Treva opened his mouth, and, for a second, nothing came out. "Wait, you— you've been here?"

"Sure, I visit all the time." Nash must have sensed that something was wrong, because he added, "Just for jobs and shite."

Marco lied to me.

Everyone knew, and they had lied, but now he'd found out what he needed to know. Marco hadn't met Nash at the Blue Pixie because he'd wanted to know Treva's friends, like he'd said. He'd already known Nash *as his employee.*

Conscious that Nash was speaking and that he hadn't heard a word, Treva interrupted, "Sorry, hold up." He didn't want to ask, but he had to know. "It wasn't an accident we met, was it?"

A cloud passed across the older boy's face. Treva could see him assessing how to respond. At first, he seemed on the verge of denying it, but then a slow grin curled his lips. His friendly façade crumbled away. "Course not. Your father asked me to look out for you."

Treva didn't let any of the queasiness that suddenly came over him show. Nash's reveal felt like a calculated move. The older boy probably resented Treva for some reason, and the brutal truth—and there was no doubt it was the truth—was his way of getting revenge. No. Treva wasn't about to give him the satisfaction of a reaction.

Nash tilted his head, a smirk still twisting his mouth. "Still want me to come over?"

It was the last thing Treva wanted. Being-face-to-face with Nash, who had pretended to be his friend, would force him to confront his own stupidity, and he didn't need more reasons for his dark thoughts to spiral out of control. "No, think I might go out for a bit."

Nash winked and ended the connection.

Treva's stomach knotted. Nash had probably been laughing at him the whole time they'd known each other, just keeping up the illusion of a friendship for the sake of a payday. *How pathetic do they think I am?*

His mother was right about Marco Steyn. Maybe he *did* make her disappear. But why? What did he want from Treva that he couldn't achieve while she was around? Whatever it was, Treva was certain that his mother wasn't dead. He would know if she was.

The front door beeped. That was Marco leaving for his meeting.

Treva was too restless to stay in his room, so he got up to wander the empty halls while he tried to figure out his next move. His footsteps echoed too loud on the polished wooden floors, crafted from finer materials than Treva had ever dreamed of seeing in real life.

He headed straight for his father's study, the one room in the apartment that was locked. He should respect that he was not allowed inside, but with all the lies, there were things he had to know.

The two metal bars crossing the heavy wooden door commanded privacy, but Treva regarded the overkill display of security as a promise of hidden secrets. Marco had reentered Treva's life under the pretense of being his father—of wanting to be a full part of his life. Lies and secrets weren't a foundation for any kind of relationship. If Marco wanted him as a son, Treva had to know what he was getting into with the 'family business'.

Treva had always been curious, and the formative people in his life had encouraged the trait. His teacher said big words about cultivating the ability to examine a situation to determine what needed to be done. That was what he was doing right now: cultivating a way into his father's study to find out what was really happening.

While Treva didn't want to risk what he'd gained in the last week, the nagging feeling that everything had come too easily wouldn't go away. His mother's lessons about being cautious must have stuck. He laughed softly. *It doesn't matter if I lose everything. Being deceived at every turn would be no way to live.*

Marco could return at any time, so he had to move quickly.

Treva tugged on the heavy handle, confirming that it was, indeed, locked. While worth checking, he had other plans. The windows throughout the penthouse were frequently left open to take advantage of the cool breeze blowing from the lake, and Treva's slow ratcheting up of the temperature on the apartment's thermostat had all but guaranteed the balcony doors for the office would be used for ventilation. The locked room had bothered Treva from the moment he'd arrived, and he'd subconsciously worked out that messing with the environmental controls might offer a way to get inside the study without having to break down the door. Nobody would need to know, and he could get the answers he needed. *I'm exactly like him—sneaking around and hiding my true actions.*

Now that his plan was set in motion, there was no sense in putting up with the stifling heat. "Zoro, reduce the temperature by five degrees," he told the system.

The system responded with a bleep that Treva barely heard on his way outside to the balcony off the living area, adjacent to the study. As he judged the short jump, he was pleased to see that the exterior office doors were wide open.

Looking down the full seven-story height to the ground, it occurred to him that if he fell, he would be seriously injured or killed. Treva's blood heated with excitement, unable to resist the thrill of imminent danger.

Since the building's security patrol was nowhere in sight, Treva climbed onto the top of the metal railing. He balanced with his left hand against the wall. A fresh breeze carried the scent of cut grass, raising the hairs on his bare arms.

No looking down. He picked his landing spot.

Bleak thoughts pressed against his mind as he prepared to leap. People would think him crazy. He had everything he ever wanted; yet, he was about to risk it, and he might be wrong. The intensity in Mr. Patrache's face came to mind as he'd held Treva's arm and said, 'promise'.

Treva leaped. Really, it was more like a big step; one hand remained on the wall for balance. As he lurched forward, his leading foot slid sideways on the railing. With a sharp intake of breath, he saw himself fall.

Fortunately, his momentum propelled him to the destination balcony. He tumbled over the railing and landed in a graceless heap on the cement. Though his palms were scuffed and knees ached, it was mostly his pride that was wounded. All the same, his heart thudded in his head. He was alive. And, just as importantly, nobody saw him pass to the prohibited area.

He dusted himself off and then slipped through the doors. The room was plain. Unlike the rest of the apartment, with its mirrors and chrome projecting wealth and strength, the finishes in here were cream and plain. A large desk was the focal point at the center of the space, surrounded by loads and loads of storage containers— presumably containing Marco's secrets.

Treva visually scanned the room for cameras or an alarm. There was nothing obvious, though there wasn't anything he could do about it now, anyway.

Mindful that he didn't have long before Marco might return, Treva started with the desk. There were some printed documents; although, Treva didn't know why his father would need hardcopies. Most looked like individual contracts written in a way that made them hard to understand.

Twenty minutes passed, and he'd not found anything that seemed useful, based on his limited understanding of what he'd read. It would probably take days to comb through the files if he maintained his present approach. So, he turned his attention to the holoprojector over the desk. On activating the log-in, he discovered a biometric scanner.

Marco wants me to be a part of the business, so maybe... It was a risk to attempt logging on, and it would be a record of his clandestine entry, but his desire for answers got the better of him. He placed his hand on the scanner.

To his surprise, the computer accepted his credentials.

Suddenly, he had access to the entire system, which appeared to only have local storage with no Net access; with any luck, that meant it wouldn't send out notice of his login. He was presented with an overwhelming number of files in what appeared to be a complex organizational system. *Shite, I don't have enough time to look through all of this!*

Then, Treva had an idea. He placed his handheld on the touch-surface desktop and initiated a download of recent activity. *Let's see what you've been up to, Father.*

He had no idea what he might find, but his mind was made up: he wouldn't rest his future on his father's designs. *Mom wanted better for me. I need to make her proud.*

CHAPTER 7

KALI WASN'T SURE that she wanted to tell the band about the offer to play on Red Ghost. Even without the promise of adventure, they were always eager to go somewhere new, so convincing them wouldn't be an issue. Her concern was that they *would* agree, and it would place them in danger. Before Luca died, she would have been focused on her mission; now, she was much more cautious about their safety.

She took a sip of the coffee Mika had fetched in an attempt to improve her mood. "Where's the band?"

Mika lay sprawled across the bed as if he didn't have a care in the world, but the tiny frown lines on his forehead gave him away. There was something bothering him, but she bet it wasn't raiding that man's mind.

He rolled onto his front and raised himself on his elbows. "Take a guess."

In the bar.

Kali was distracted by the tiny flecks of amber and hazel gathered around the pupils of Mika's astonishingly green eyes. Sometimes, she glimpsed an intensity of feeling that he generally hid.

She took a deep breath—might as well get it over with. "We need to talk."

"Yes, I used illegal telepathy, but it was necessary and justified." Mika rolled his eyes.

"I didn't mean that, but since you brought it up, we need to talk about that, too. You signed a binding document to say that you wouldn't use it under *any* circumstances. A breach of the rules could lead to you being locked up for life."

Mika just stared at her. There was no sign of anything other than anger now.

"I can't keep secrets from the TSS, Mika. You know that."

"Do what you have to do."

Kali sighed, irritated that he didn't seem to understand the severity of what he'd done or the difficult position he'd put her in. "We need to find the others. There is something that I might as well tell you all together."

Mika sat bolt upright. "I *knew* you were hiding something!"

"What do you want? An acknowledgment that you're a great detective?" Once she told them, she would have to decide what they did next.

"Of course not." He was silent for a few seconds. "Okay, go on. It would be nice to feel appreciated for once."

Kali shook her head, unwilling to be drawn into joking when she was still annoyed.

Mika saw her expression and jumped up, immediately heading for the door. "Let's find the others."

If she reported him to TSS Command, the matter would be out of her hands. He might only get a warning, but she doubted it. They would take the matter very seriously if any Agent had broken the rules, but since Mika hadn't been formally trained, they might be more lenient. The other problem was that she was pretty sure he wouldn't hesitate to do it again under similar circumstances.

For now, they had a crucial decision to make, so Kali would leave it until later. She joined Mika, hoping that the others would be reasonably sober.

They were easy to find in the main room. There was the deserted stage at one end and the sort of soft music that Kali grew up listening to, playing in the background. The band members sat at a table in the far corner. They didn't look happy, which was good, because it meant they hadn't been drinking for long.

Vaira was the only one not seated. She strolled in through another doorway across the bar at the same time as Kali and Mika entered. "We wondered where you two had got to."

Owen uncurled from a low, uncomfortable-looking chair. "You're late, and we were worried about you."

She ignored him, but was that a tinge of guilt she detected in his expression? If she didn't know any better, she'd think he was sober.

Caryanne remained seated and smiled up at them. Her eyes were slightly unfocused, but that was usual for her. Next to Caryanne, Honk struggled to rise from his chair. He lost his balance and toppled, falling awkwardly to the floor. It happened too quickly for Caryanne, who was the nearest, to have any hope of saving him.

Kali almost reached out with telekinesis before remembering the risk of blowing her cover. Honk was unscathed as he levered himself off the floor.

Kali shook her head. Perhaps she should try drinking to see if it helped her to play the bass better. Another look at Honk's vacant expression, and she decided to work harder on learning the technique instead.

Despite Honk's very typical behavior, there was something different about the band. Had they been worried that she wasn't coming back? Either they cared more than she thought, or they'd realized she was the only bass player they were likely to get out here.

The place was too empty and quiet to have a private conversation without risking their cover. They had better take some basic precautions.

Kali headed to the deserted bar at the far end. "Just

going to ask them to turn the music up."

"This shite?" Vaira asked, clearly incredulous that Kali might actually want to listen to ambient sounds. "No wonder she can't play."

Kali heard Mika say, "I think it's more to muffle our conversation than for enjoyment."

When Kali returned with drinks, Mika was in the middle of describing what had happened earlier. He included the illegally gained telepathic information as if it was normal to raid someone's mind. His casual attitude irritated her all over again.

"The guy—Rolle—wanted to get the girl onto a transport ship, which was going to a planet called Red Ghost. It was on the list of places Tregaren visited frequently."

"Is that a place?" Caryanne asked, demonstrating how little attention she paid to anything outside her bubble.

"Anyway, there were two other women he took before Carla—"

"That was the name of the attacked woman," Kali clarified in case Mika hadn't told them.

Mika scowled at her interruption. "So, the others were put on transport ships destined for the same place. I don't know if it was this transport ship or another."

"All right, sounds like we need to check out Red Ghost," Owen said. "I'd better get a few drinks in, then. Who knows what passes as alcohol out there?"

Mika shook his head. "It's difficult to get permission to visit the planet. Any ship docking there has to have a valid visa, and those are impossible to get unless you can prove you have legitimate business. We might be able to get someone to vouch for us."

"Can't Andy get us one?" Caryanne asked.

Mika shook his head. "The planetary authorities aren't likely to cooperate with the TSS. I imagine they are criminals, and by demanding visas, they can keep out the TSS and anyone else they don't want."

Everyone started talking in excited voices. It was as if everything was a game. Kali wondered what it would take to get them to take things seriously.

Caryanne cocked her head to one side. "Oh, I'd love to go somewhere secret."

Mika frowned "I don't—"

Kali knocked on the table to get everyone's attention. "It is my decision where we go next, nobody else's."

Mika scowled at her. "There has to be a way to get to Red Ghost. I'm not willing to give up so easily." When Kali didn't respond, he glared and carried on, "Why are you so reluctant to investigate? Our mission has always been to find these women."

"*My* mission. You're not a member of the TSS, despite the way you sometimes act." Kali stopped herself from saying more.

Mika looked around the group, meeting everyone's eyes. "We need to go to the planet—"

Kali knocked on the table again. "We can't justify acting on information obtained illegally." Mika clenched his jaw, his shoulders tightening, but before he could say anything, Kali continued, "I may be called upon to explain my decisions, and that explanation won't cut it."

The band stayed silent, watching Mika and Kali. She realized too late that they probably didn't know how illegal Mika's use of invasive telepathy had been.

Mika stood. "I told you what I saw in his mind. If there's a chance of my mother being there, I won't let rules and procedures stop me going to Red Ghost."

When he looked at her abruptly, she guessed there was more than he'd told her so far.

She sighed. "Go on. You might as well tell us everything."

Mika didn't hesitate. "Tregaren was here for something else." He glanced at her. "You were right about him. Rolle had seen him in the past when he was asking the locals about unusual activity in the jungle."

Kali was still trying to find a reason not to go, but it was difficult to think of anything that could justify abandoning Mika's mother or the other missing women.

Owen suddenly leaned across the table and put a hand on her arm. "What are you avoiding, Kali? Do you feel guilty about Luca?"

She stared at his long fingers and found herself saying, "You know." That was all that came out and she tried again, "You know." As if that made any sense to anybody.

Owen smiled sadly. "I do. You can always join me in numbing the pain. I have a thousand and one ways."

Everyone looked at him, but it was Mika who spoke. "What do you mean, Owen?"

"Kali doesn't want to put us in danger after what happened to Luca." Kali opened her mouth to argue, but Owen continued, "Fok, even I wish I could have done something to stop it." He looked at her. "It wasn't your fault. Nobody blames you."

Kali blinked, refusing to let tears fall. She could have coped with a personal attack, but Owen's unexpected understanding left her not knowing how to respond. She wasn't sure how loss could sneak up on her time and time again, but Owen was right. She'd come to the same conclusion a short time ago.

"It was my fault." The words surprised her because she'd not been thinking that. It felt like someone else was speaking and yet, the words were true. "It was my fault, or it feels like it was. I should have been able to protect him, and should have seen what was going to happen." She opened her mouth and at first, nothing came out but it felt as though the words might choke her if she didn't force them. "I foking hate being powerless."

"You weren't powerless; you killed Tregaren." Owen sighed. "While all I've ever killed is a song." There was a bitterness in his tone that snapped her out of her own misery.

Mika's hand touched her shoulder, warm through the cotton of her t-shirt. "I feel the same. You were right, what you said earlier, but Tregaren was my father. I shouldn't feel responsible for what he did and yet, it's impossible not to especially when I helped him abduct those women." Kali turned and found Mika staring at the table. "I didn't like him or want anything to do with him despite the blood between us. It was a forced connection that he made against my will. I can't change what happened in the past, but I need to make things right. Without that… "

Tears fell onto Caryanne's cheeks, but she didn't make a sound as she stared at Mika. Vaira put an arm around the other woman and murmured something Kali couldn't hear.

"I didn't know about the backdoor into my mind." Mika looked up. "But, I'm alive. I need to find my mother and help those other women before I can start to deal with the rest of what happened."

Kali found herself saying, "I do feel responsible for Luca's death, because I was, and I don't want to risk any of you. I don't think that you were aware of the risks when you agreed to help me with this mission, but if we follow this lead and go to Red Ghost, I'm afraid of what we might find there." She looked at them all in turn. "I don't want anyone else to die."

With one arm still around Caryanne, Vaira spoke, "We've seen what can happen firsthand. Luca died, so you can't say we don't know the potential danger. It's partly because of him that we want to do this. We want to make sure that he didn't die for nothing."

Caryanne was nodding even though her eyes were full of tears. She had made her choice, just like the rest of them.

Kali took a deep breath and let it out slowly. "Earlier tonight, we received an offer to play there."

There was a long silence before Owen spoke. "That's a bit of a coincidence, isn't it? What if they know who we are and it's a trap?"

Kali shook her head. "I gave him a mental nudge to get the invite."

Mika's expression became thoughtful. "Besides, we are

following Tregaren's trail, which is why we're in the right place. It's not such a long stretch that we should encounter the same people and that they believe we are what we appear to be—a traveling band, eager to entertain the masses."

Kali sighed. "I need to talk to Andy before we make any definite decisions."

Mika frowned and started to argue.

Kali could understand his concern, but there was nothing she could do about it. "Give me ten minutes, okay?"

Mika looked away. He probably knew that she was trying to decide how much to tell Andy. Perhaps, he finally understood what a position he'd put her in.

Kali went up to the hotel room to speak privately with Andy.

He answered immediately. "Hi, are you okay?"

"Hey." She decided to get straight to it. "Tala appears to have been a convenient planet to find women with potential abilities. There's a planet called Red Ghost, which has numerous transport links there." She explained some of what had happened. "We've been offered a music gig there, and so it works out perfectly. A little too perfectly, actually."

Andy was staring at something off-screen. She guessed that he was in the process of pulling up information.

He frowned. "There isn't much intelligence, which is one reason you initially avoided Red Ghost."

"Yes, and that we needed an impossible-to-get visa. I don't think the risks have improved but there is an opportunity to visit without arousing suspicion."

"We're going to struggle to help if you get into trouble out there."

"I know. What do you think?"

"It's your call. Is it worth the risk?"

Kali thought through everything that had happened. "I don't think we can ignore the fact that Gifted women are still going missing."

Andy inhaled deeply. "Okay."

"Besides, the band members aren't going to take no for an answer—particularly, Mika."

"Still, you wouldn't take the risk unless you were sure you needed to go."

Kali smiled because it wasn't a question. "There's something else." She hesitated, torn between telling the truth, which would have to come out at some point, and staying silent for now. "Mika used telepathy to take the information from the criminal's mind."

Rolle had been guilty of a crime, and so, technically, she would have been within her rights to examine him. But that wasn't the point.

Andy nodded thoughtfully. "Okay. I'll need to speak to someone more senior, but for now, carry on with the mission."

"Thank you." Kali ended the call, wishing that it wasn't too late to take back what she'd shared. It felt like things had just moved out of her control.

She would accept the offer for the band to play on Red Ghost. With any luck, they'd be one step closer to uncovering Tregaren's secrets.

CHAPTER 8

AFTER TAKING A short walk around the neighborhood, Treva returned through the security gatehouse. He assumed that his father's computer system had flagged his login, but he figured that having an alibi that he'd been out on a walk during the break-in might be helpful, just in case. Of course, the time stamps wouldn't line up quite right, but it might delay things while Marco ran some checks.

Most of the security guards already knew who he was and didn't bother to check the pass stored on his handheld.

On his way by, he smiled at the guard on duty. "Hey, has my dad returned from his meeting?"

The stocky man grinned. "Not planning on doing anything you shouldn't while the old man is out, are you?"

Treva felt his cheeks warm. It had crossed his mind to go somewhere else if Marco was already back home.

The man checked his screen. "Don't worry. He went out at 14:15, and he's never back before 18:00." He winked.

Treva muttered, "Thank you," as he ducked his head and sped away up the drive to the apartment block. He still had time to start going through the files on his handheld before Marco returned for dinner.

He didn't see anyone in the elevator, and once the front

door swung open, Treva entered the apartment quietly. Despite being told that his father was out, Treva couldn't be sure that there wasn't a cleaner or one of Marco's friends.

The apartment was silent, except for the hum of the air filtration system. He crept down the hall to his room.

Safely in his sanctuary, he locked the door. Just for a moment, he pretended to be a typical teenager hiding out from his parents in his bedroom. *If only.*

Kicking off his shoes, he prepared to open the copied files on his handheld. He half-expected them to have some sort of protection or self-destruct. It was difficult to believe that Marco didn't have safeguards in place, aside from being air-gapped from the Net. Even if automated security measures did destroy the device, he told himself that he would cope; he'd been without a decent handheld for most of his life. He held his breath as the first file took far longer than it should to open.

Row upon row of text appeared. Treva's hand started to ache. He was clutching the device so tight that if he wasn't careful, he was likely to break it into pieces. He forced himself to loosen his grip.

As Treva stared at the meaningless data, he wondered if it was in some sort of code. He couldn't understand the letters and numbers. So much for an immediate revelation about Marco's guilt or innocence.

The first column held future dates; that much was clear. Next came a jumble of letters and then more letters. One column denoted large amounts of credits, and next was a list of names. Treva recognized a few as the names of planets. Red Ghost appeared time and time again.

Treva looked it up. A deserted planet in a nearby system with no industry and few people. He stared at the list for a long time, letting his mind go blank. It was obvious that if one column was a list of destinations and another the names of ships, then Treva had a list of ships, with their routes and destinations. Except, if there wasn't anything on

Red Ghost, why were so many shipments being directed to that location?

A remote planet like Red Ghost sounded like a good place to get rid of someone. It would be easy, with ships docking on a regular basis.

Wouldn't it have been easier to kill her? He suppressed the thought, determined to believe that his mother was alive.

Treva opened another file and almost immediately closed it when he saw the contents. Somehow, looking at Marco's bank account felt more personal than his business files. The vast sums explained why everyone at the Blue Pixie treated Marco with such deference. Only wealth could command that kind of respect, and there were only two ways to get that rich: be born into it, or engage in illegal activity. And Marco definitely wasn't highborn.

The Blue Pixie. The packages. Nash recruiting him. Marco was behind it all.

If Marco had lied to him about Nash and the Blue Pixie, then there was nothing to stop him from lying about other things. The only question was, did he have his mother killed or taken away?

I'm so sorry, Mom.

Treva's eyes burned, but he wouldn't cry—not before he was certain about what had happened. The answer was somewhere; he just needed to find it.

—

After a couple of hours of poring over the figures, searching for patterns, he was nowhere closer to discovering anything useful. Treva thought that he'd do better after something to eat and went to fix a snack.

On his way back from the kitchen, Treva heard Marco's raised voice; he hadn't heard his father return. *Does he know I'm here?*

Eager to eavesdrop—and do anything that didn't

involve going back to those lists of figures—he moved quietly toward Marco's forbidden office. He stepped onto a thick hallway rug so that any sound he might inadvertently make would be absorbed.

The office door was wide open and Treva could see an arm and shoulder from his position in the hall.

He definitely doesn't know I'm home.

Treva supposed Marco was used to living alone and had no idea how sneaky teenagers could be. *Like father, like son.*

He stayed close to the wall and as far back as he could while still being able to hear what was said. As he listened, he realized that there were actually two voices, not just his father's. Although the two voices had the same tenor and accent, Marco's was louder.

"The *Oxana* has been delayed by engine trouble. They won't deliver until the third."

"Is their return cargo a special delivery?"

Special delivery! Is that drugs, or something else?

"Yes, but it can't be helped. I don't have anyone capable of taking over. It'd be nice if I could get the boy up to speed, but he really isn't ready yet. He's spent too much time influenced by his mother, but I'm working on him."

Treva stared hard at the floor as the words rang in his head. He wished their meaning wasn't so obvious. The more he tried to pretend he didn't understand, the clearer it became. *Marco doesn't want a son. He wants a loyal employee.*

After Nash, Treva had no intention of being used again. He silently returned to his room. It was time to put his half-formed plan into action.

—

Only as he approached the door to the Blue Pixie did it occurred to Treva they might not let him in. He was three years too young and didn't have anyone to vouch for him.

They could just turn him away, and he'd have to think of another way to get what he wanted.

Nash never seemed to have any trouble getting into anywhere. However, everybody at the Blue Pixie knew Nash, as he'd apparently been working there for years. Today, though, Treva was feeling the crazy side of reckless and was willing to give it a try on his own. So, ignoring the jittering in his stomach, he squared his shoulders and marched to the entrance.

The two bouncers were deep in conversation. Treva's heart hammered as he saw both men were the size of a small shuttle, but he reminded himself that he didn't have to fight them.

His heart was thudding so loudly that he was worried they'd hear it as he marched forward without making eye contact. The hair on the back of his neck stood rigid, but then he was inside.

Feeling elated by his success, Treva strode into the bar area and stopped. He could only make out dark shapes until his eyes adjusted to the laser-lights that lit the interior. There was so much that could go wrong. The pirates shouldn't be there since Marco had demanded they leave, but Treva had no idea how else to get in touch with them. Despite the odds, he had a feeling that Herja had enjoyed taunting his father by drinking in the Blue Pixie. Treva wanted to know that someone—anyone—was willing and able to stand up to Marco.

One step at a time, he told himself. It was too overwhelming to think of the whole plan. The first phase had been executed successfully; he was inside the Blue Pixie, hopefully without his father's knowledge. Although, he could always claim to be looking for Nash.

There was a handful of staff and although any one of them might report his presence to Marco, they all looked too busy to care. It took Treva a few seconds to locate Herja because she was surrounded by large men. Her laughter carried through the din before he spotted her.

Treva's heart skipped a beat. He couldn't quite believe that she was still here after the other night despite his hopes.

Treva swallowed as the second phase of his plan became possible. This could get him into all sorts of trouble. If his father found out... never mind that. He was giving up everything, but Treva couldn't forget about his mother. He had to do something, and so he moved toward the group.

What if they discover who I am? The pirates could easily hold him for ransom or kill him outright. *Mum must have been afraid of something like this.*

A large man stepped into his path to block his way. "What do you want?" His tone was almost friendly, but there was no getting past the bulky body.

Treva looked around him. All the men were hard-faced, with weapons on display. They smelled as if they'd washed in beer, and Treva wondered how long they'd been drinking. It was enough to give him second thoughts, but if he was going to find his mother, he needed to speak to the captain.

"I need to..." He tried not to stammer as, one by one, the group turned to look at him.

A woman's voice said, "Let the boy through. What harm is he going to do, you bunch of foking barbarians?"

A path cleared in front of Treva. The captain he'd been so desperate to speak to was a couple of meters away and staring at him. He tried to hide his fear, but it took all his courage to meet her dark green eyes. They were the color of the rocheen plant, which grew near to the artificial lakes on Glaendor. She was beautiful, which only made things worse. Treva tried not to let his gaze linger on the gun and the two knives at her belt.

"How can I help you?" Her voice was rich and smooth.

Unthinking, Treva almost blurted out who he was and who his father was. Stars, he wanted to get out of this alive, and it had been clear from the confrontation he'd witnessed that the two didn't like each other. More than that, Treva remembered his father's accusation that they had attacked his ships. The fact that he wasn't supposed to know anything about those ships helped him to focus. Marco was lying to him, and he couldn't trust him.

Treva took a deep breath, knowing that if he got this wrong, he might never find his mother. "I want to offer a trade." Even though he'd tried to speak quietly, everyone was listening to every word.

Someone asked, "What does the lad want?"

They must all be wondering the same thing, but at least they weren't hostile. There were a few sniggers, but Treva ignored them. This was too important to get side-tracked by what people thought.

He had got this far, and so he said, "I want to go to a planet called Red Ghost."

"Never heard of it," a different female voice said.

Startled, Treva looked around and saw that there were a few women amongst the men. He hadn't spotted them because their clothing was the same, and most had short haircuts. The one who'd spoken had laughing eyes and a cheeky smile; she wasn't much older than Treva. His face flushed under her gaze.

When he looked back at the captain, he found that she was studying him. He'd seen the same calculating expression on his father's face, but this was a stranger and a pirate.

The man next to him said, "What thing of value could you have to trade? Best go now, boy."

Treva had the distinct impression that they had been humoring him so far. They probably thought that he was wasting their captain's time and their patience was running out.

The intense scrutiny made Treva's face feel even warmer, but he didn't back down. "It *is* valuable."

"What?" This voice was full of scorn. "You've brought your mother's jewels to sell?"

The captain's eyes had lost their amusement when he hadn't left. "What are you offering?"

This was the tricky part. He needed to get her alone to talk. If not, there was a danger that word would get back to his father, especially as Treva suspected that his father owned the club. In which case, the bar staff would be loyal to him.

"I will tell you in private."

"This is my crew. If you were lucky enough to be allowed passage on my ship, these are the men and women you would travel with. But, to be invited on board you need to offer something worthwhile."

Treva could tell that he'd pushed too far and she thought he was trying to dictate the terms without reason. She didn't know how sensitive the information he held was.

"I didn't mean to cause any offense. It's just that there are ears everywhere in this bar." He looked meaningfully toward a man who had been polishing glasses for far too long.

The captain considered what he had to say, while the man next to her whispered in her ear. It was the same man Treva had seen during the confrontation with his father. Someone she trusted to keep close and give her advice?

"I just need to talk to you, that's all." Treva injected a pleading note into his voice.

She nodded but was still listening to the man who talked so low that Treva couldn't hear what he was saying over the background music.

Herja set off for the exit. "Okay, follow me."

The man shook his head, clearly not pleased with her decision. Treva hurried before she changed her mind, weaving through the tables and out the side door.

He stepped onto the dirty pavement a second before he was shoved against the wall of the building. Air left his lungs and pain exploded down his spine. His feet couldn't get any traction and the compression of his neck set off an explosion of panic.

Treva found himself staring up at Herja's advisor. "You were with Steyn the other night." Treva hadn't seen the man follow him out.

His legs were shaking, but his thoughts were clear. "I pick up packages for him. That's the reason I need to talk to you." It was hard to get his words out.

"Gosta, stop choking the lad and let him breathe. He hasn't done anything."

"Yet," Gosta muttered under his breath.

He was so close that Treva couldn't fail to hear him or smell the sweat from his armpits.

Treva squirmed, trying to break free, but it was useless. "I know the routes of his ships. You said..."

"You stole information." The captain watched him carefully.

Treva didn't think that stealing should be a problem since that's what pirates did and so decided to be honest. "I need to find my mother. She was kidnapped and possibly taken to a planet called Red Ghost." When the captain didn't respond, he added, "Please, I'm desperate."

"I see you mean what you say, but how do I know your information is good?" She was studying his face and he was suddenly certain that she'd be able to tell if he lied.

Treva thought rapidly. "I could tell you about the ships that are due to leave today, and you could check them out."

"You will give us everything, and we will decide whether or not to take you with us." Before Treva could protest, she added, "As you can imagine, I don't run a passenger ship, which means that we might or might not head to Red Ghost at some point. So much depends on our other commitments, and it's up to you whether you want to take that chance."

It wasn't what Treva wanted. He realized that it had been unrealistic to think he could persuade the pirates to do anything they didn't want to do.

Gosta released him. "Perhaps you'll get lucky."

Able to breathe more easily now, he met Gosta's gaze

head-on. "You'll see my information is worth your while and then you'll help me."

Herja laughed. "Ah, the arrogance of youth."

More like desperation.

Gosta pressed his hand to his ear and straightened. "Trouble's on its way. Let's go, people!"

The men and women who had surrounded them earlier came out the door in ones and twos. They melted onto the walkway in silence, and it was as if they had never been there.

Treva blinked, and when he looked around, the captain had disappeared, leaving him alone with Gosta.

He felt Gosta's hand on his arm, guiding him. The distinctive sound of pulse gun fire sounded from inside the club.

"Come on, lad. You wanted an adventure. You got it."

There was no chance to say goodbye to anyone and no opportunity for second thoughts. Everything was happening far too quickly as Treva followed Gosta into the black of the night.

CHAPTER 9

HERJA KNOCKED BACK the fourth—or fifth—shot and closed her eyes, concentrating on the way the burning liquid warmed her throat. She grimaced, hating the taste but loving the way her body surrendered to the fiery sensation and the heat made her limbs feel liquid.

A soft bleeping and the constant whir of a fan close by were lulling her to sleep, but something had disturbed her. She squinted to see that the light had brightened on the *Hyperion's* flight deck.

"Turn it down," she grumbled, unable to muster enough energy to move.

Gosta's sour face appeared above. If not for him, she'd be fast asleep by now.

"Interior lighting down," she instructed the computer, finally realizing that she didn't have to move.

The harsh glare lessened, allowing the blue-green of subspace to wash across the deck exactly the way she liked it. Herja didn't want to be anywhere else. She'd been flying so long that she was more comfortable on this ship in subspace than anywhere else. It was her home.

She sighed. *Alcohol always makes me too sentimental.*

Gosta walked up to her and crossed his arms, making his serpent tattoos ripple. "Steyn is too powerful. We shouldn't piss him off."

She scowled despite the effort it took. "Psh, we've intercepted a few ships. If we didn't, others would have."

"Acting on this new information would go beyond that, and you know it."

"Oh, that." She smiled. It was so much easier to smile. "Where would the fun be in that? Besides, he'll never see us coming." She paused as something occurred to her. She knew him too well. "But that isn't what's really bothering you. You don't want the boy on board?" She wasn't about to tell him that she hadn't planned to bring him along, and it had been an accident. "Why?"

Gosta grumbled under his breath, but she waited until, eventually, he said, "You can't really think his information is going to be any good?"

"Why not? He was with Steyn the other night." She wasn't sure why she was bothering to argue; half of her agreed with him. "I think the boy was the only reason things didn't get violent that night."

Gosta glowered. "I thought we'd agree that we weren't going to look for trouble anymore."

She ignored the comment. "I saw the way Steyn looked at him, and I'd stake your skinny ass on the fact that he's more important than Steyn wanted us to know."

"Even more reason to leave him behind."

"Perhaps you're right, but it's too late now. And, besides, we can always get rid of him out here if he becomes too much of a risk. Nobody knows he's with us."

Gosta shook his head slightly. "You might convince the others of that, but not me."

She propped herself up on the console and reached for her glass, which wobbled precariously. "You know how desperate we are. We have to do something drastic."

"Piracy isn't drastic enough?"

Herja surprised them both by laughing. Stars, she was tired. If only she could have a few days off to recharge, then she'd be able to think more clearly. One thing was certain, they needed some luck soon.

She pointed at him. "Gosta, we can't afford to find ourselves stuck with another haul of farming supplies. We need a better approach. And if we find a way to hurt Steyn at the same time, it's a bonus."

"That bad haul has been troubling me," Gosta mused. "Why would Steyn's people even bother transporting farming equipment? Was it just a decoy from their real operations?"

Herja shrugged. "Perhaps. Or maybe not. Really, we don't know how large their operations are. They might legitimately be using it for agriculture to colonize a world all their own."

He met her gaze. "Perhaps it's time to think about alternative ways to deal with them."

If anyone but Gosta had said that, she would have seen it as a challenge, but he was too dumb and stubborn to lie or try to manipulate her. She'd guessed some of the crew were unhappy, but she was surprised that it had gotten to the stage where anyone would talk openly. That didn't mean she was willing to acknowledge their complaint.

"Steyn's not stupid. He's going to take precautions after losing two ships, but there's no way he has the resources to protect all those vessels—not with the numbers he's sending out. He's spread himself too thin, which was why we got lucky last time. Our biggest problem is finding them—"

"I have a bad feeling about Steyn. It'd be better to leave well enough alone."

"We don't have a lot of options."

An alarm shrilled to Herja's left and she silenced it with a sweep of her hand. It was time she checked on the crew, anyway. "Get some rest so you can relieve me in a few hours."

Herja never left the flight deck without a senior member of the crew to monitor the systems and make sure everything was okay. Despite the ship's advanced navigation system, things could go wrong quickly, and the sensors could only detect so much. It was a policy that had saved them on numerous occasions.

Gosta gave her a knowing look as he passed. A look that was intended to remind her that he knew her as well as she knew him.

She watched until the doors slid closed behind him. Then, she watched him on the interior security video feed to make sure that he went straight to his bunk on the deck below. She wanted him fresh and ready for whatever the next few hours would bring.

She grimaced. If only they didn't have to bother with the outside world, she thought she could be happy surrounded by their small crew.

Herja's mind drifted to the boy. Despite what she said to Gosta, she didn't like messing with organized criminals like Steyn. He had too many resources at his disposal, not to mention powerful friends.

She was under no illusions about how vulnerable they were out in space. It wouldn't take much for the TSS or Tararian Guard to hunt them if they could be bothered to come out this far. Then again, they couldn't avoid risk.

They needed to target the rich and powerful to take anything worthwhile. It would be nice to think that they were redistributing wealth, but nothing was that simple. Herja was no hero, stealing from the rich to give to the poor, but she wasn't the monster they made her out to be, either. She would rather target people like Steyn than those with less blood on their hands.

Steyn's ships made an ideal target—morally, and because of the riches they normally carried. Their last haul of farming equipment had been disappointing; that was her excuse for listening to what the boy had to say. They needed a quick win, and despite the risks, she was happy to go after another Steyn ship.

Herja wanted to smack herself for not anticipating that Steyn would attack when they were planet-side on

Glaendor. She'd goaded him by drinking at the Blue Pixie night after night; he must have been distracted, not to have retaliated sooner. Marco Steyn wasn't the sort to ignore anyone getting one over on him. They hadn't finished their re-provisioning, but she always kept enough on board to get by; there were too many times when they'd needed a quick exit.

Now we just need to find Steyn's ships with something valuable on board.

—

After Gosta returned to the flight deck to relieve her, Herja went down to the cabin the boy was sharing with Idra and Kinder. If nothing else, spending the voyage with the two should put him off a life of piracy.

Herja supposed that he was bright enough to work out how to get home if they decided to drop him on a planet somewhere. It would certainly be safer than traveling with them. With that in mind, she intended to find out what he knew.

When she arrived, the boy wasn't there. Kinder pointed her in the direction of the galley.

Upon entering the galley, he was seated alone, looking small and dejected. She suppressed the pang of sympathy that escaped her no-nonsense defenses and tried not to think about how desperate someone had to be to ask for passage on a pirate ship. He didn't seem the romantic sort that thought piracy was a fun way to meet girls, although she hadn't missed the way he'd looked at Idra.

Poor lad. Idra will chew him up and spit him out.

Herja slid onto the bench seat opposite, deciding it was time to learn more about her informant. "What's your name? You started making demands, and we missed the pleasantries."

For an instant, he looked up from his hands before his gaze dropped down again. "Treva Marsh."

Herja was surprised that she believed him. She didn't have the gift of telepathy, but she could read people. Treva was like an open book. The things he'd said about his mother had rung true as well.

"I'm Herja. Welcome aboard the *Hyperion*. Now, can I see the flight plans?"

He pulled out a brand-new handheld—better than the one she owned. If he wasn't careful, he'd lose that within the first few days with this crew.

Herja peered at the device's screen, too small to make out the complex information tables from a distance. "It's okay, you can project the details."

Treva checked over his shoulder, as if there might be something more dangerous than a pirate on board.

A column of light shone from the device, displaying a magnified version of the information. The details about the first six ships were from the previous month. She recalled that at least one of the flight paths and timing was correct, but that didn't prove anything. He might have had access to that information retrospectively. It was the ships scheduled to leave in the following days that interested her. If he was right about those, there was a chance that the rest of the data would be both accurate and useful.

She considered the likelihood of a trap, despite the trusting innocence Treva projected. Herja knew from experience that betrayal came in all sorts of packages. Her instincts were generally sound, and there wasn't anything making her seriously worry.

He hadn't given her everything, not yet, but he would. There was no point threatening him until she was sure it was worth it. He would find out that his continued survival depended on his ability to please her, at least until she could get rid of him.

Herja had been aware of Kinder entering the galley and wondered if he'd come to check on them. "Make sure little Treva doesn't get into any trouble," she said to him. Kinder froze, in the middle of stuffing a pastry into his mouth.

Herja kept her smile. "Slow down, nobody's going to take it from you."

She left to the sound of Kinder choking. She shuddered. Sometimes she felt like the crew's mother. Now, if only she could stop picking up orphans.

CHAPTER 10

"RED GHOST," KALI muttered, not sure what she was looking for.

She scowled at the bright, dusty landscape. What they'd seen of the planet so far made her uneasy. Something was off, but it was hard to identify exactly what was bothering her.

Even though they'd acquired the necessary visa, the authorities had still locked down the *Sepiantia*. That had been the start of Mika's foul mood, which had rubbed off on Kali. Worse, the authorities had waited until their ship was within range of the planet's weapons to initiate the lockdown; unsurprisingly, they had some serious weapons. The crew of the *Sepiantia* had no choice but to surrender control of the ship.

Perhaps Kali shouldn't have chosen their time in transit to confess to Mika that she had spoken to Andy about his illegal use of telepathy. She was already feeling awful, and it had felt underhanded not telling him. He hadn't taken it well. There hadn't been a confrontation, but he hadn't spoken to her since, not that she blamed him.

Now, planet-side, she needed to figure out how in the stars she was going to make the most of their temporary visa to conduct her investigation while not arousing suspicion. Their current hike through the barren countryside surrounding the town wasn't how she'd hoped to spend the morning, but Kali's primary concern was finding the missing women.

Vaira turned in a full circle, both hands on her hips. "They should have called it Dead Ghost. There's nothing alive out here." Her tone remained cheerful, despite the complaint. However, considering that the woman hated walking or doing any type of exercise, Kali had no idea what she had to be so happy about.

Kali turned to examine her footprints in the dusty soil. They remained undisturbed.

Vaira was right; not a single plant grew on the arid land. Even the air was dry. It scoured the inside of Kali's nostrils whenever she took a deep breath. It felt as if the planet was trying to suck every last drop of moisture out of her. The deep, narrow cracks crisscrossing the landscape further illustrated both the dryness and massive temperature swings from day to night that contributed to making the planet so inhospitable.

Squat, abandoned buildings dotted the horizon. Each was narrower at the base than the top, almost reverse pyramids. The sun hung low in the sky, casting a golden light and long shadows. As soon as it dipped below the horizon, the temperature would plummet; they'd been warned it would be freezing after dark and to plan accordingly.

Honk crouched, staring at something in the dirt. Perhaps he was feeling queasy. Unlike the others, he suffered from hangovers, and since he continued to drink every night, most mornings were unpleasant. Kali wondered what it would be like to be either drunk or hung over. Looking at Honk's furrowed forehead and pale features, she decided that she would rather not find out.

She studied the tracks next to hers. The dust held the shape of a paw-print. How would any animal survive out here? There was nothing to eat or drink. Not a thing had moved in the forty minutes they'd been outside the complex, where their accommodations were located.

More disturbing than the lack of life was the constant whispering. Kali knew that the sound was nothing more than the breeze circulating around the strangely shaped buildings, but it was eerie all the same.

"Has anyone seen any footprints other than ours?" Mika asked. It was the first thing he'd said since they set off.

"People footprints?" Owen continued to blink rapidly as if his eyes couldn't get used to the brightness. "I can see lots of paw-prints and animal tracks. I'd really rather not meet whatever creature that one belongs to." He pointed to a large depression with gouges, which could only have been made from claws.

"Where do you want to look next?" Kali directed the question at Mika, who was scuffing the soil with a booted foot.

She wasn't surprised they hadn't found any trace of captives or identified anywhere they could be kept. They were searching an entire planet without any equipment, thanks to the planetary authorities. Mika didn't answer her question, and she remembered that he wasn't talking to her.

Owen bent to pick up a small stone. "Could they be somewhere underground?"

There was something different about Owen. He was alert and interested, playing an active part in what was happening. It was as if he had finally plugged himself into the world.

She shrugged. "Anything's possible, but there should be *some* indication of activity."

At least, as far as they could tell, only this one small area of the planet was inhabited, which didn't mean that the women couldn't be kept elsewhere. In fact, it was likely the criminals would pick an isolated area, since they had the entire planet, but there was no indication of where that might be.

Not for the first time, Kali wondered if they would be allowed to leave after they had finished playing the gig. They were trying to delay the performance for as long as possible, because there was no telling what would happen once they were no longer useful. If they were popular, they may be asked to play for longer—and have little say in the matter.

There's no pressure to play that foking bass competently, then.

"Let's go for a walk, she says," Vaira muttered. "See the sights, she says."

Kali rolled her eyes. "We agreed that we needed to see as much as possible of the planet. I didn't need everyone to come along."

"Yes, well, we might be seeing it for a lot longer than we would like, by the looks of things."

Kali suspected that they wouldn't have been allowed to wander anywhere if there'd been any danger of them discovering something suspicious. Although, based on the lack of interesting landmarks, it seemed unlikely that anyone would ever want to wander around for the sheer fun of it. Still, it would have been foolish to come all this way and not try to discover the planet's secrets. Besides, the criminals running this planet—because she had no doubt that's what they were—might have left their prisoners somewhere obvious if they didn't intend to let the *Sepiantia* leave.

Mika frowned as he studied his handheld. "That's weird. There's nothing about these buildings or who built them." His frown deepened. "The gang who act as the planetary authority are a secretive bunch, but they don't seem very intelligent. I thought I'd be able to find out *something*."

Honk ambled over, looking especially pale next to everyone else's reddened faces in the heat of the day. "I didn't like the way they insisted we play tonight." He grinned. "Foking genius of you to tell them that Owen would sound like a wounded bird. They believed that he needed time to acclimatize to the atmosphere."

Kali smiled. "Yes, that was quick thinking. But it was strange that they accepted the excuse."

Honk wandered off, muttering, "Genius."

She was hoping that when they did finally play that things would go better than their gig on Tala. If their performance wasn't well-received, she had a feeling the consequences might be serious.

Kali wandered close to the nearest building. "Perhaps you could get friendly with some of the natives?" she suggested to Caryanne.

"Why pick on me?"

Not wanting to point out that Caryanne was the most promiscuous out of all of the band members, she said, "You have the most innocent face."

Vaira laughed. "Is that why? Actually, she'd make a useless spy, since she can't remember anything."

Caryanne stuck her nose up and folded her arms. "I never said I wanted to be a spy."

Owen smiled at Kali. "Leave that to me." She opened her mouth to tell him that she'd been joking, but he said, "Did you see the woman with long auburn hair?" He wandered off toward another building, deep in thought and clearly not wanting an answer.

Kali could only recall one woman with hair that hadn't been in an updo, but she'd been a vicious creature. She hoped that Owen didn't mean her; he'd never survive if he disappointed her. Perhaps, he'd known that Kali was joking and was responding in kind.

Mika kicked at a rock. "I don't like it. This whole place gives me a bad feeling." He scanned the horizon, with a frown etched into his face that Kali worried might become a permanent feature. She wondered what he was annoyed about apart from losing control of his ship and her reporting his use of telepathy. *Okay, so maybe that's enough.*

The breeze picked up, lifting dust from the ground, and the whispering increased. Kali rubbed her nose; it was dry enough to crumble.

Something wasn't right. "We need an alternative way off-planet, especially if anyone decides to take issue with us being out here."

Mika continued to kick at the ground. "I'm not leaving without the *Sepiantia*. Have you seen the grapples they have on her?"

Is he speaking to me again?

"Well, they never said we couldn't explore," Honk stared off into the distance.

Kali shook her head. "It was implied when they locked down our ship and told us not to cause any trouble."

"What? You don't think they want us to explore?" Vaira said in a tone that might or might not have been sarcastic. "What could they possibly have to hide?"

"We'll soon find out." Mika pointed at a cloud of dust.

"Where in the stars did they come from?" Vaira muttered.

Kali squinted and saw a group of determined men marching in their direction. She counted five, and they were armed. Their little group didn't have a single pulse handgun, let alone something that would do serious damage in a firefight. They hadn't been allowed to take any weapons off the ship, and since they were supposed to be a band, it had been hard to argue. They were as vulnerable as Luca had been, although they did have Mika's and Kali's abilities to keep them safe.

Kali made a mental note to check the spot near to where they'd first been spotted. They must have been underground.

Kali looked at Mika. *"Get ready in case the situation gets desperate."*

He nodded once, and she sensed his determination to protect the others. He must be thinking of Luca, as well. It occurred to her that she wasn't entirely sure what he could do. His training under Tregaren had been unorthodox.

As the group got closer, Kali recognized the man leading the group—Diamond-Boy. Nobody had told them but from the way he acted, he was in charge. It didn't matter that he was the smallest in stature, she wouldn't underestimate him. His aura was bright, although there was no indication that he was aware that he was Gifted.

Owen opened his mouth to say something but closed it again. The group was almost on them, and he obviously didn't want to be overheard. He moved to stand shoulder-to-shoulder with Mika.

The men stopped, and the cloud of red dust expanded to cover Kali's group. Caryanne started coughing. Out of the corner of her eye, Kali caught Owen grinning. She followed his gaze and realized that one of the men was, in fact, a woman.

"What do we have here?" Diamond-Boy sneered, not bothered by the layer of grime that coated his skin. "I thought I told you lot not to go causing any trouble."

"What trouble? We were walking. You never said anything about not walking." Kali wanted to ask if they were prisoners but was afraid of the answer. "It would be rude to visit a planet and not see the sights," she looked around, "such as they are."

"As if I'm going to believe that pile of shite." He swung an arm wide. "There's nothing to see—just dust and empty buildings."

Mika raised his hands in a placating gesture, but the set of his jaw suggested that he was ready to start a fight. "We see that for ourselves, now."

"Don't push it. They're armed and we're not," Kali said. *"We don't want to put the others at risk."*

Mika glared at her and she nudged him. She didn't want Diamond-Boy to get suspicious. She remembered that anger all too well, because she still felt it. She resolved to talk to Mika once they were alone. For now, the priority had to be to calm things down.

Kali checked the weapons on display, considering using telekinesis to disable them. If she'd been alone or even with just Mika, she would have been willing to fight, but the chance of the band getting hurt was too high. They weren't supposed to be involved in combat situations.

"*Mika, we'll come back when they're not watching us.*"

"*They'll be watching from now on. They're suspicious.*"

"*I'm sure we can think of something.*"

"*You're being too cautious. You didn't want us to come here in the first place. We aren't going to find out anything unless we take a chance.*"

"*Let's not do this in front of the enemy. We need to have this conversation in private—later.*"

Diamond-Boy was watching Mika carefully. "When are you going to play? My people need some good entertainment. That's what you were invited to do—entertain us. Everyone knows there's a band, and they're expecting great things."

Kali tried to control the flutter in her chest at the thought of going on stage under those circumstances. *Don't be ridiculous. It won't matter if you are dead.*

"We aren't the reason for the delay," Caryanne said with a tilt of her head and a serene smile. "We have to wait for the instruments to acclimatize to the planet, else there's a danger that we will not perform well."

Kali had been right earlier—she did have the most innocent face.

Diamond-Boy gaped. "Are you serious? Instruments need a vacation! I thought it was his voice that needed time?"

"The sound is trapped inside, and it'll come out wrong if you're not careful." Caryanne spoke with such sincerity that Kali believed her.

Honk swayed and almost fell. He was saved by Owen's strong grip on his arm.

Diamond-Boy glanced their way, before returning his attention to Mika. "If you hadn't been so highly recommended, I'd wonder if you could play at all." He leaned forward. "I wonder how well you'll perform playing for your lives."

One of Diamond-Boy's men laughed. "Without transport, we can do what we like to them."

A shiver went down Kali's spine as she looked closer, recognizing the man, Adam, who had lured them to Red Ghost. The scarf that covered half his face to protect him from the dust didn't disguise his voice.

Mika tensed, but Kali automatically put a hand on his back. He glared at her, not happy at the reminder that he needed to control his temper.

"Mika, we can't risk the others." She tried to send a soothing vibe. *"We'll investigate later, I promise."*

He stared at her for a long moment before his eyes narrowed, but he didn't say anything. Kali needed to end this conversation before things became heated again.

It was a miracle that Owen hadn't said more, or Vaira, who was usually quick to intervene with cutting words. Fortunately, Honk never got involved in much, and mild-mannered Caryanne just smiled as if she didn't have a care.

"We've seen enough of the sights. How do we get back?" Kali looked at Diamond-Boy and smiled.

He scowled. No, he hadn't bought her attempt at innocence for a second. Perhaps she should have left it to Caryanne.

CHAPTER 11

TREVA THOUGHT THAT his mother would be proud of the way he'd adapted to life on board the pirate ship in just two days. Well, except for the pirate part. She would not have been impressed with his choice of transportation. If... *when* he found her, she would have to forgive him for the choices he'd made.

Most of the *Hyperion*'s crew merely tolerated him, but he'd started to foster a friendship with a handful of the younger pirates. They seemed particularly entertained by him. Perhaps they didn't know what to make of the boy who had never traveled in space before. That was just one of the reasons Treva kept his head down, and when they gave him the worst jobs, he worked hard and didn't complain.

At present, he was stuck cleaning the recycler—a vile device that looked like it hadn't been serviced in years. He wrinkled his nose, sure that it would recycle *him* if he fell inside. *Why aren't they designed so they are easy to clean?*

The unappealing task was a reminder that his control over his life had dwindled since he'd approached Herja and sold out his father. *That's what happens when you betray someone—you're at the mercy of anybody who's willing to help you.*

He'd been so focused on what he had to do next, there'd been no time to consider whether he'd even wanted to go off on a wild adventure. Well, he'd gotten into one, whether he wanted it or not.

Treva didn't want to think about what he'd given up in the search for his mother. So, he set his jaw, determined to do whatever it took to find her.

Herja and Gosta were always busy on the flight deck, which was off-limits to anybody but the most trusted of the crew. It meant that Treva couldn't find out anything. Aside from when they gave him new, increasingly annoying assignments, he thought they might have forgotten about him. In some ways, being ignored might be good.

Treva didn't know whether they planned to act on the information he'd supplied. He kept track of the jumps to subspace, but he had no idea where they were going.

Not wanting to be alone with his thoughts, and with nothing else to do, he headed to the galley. There was always someone in search of a meal, and since everyone was expected to feed themselves, there was always someone there.

Big Kinder was sitting with Idra and a woman that Treva had seen around, but they'd never spoken. The three stopped talking as he drew near. They all held their hands close to their chests.

Treva looked around the group, trying not to let his eyes linger on Idra. "What are you doing?"

"What does it look like?" Kinder said. When Treva's expression remained puzzled, he added, "Playing Fastara. What else would we be doing off-shift?"

Treva stared at the plastic cards fanned out in Kinder's right hand. Colorful symbols covered the back. There was nothing in the galley to explain what Fastara entailed.

Kinder laughed. "Look, he's never played before." He winked at Idra. "Do you want to learn, boy?"

Treva ignored that Kinder had called him 'boy', having got used to it. He hesitated, not sure he liked the look that passed between the three. "Okay, but I don't have any credit for betting."

Kinder looked disappointed but Idra said, "There are things more valuable than credit on a ship."

Before Treva could make his boundaries even clearer, the ship shuddered as they dropped back into normal space. Treva went to look out of the viewport while the others laughed at his excitement. He never got tired of staring out into space, whether in subspace or out of it. Both were beautiful in their own way. Now, the swirling blue-green had been replaced with blackness and bright stars.

When he eventually returned to the table, he found Kinder and Idra arguing over the cards. The other woman rested her head in her hands and watched.

Since they were becoming more heated, Treva took a chance and interrupted, "Is somebody going to show me how to play?"

They both scowled at him, and Idra said, "I suppose."

With a last scowl at Kinder, she produced another deck of plastic playing cards, fanning them out to display a series of symbols in different colors on each card.

Idra explained how the game worked but Treva didn't understand much of what she said. It was nice that she was talking to him though. When Kinder tried to clarify some points, he made it more confusing. They all teased him, but as far as he could tell they didn't try to take advantage. Treva still lost his first game spectacularly and when he did win a hand, it was because he'd inadvertently cheated.

Kinder laughed. "I've never met anyone who plays Fastara so badly."

"Look, I know that I'm different, but you won't have to put up with me for long."

Kinder laughed. "You fit in fine."

Treva felt lighter and had to blink a few times to clear his vision. He hadn't realized how badly he wanted to fit in somewhere.

"Why, where are you going?" Idra asked.

It startled Treva to realize that they didn't know. Herja and Gosta hadn't told them about his mother. He shook his head, worried that if he told them the truth they would think him stupid.

He felt a light touch on his arm. It was Idra.

She smiled. "It's okay, you don't have to tell us."

Treva wanted to tell them. It was just that he didn't want them to think that he was weird and yet, if he didn't take a chance, they would only know what they'd seen so far and he didn't think he'd impressed anyone. It didn't really matter if they thought he was silly or spoiled and it was irrational that he wanted to be liked. In a hesitant voice, he explained how his mother had gone missing a few weeks ago and he was hoping to find her on Red Ghost.

Idra said, "That's awful."

Kinder nodded and opened his mouth to say something but an alarm started to shrill, causing curses from the small group. There was a commotion from the table behind and Treva looked back to see discarded cards and food. Everyone headed in different directions, leaving Treva in the same spot, wondering if he should know what the alarm meant.

"Hey," he shouted, but they'd already gone.

Treva went into the corridor, where everyone seemed to have someplace to be as they hurried in different directions. Nobody spoke, and Treva spotted some people wearing EVA suits.

Are we under attack?

Treva frowned, not sure what was going on or why nobody was telling him what to do. He had no idea if this was a drill or something serious. He was struck that the crew were military in their efficiency, which wasn't what he'd expected.

"Get a move on." Treva turned toward Gosta's familiar voice, grateful that he hadn't been forgotten all together. The tall man gestured for Treva to follow him.

He didn't hesitate, wanting to know what was happening. Anything was better than to be left standing around in ignorance.

Gosta rushed through the corridors. Treva had to jog to keep up with the man's giant strides, and they were both breathless by the time they reached Herja.

She was in command on the flight deck. Dressed in a black pressure-suit minus helmet, she was talking into the comm unit. Her voice was calm despite the flashing lights turning her face red. The alarms were silent here, although Treva was sure that was only because someone had turned them off. The only sound was Gosta's footsteps over the background mechanical hum.

Treva looked around. For some reason, he'd imagined that the flight deck would be cramped and full of seats, but there was enough room to freely move. Treva was drawn to the expansive viewport along the forward bulkhead where stars and planets claimed his attention.

He was vaguely aware of Herja focused on the controls. "We've engaged the starship *Shockwave*."

Treva stiffened. *That's one of the ships on my father's list.*

Gosta opened a storage locker and pulled something out, which he held out to Treva. It was a silky metallic fabric. Next, he tossed a helmet onto the chair in front of Treva.

"Best get into the suit, boy. You'll be coming with me."

Treva's eyes widened. He had never even seen an EVA suit in real life prior to a few minutes ago. He had certainly never dreamed he would one day wear one, and he wasn't sure that he wanted to start now.

"Come on. It's easy to get into. Unless you want to board without any protection. I have to say, it wouldn't be my choice, not after we scramble her systems."

"Board! Oh, stars!" Treva grabbed the suit and held it up.

If only his hands would work properly. Thankfully the

fabric was stronger than it looked, and after a couple of false starts, he managed to get his arms and legs in the correct places.

At some point, while Treva was struggling into his suit, Gosta had donned his own. Now, both Gosta and Herja were busy so, Treva returned to the viewport to see if he could make out anything different from this angle, and there it was. A large ship, easily twice the size of theirs, visible to the left-hand side. *We aren't going to attempt to take that, are we?*

"Everyone ready?" Herja asked over the comm.

"Affirmative," came a response.

Treva didn't recognize the voice. He barely knew the crew. Gone was the relaxed camaraderie and joking that he'd observed for the past two days. The promise of piracy had revealed a professionalism that he'd never suspected, from what he'd seen so far.

Gosta nodded to Herja, who smiled in response before putting her helmet over her head. She jerked on a lever.

The lights flickered, and an audible alarm sounded. Herja silenced it without looking at it, or the readings that filled the viewscreen.

Gosta also had his helmet in place, so Treva hurried to secure his own. He tried not to panic as it swiveled without catching before he managed to click it into a locked position on the second attempt. There was a moment of claustrophobia before he got his breathing under control.

Gosta's voice filled the helmet, "Don't worry, boy. The suits are a precaution. That's how we try to do things—safety first."

Treva wanted to point out that he sounded more like one of his teachers than a pirate, but he didn't dare. Something told him that Gosta's patience was thin.

Someone spoke in his head, which he realized after a moment was the helmet's comm. "Boarding."

Were they boarding the *Shockwave*? Already? But there hadn't been a battle, had there? Still with no clue of what was going on, when Gosta signaled for him to follow, Treva thought he'd better obey.

"Can you hear me?" Treva asked as he jogged down the corridors behind Gosta. When there was no answer, he tapped the large man on the shoulder and mimed talking.

Gosta grabbed his hand and flicked a switch on the wrist of his suit. "No talking unless it's vital."

His ears felt as though there had been a change of pressure, but Treva didn't dare test out the microphone in case everyone heard him. He thought he could detect distant chatter.

Treva lost his bearings with his vision limited by the helmet and all the corridors looking the same. Eventually, they climbed through a hatch into a narrow umbilical that must connect the two ships. It swayed slightly whenever they took a step, and the end looked as if it was kilometers away.

Gosta didn't check to see if Treva was following. He seemed to be in a hurry to get to the other ship. Treva would have hung back, but he didn't want to linger in nearly open space and so, he stayed a step behind.

Treva's breathing was too loud in the helmet and he wanted to pee. He felt he could breathe again only when they reached the other side and emerged through a hatch onto the larger ship.

Drawings covered a plain, grey wall. Some were rude, and there were initials and scribbles. There was nothing that suggested any imagination, and Treva was glad he wasn't traveling on the *Shockwave*.

"Clear."

"Two on the left with weapons."

"Lower deck secured."

Are these really the same people that I've been with for the last couple of days?

Gosta removed his helmet, and Treva tried to take off his but it was stuck. After some fiddling around the neck, he found the catch. He pulled it off and immediately felt as if he'd shed a few kilograms. He sucked in deep breaths reassured by the slight odor of artificial air.

Gosta laughed at Treva's dazed expression. "I thought you knew we were pirates, lad. Didn't it occur to you that we would capture ships?"

"But how?"

Gosta tapped the side of his nose but then told him anyway. "Catch-All—it's a device that cycles through the encryptions until it gets a match." Gosta was full of pride. "It temporarily overrides basic commands, like door locks, by piggybacking on the automation protocols for docking."

"What?"

"It tricks the system into thinking it's going into remote autopilot."

"You take over the ship?"

"I wish." Gosta shook his head. "Sadly, it's not enough to fully take over the ship, but it causes chaos so that a boarding party can gain access."

A couple of pirates ran past, heading back to the *Hyperion*.

Gosta tapped Treva's shoulder. "Make sure you stay close to me."

Treva was too afraid to do anything else. People were moving in all directions. Everything was hectic, but at the same time, everyone else seemed to know what they were doing.

Stars, is that rifle-fire? Treva ducked when he heard the distinctive sound coming from ahead. It was only because Gosta was so calm that he resisted throwing himself to the deck.

Booted feet passed as they ducked into yet another corridor. Treva gawked.

Why had Gosta brought him over when he wasn't armed and had no experience in combat? He was relieved they hadn't given him a weapon, since he wouldn't have known what to do with it. If they expected him to use one, they would all be in trouble.

As they moved further into the ship, Treva noticed that everyone had taken their helmets off. They started to pass people wearing a green uniform Treva didn't recognize. Most weren't much older than him and looked frightened.

One man argued with a pirate that Treva remembered was called Kurra. They'd spent some time cleaning the lower corridor together. Treva had the impression that for Kurra it was a punishment for some minor infraction, whereas for Treva, it was a job he'd been given.

Gosta didn't slow, and he ignored everything going on around him. Treva stayed right behind him, worried that nobody would recognize him in the generic suit. If he got separated, the pirates might think he was a part of the other ship.

Most of the *Shockwave*'s crew lined the corridors with their hands in the air. They looked like ordinary people; some were shaking and understandably terrified.

It was only now, seeing the effect on the ship's crew, that he realized what being a pirate meant. *Stars, this is all my fault.*

He hadn't known they were going to attack the ship, or else he might not have given Herja the information. *What did you think they were going to do? They're pirates!*

He had to admit, that while he hadn't considered the details, he'd known very well what they planned. Stealing ships was a serious business, and probably, not so different from what his father did.

How did I end up here?

Treva was swept along with Gosta and everyone else. He still didn't know where they were going but was starting to get a bad feeling.

Gosta must have seen Treva's expression, because he slapped him on the shoulder, sending him stumbling. "You need to know about this business. Nobody gets to play it safe in this game."

An alarm, which Treva hadn't been conscious of, cut off abruptly, along with the shouting and distant pulse-fire. A calm descended over the entire ship.

Gosta sped up. "Come on, let's get to the flight deck."

Treva froze as he wondered what happened to the crewmembers of captured ships. If they took the ship, what would they do with all those people? Surely, they couldn't keep that many prisoners. He swallowed. *If they killed them all, those lives are on me.*

CHAPTER 12

TREVA STAYED BEHIND Gosta's larger frame, trying not to gawk as they walked through the ship. He didn't recognize any of the bound men or women, but that didn't stop him from feeling guilty for his part in their capture.

They sat in corridors. Hands and legs secured in metal shackles. It looked very primitive to Treva, though he knew nothing about restraining people.

He wondered again what happened to the prisoners captured by pirates and felt a wave of nausea as a range of possibilities came to mind. *Aren't pirates best known for spacing people? That's what they report on the news.*

Gosta glanced over his shoulder at him. If he had some idea of what Treva was thinking, he did not say anything. The words that formed in Treva's head refused to come out and so he stayed silent.

They'd reached the lounge on the larger ship they had boarded, the *Shockwave*, where Herja joined them. It was the biggest space Treva had seen on either vessel, with a range of different shaped chairs, all in the same shade of grey. Gosta and Herja remained standing and so did Treva.

Herja looked at Treva. "No regrets?"

Despite his earlier train of thought, the question surprised him. "I still have to find my mother." It was a childish answer, but it was genuine.

"At any cost?"

Treva didn't hear any judgment in the question—just interest. Not finding his mother and never knowing what happened to her wasn't something he could live with, especially as he felt responsible.

When he finally answered, it was with the truth. "Yes."

Herja nodded. "You need to be certain about what you want. The cost is often higher than you think."

She turned to greet others who were now drifting in, answering a call that Treva hadn't known about. Kinder was there, but Idra was nowhere to be seen.

When Herja addressed everyone, Treva didn't understand the language. The sound rose and fell until he almost thought that he could understand if only he could concentrate a little more. The odd word sounded vaguely Taran, but not enough to understand the meaning of the sentence.

The pirates gave Herja their full attention, operating with the same military-like precision he'd observed from the moment the first alarm sounded. Treva had thought they would only care about a quick profit; not that they would have any discipline or work ethic. The media portrayed them as vicious killers who enjoyed inflicting pain on hard-working people.

Why didn't I find out more before asking to join a pirate ship? It had been desperation. He could almost hear his mother's exasperated voice, telling him that he needed to think of the consequences before he acted.

Idra slipped in at the back. Treva straightened and tried to make eye contact, but she was too focused on Herja. He tried not to feel disappointed.

Then the corners of her mouth lifted into a smile and she winked at him.

Did I imagine it? No, not all pirates were bad.

Herja was staring at him now, and he found that he could understand her again. "Stay with Gosta."

Treva nodded. He probably should have said something, but he didn't trust his voice or want to draw any more attention to himself than he already had. He had never been in a situation where he had felt more out of his depth, even in his dealings with Nash and the Blue Pixie.

Gosta gestured, and Treva followed him down to the ship's hold.

Two helmeted pirates guarded the door. They stood aside to let them pass when they saw Gosta. Treva blinked rapidly as they entered a bright chamber. Once his eyes adjusted, he saw row upon row of storage containers. A couple had been pried open. Unable to resist, he went to examine the contents.

Inside were small packets. Treva stopped breathing. They were identical to the packets he retrieved with Nash, during his evening runs in what felt like a lifetime ago. The bitterness that he always felt when thinking of Nash was pushed to the back of his mind as he considered what it might mean.

Gosta picked up one of the packages. "The Marco Steyn specialty." He watched Treva through lowered eyelids, no doubt interested in his reaction. "His own brand that's worth a fortune on some planets."

"What do you mean?" Treva asked as he cringed inside at the mention of his father.

Treva remembered handing those same packages over to the manager at Blue Pixie, which meant that he'd been right about the Blue Pixie belonging to his father. It wasn't like he was unaware that the man lied. This was just more confirmation of what he already knew. *So, why does it feel like a knife in the heart all over again?*

It came back to the fact that his mother had been right about the danger that his father posed, yet he had refused to listen. He'd been too eager for that connection with a man he didn't know. Because of his stubborn selfishness, his mother had vanished. It was his fault. More than ever, he needed to get to Red Ghost.

"Steyn's own brand of chemicals, worth far more than they cost to make." Gosta had a fierce expression on his face. "Chemicals that enhance physical prowess. Do you want to try some?"

Treva shook his head. Stars knew he could do with some physical enhancements. He might be young, but even he knew that they wouldn't be illegal unless there was a serious downside.

"Good choice. You're not as stupid as you look."

Treva thought that he'd been pretty stupid, but he wasn't about to point that out.

Gosta picked up one of the packets, testing its weight. "This stuff has wiped out the infrastructure of cities. Once it's available, people can't resist trying it—just once. Everyone has a reason to be stronger and faster, regardless of the consequences."

"What are they?" He had to know how bad it got.

"I can't claim to understand it, but I reckon everyone's heart only beats so many times before it stops. This speeds up everything. It's better to flame out than wash away and all that."

Treva frowned, wondering how many people his father had killed. For a mad moment, he wanted to confront him and ask why. In the end, though, it didn't matter; he'd barely known the man, and now he knew it wasn't worth having him in his life.

Feet pounded on the metal rungs outside. Moments later, Herja strolled in, accompanied by a couple of her trusted people.

She grinned. "Have you cataloged the cargo yet?"

Treva swallowed. Herja rarely looked happy and he had the impression that she was annoyed despite her smile.

"Just about to start," Gosta answered. "It'd be easier if you could get these unlocked so we don't have to break into each one."

"Umm, not sure that's going to be possible."

Treva couldn't stop himself from asking, "What have you done with the crew?"

Herja smiled. "Ah, I see our reputation precedes us. Good, that's how I like it."

Treva felt the blood leave his face. Even though she hadn't answered the question, he feared the worst. It didn't seem to matter what he did, people got hurt. The pirates could have found the ship without his help, but he'd made it easy for them.

Should I tell them I'm Marco Steyn's son? He didn't know what they might do with that information. Ransom him back to his father?

Searching for a distraction from his thoughts while Herja and Gosta had a conversation in that strange language, Treva wandered deeper into the hold, passing row upon row of storage containers.

They can't all be full of drugs.

Unable to find anything except for more of the same, he made his way back. Almost there, he heard Herja's voice. She'd slipped back into the standard New Taran dialect he could understand. He stopped to listen, hardly breathing.

Her voice was low, but it carried along the metal walls. "We will open the boxes, anyway. It will just take less time, if you tell us how."

A man cleared his throat a few times before saying, "I will input the code, if you don't hurt me."

Treva didn't recognize the voice.

"Take him back up."

The sound of feet moving away made Treva start forward, hoping to catch a glimpse of the stranger. He stopped, just out of sight, when he heard Herja speak.

"We don't have any choice."

Worried that the conversation might be about him, Treva didn't dare move

"Our people have to be the priority," Herja continued.

Gosta replied, "I know. I hate the thought of adding to the mess out there but people have a choice. We aren't forcing anyone to use the drugs."

"We need the credits." She sounded as if she were trying to convince herself. "Selling farming equipment isn't going to get us very far."

Gosta replied in the language Treva couldn't understand.

When the two fell silent, Treva took the opportunity to walk back as casually as possible, worried he would be discovered if he stayed where he'd been eavesdropping. To ensure they'd hear him coming, he scuffed his feet on the rubber floor before he turned the corner and came into view of the others.

The idea that he was now in a worse position than if he'd stayed with his father gnawed at the back of his mind. The pirates were proposing to sell the drugs they'd stolen from Marco. It was exactly how he should have expected pirates to act, but he couldn't help feeling disappointed all the same. He wondered if there was anything he could do to stop them. *Those drugs should be off the streets. Have I only made things worse?*

Treva had started to feel as though he fit in on the *Hyperion*, but in the end it didn't matter whether they liked him or not. He wasn't staying. The reality was that the pirate ship had got him away from a tricky situation. He didn't want to get involved in selling drugs, and they weren't going to take him to Red Ghost. He would find another way to get there alone.

Treva resolved to do what Herja wanted and wait for his opportunity. If he got a chance to get rid of the drugs and reduce the harm caused by his father, he would.

CHAPTER 13

KALI PEAKED AROUND the curtain covering the stage. She only had a limited view, but below her, a sea of predominantly male heads bobbed. They seemed to be in groups, though none showed any sign of friendliness; worse, they didn't appear even mildly drunk. She was hoping that they would be too out of it to notice how bad her playing was.

It felt as though the entire planet had come to see them perform, and not one person seemed happy about it. The usual excitement that Kali had experienced from the audiences at every other gig was missing, and that worried her. Most were scowling, which made her sure she was going to feel like a sacrificial victim when she walked on stage in a few minutes.

Mika had said to wait until she played a large venue to get nervous. Well, it looked like this was the night. The stage wasn't the grand structure she'd had in her head for the occasion; it appeared to have been put together from leftover panels and scrap.

The way that Diamond-Boy had talked, this gig would be an entertainment highlight on the planet, and such events were few and far between. Kali was certainly feeling the pressure to make sure everyone had a good time.

What are all these people doing on Red Ghost when there

doesn't appear to be any industry?

Leader and dictator, Diamond-Boy, had made it clear that there was no point trying to find out anything. Nobody was allowed to talk to them—at least not without suffering serious consequences. Kali didn't want to put anyone in harm's way, but she realized she might not have a choice. They were definitely hiding something, and Tregaren's ties to the planet were too strong for her to assume their secrets were wholly unrelated to the missing women.

An impromptu cheer came from the audience, sounding like there were hundreds of people out there. Her heart picked up and she wondered why she kept doing this to herself. *It was a stupid idea to think that I could learn to play this bomaxed bass.*

Her parents would laugh if they knew that she—the former kid who could barely tap her foot to the beat—was pretending to be a musician. Now, she was about to go on stage to play for their lives. *Life certainly has a sense of humor.*

Kali would have been more worried about playing if she wasn't so concerned about Mika, who'd ventured out alone. He'd announced that he was planning to head out to where the men had intercepted them earlier. Kali hadn't wanted him to go, not alone, but there was little she could do to stop him. If she had refused, he would have just snuck off without telling anyone.

The lights went down. Even the hostile audience quieted, faces turning to the stage. Standing in the dark wings, Kali thought she might have become paralyzed. The stage was far bigger than any she'd played on before, and she wondered how the band would keep from losing each other.

She jumped as Owen sidled up to her. "There's a woman who won't be able to resist me after she sees me play tonight."

"No, you can't. Not here." Why couldn't he focus on what was important for once?

He laughed softly. "It's not what you think. I might be able to find out something."

Kali frowned. "Owen, you haven't been drinking."

"I haven't touched a drop since we arrived. That's what I'm trying to tell you; it's time I took some responsibility for saving those women. It's what Luca would have wanted."

Familiar intro music started up. Kali's heart took it as a cue to hammer so hard that it felt as if it was coming out of her chest.

Owen smiled. "Trust me." He stepped back into the darkness.

Kali was left blinking after him. What did he mean—'trust me'? Was the girl he was talking about the same one with the long hair and vicious scowl? She would speak to him afterward.

Kali was aware of Vaira coming up behind, but a shove caught her by surprise. She stumbled forward and glared over her shoulder at a grinning Vaira, but it was too late; she was already on the dark stage.

What is it with these people? I don't need a push to get out there! I can do it. The trouble was, she wasn't certain that she would, not when everything inside her wanted to run away.

Rock star. Rock star. I am a rock star. Kali took a deep breath and stepped over to her spot like she was a real musician—confident, assured, talented.

The intro music was deafening. Then, suddenly, everything was bathed in light. She blinked rapidly, trying to force her eyes to adjust.

Kali concentrated on the bass' strings and was only half-conscious of Owen sprinting across the stage. She stumbled over the rhythm when he stopped in the middle and started swaggering. Sticking out his chest, he glared at the audience. She grinned as he invited them to take a pop at him. Next, she sucked in a breath, remembering how the crowd had looked and afraid that someone would leap onstage to punch him.

Owen continued swaggering around, using the microphone stand to hold himself up. He was acting for the audience—or captors, whichever they were.

She half-watched, mesmerized as Owen lost himself in the music. He didn't seem to care whether the audience responded to him or not. She was unsure whether he knew what he was doing or if for him, it was like playing in a dream. It was little comfort that, sober or off his head, he played better than her.

At least watching him distracted her enough to get her nerves under control. It also helped that the audiences' attention was on Owen and not on her.

Kali attempted to feel her way into the song. The rhythm was there, and when she didn't try too hard, she caught it for fleeting moments. For the first time, she understood the temptation to get drunk to see if it would make her play better. She recognized the danger before she'd even finished the thought. What would Andy do if she became a musician and gave up the TSS? Like that would ever happen!

Her fingers found the elusive notes, and she was elated. For once, she was with the rest of the band until a few seconds later, she stumbled and fell behind again. This time it was easier to find the rhythm. Kali forgot about the danger as she concentrated on this part of her job.

The attitude of the audience had changed. Kali felt it, even while all of her attention was focused on the sound coming from her instrument.

She understood. The crowd had needed to be sure they were in for a good night before they'd commit to enjoying themselves. Owen had worked his magic and it had gone a long way to establishing the band's credibility.

He was sweating so much that a sheen was visible on his forehead and cheeks. He drove himself to higher and higher notes and covered the entire stage numerous times during one song.

Finally, the last song came to an end, and the floor shook

as the audience clapped, cheered, and stamped their feet. Kali hoped the stage wouldn't collapse. Her mouth dropped open, shocked that they had not just liked, but *loved*, the performance. *We did it!* Perhaps she could play the bass, after all.

The noise was deafening. This wasn't the same hostile crowd of ninety minutes ago.

Owen bowed and threw plectrums into the crowd. Caryanne waved as if she was royalty, while Vaira grinned from ear to ear, and Honk tried to pretend that none of it mattered.

The band had to play two encores before the crowd seemed satisfied. By the end of the second, Kali was exhausted from the high level of focus it had taken to play their more obscure songs. She could barely fake playing the bass guitar for the songs she knew well, let alone the others. By the time she stumbled off stage, she would have collapsed straight away if not for a visitor.

Diamond-Boy was flanked by two men a step behind him. The broad grin on his face didn't extend all the way to his eyes, bringing back Kali's worries in a rush. She couldn't help thinking how uncertain life was. *One-minute things are going great, and the next...*

Kali said, "What's your real name?"

She had no idea why she'd asked the question. It was hardly the most pressing issue. Maybe she was trying to deflect him from whatever he was going to say.

As expected, Diamond-Boy didn't answer but moved closer with eyes fixed on Kali. The two men behind remained where they were as if they'd rehearsed the same scenario many times. Diamond-Boy stepped into a spotlight of colored light and had to shade his face with one hand.

He leaned into the shadow. "Everyone enjoyed the gig so much that I'm asking you to stay a little longer."

It was not a request. The band hadn't planned to be so popular and now, Kali wondered if it had simply bought them some time or trapped them indefinitely.

They would have to free the *Sepiantia* from its docking locks somehow, as well as find out what Red Ghost was hiding. It wouldn't be easy. Kali wondered if it was too late to try to cultivate some trust with Diamond-Boy. First, he had to believe that they were exactly what they said they were. That did not mean agreeing to his every demand.

Kali smiled. "Have I got this right? We came in good faith to do a job, but now you're telling us we can't leave when we please?"

Diamond-Boy looked around, taking in the faces of the band, one at a time while Kali held her breath. "Where is your manager?" When nobody answered, he smiled slowly. "You lost him."

Kali shrugged.

He leaned forward, his smile now reaching his eyes— but filling them with venom, not mirth. "That's okay, because *I* found him."

Oh, no. Mika, what have you done? Kali's heart sank further. *So much for convincing him that they we're just a band.*

"Is Mika okay?" Caryanne's voice came from behind her.

"That depends on you. Are you going to give us any trouble?"

Before anybody could answer, Kali asked, "How long do you want us to stay, exactly?"

"Oh, I don't know... perhaps a couple of weeks? Or perhaps, months. Until this lot gets bored with you." He grinned, and she had the unpleasant feeling that he had no intention of ever letting them go—at least not alive.

When they were no longer useful, they really would be in danger. For now, it was best to go along with things, until they could find a way to change the power dynamic.

"Can we see Mika?"

"Behave yourselves, and I'll see what I can do."

CHAPTER 14

HERJA STARED OUT of the viewport as they approached the
Vector. At a guess, the ship was waiting for its jump-drive
to cool down. She was shocked that the ship was precisely
where it was supposed to be.

Treva's information had seemed too good to be true.
Herja had learned to be wary of easy solutions, and the
ability to locate targets was straight out of a dream. And, to
think that she almost sent him away. The only reason she'd
listened to him at all was that she'd seen Steyn's reaction
on realizing that the boy was present during their last
contact.

The odds of the *Vector* being in this location by chance
were so remote that it wasn't worth considering. The
Vector was the second ship they'd found using Treva's data,
proving beyond the shadow of a doubt that his information
was reliable.

If they could find Steyn's ships whenever they wanted,
they had a chance at survival. Herja just needed to take
advantage of the situation before Steyn discovered Treva's
theft and changed his routes.

Would Steyn know who had betrayed him? It depended
on how well Treva had covered his tracks, but since he was
only a boy, it was unlikely that they'd have long.

What will Steyn do when he discovers that Treva is the culprit?

If she was right about his identity, Steyn was bound to feel betrayed, and they couldn't anticipate how he'd react. When he found out who was harboring Treva, the boy would rapidly become a liability. Although, she supposed that Steyn had enough reason to come after them regardless of who was on board. There the added complication that Treva was telling the truth about his mother. She could read that much from talking to him.

The woman was missing and Treva wanted to find her. It wasn't hard to imagine what might have happened. Perhaps, she ought to find out why Treva was so convinced that there were any answers on Red Ghost. She'd never been to the planet but everyone knew of its reputation. They would need a good reason to risk having contact with the gang that controlled the small world. Herja paused— was she actually considering it?

For now, she had more pressing concerns, and she still had to decide what to do. She paced the flight deck. Although Treva's information might become redundant at any time, it was too soon to carry out another raid, which was precisely why she was considering it. Nobody would imagine there'd be another attack so soon after the last one. Herja had built her reputation on doing what was least expected.

Always be unpredictable.

A magnified image of the *Vector* filled the front viewport, though it was only from a distance that they could appreciate the scale of the kilometer-long vessel. Its size was a vivid reminder of the implications of getting the attack wrong.

According to Treva's information, the *Vector* carried weapons and valuables as opposed to drugs that she didn't want to sell. Although, what constituted valuables, she didn't know. It could be precious metals or food but if so, why not label it? They would find out soon enough because she'd made up her mind. For better or worse, they would attack the unsuspecting ship.

Herja couldn't have asked for a better crew, and if anyone could pull off the raid, they could. Gosta claimed responsibility for the discipline on board, but she knew better; they were the best people and operated with such efficiency because they were intrinsically motivated. They had a purpose.

Treva was the one unknown factor, which was why she'd assigned Gosta to keep an eye on him. She couldn't presume he was what he appeared to be, even though her gut—which never let her down—told her that he was. Despite the resources needed to monitor him, so far, he had proved worth the risk to keep around.

Herja activated the comm. "Gosta, where are you?"

He didn't respond, but a few seconds later, he appeared with Treva in tow. "You called, my queen?"

She raised an eyebrow. "Less sarcasm and more action." Turning her attention to Treva, she said, "Has anyone explained what's happening?"

He shook his head, which didn't surprise her. Everyone was too loyal to let anything slip without her permission. He was ridiculously innocent as he met her gaze, but the boy took far too much notice to entirely fool her with that act.

"We are going after ship five on your list."

"*Vector*," Treva said from memory, proving that he warranted watching. After a pause, he looked down at the deck. Herja smiled; it was too late, and he knew it.

"That's right, but what I need to know is, how accurate is your data?"

Treva's face reddened as if she had questioned his integrity. She watched with interest to see what he would say.

He frowned, appearing to consider her question. "As far as I know, unless something got changed because of... you know... the last ship, it is correct."

It was a good answer, since he didn't claim to know everything, which wouldn't have been realistic with so much out of his control. Herja was not ready to trust Treva, mainly because she had a feeling that he wasn't being totally honest with her. It showed in nervousness when there was no reason to be worried.

"Alert the crew. We're going to board."

If Gosta was surprised, he didn't show it. He'd probably guessed what she was planning since sometimes he showed an uncanny insight into the inner workings of her brain. One morning she was going to stay in bed and get some much-needed rest while he ran the ship.

Herja activated a warning signal, which turned the lighting throughout the ship to red. It would alert the crew that they were near an enemy vessel. Most would guess their next move, but to be safe, Gosta would pass on her orders.

Treva stood as if waiting for her to tell him what to do. He probably was, but she didn't have a job to give him. It wasn't as if he had any useful skills, and so, she ignored him for now.

She hated waiting. When there wasn't anything to do, it made her feel out of control and a little anxious.

They needed to approach the other vessel quietly, running as dark and as stealthily as they could without possessing military stealth tech. Their spoofed signals only went so far, but it was surprisingly easy to sneak up on a vessel in the black when they had no reason to be on alert.

Gosta sent out a simple message to the crew that everyone would understand, "Ready." He left the flight deck to ensure that all hands were where they should be.

When they were close enough, Herja opened an audio-only communication with the *Vector*. "This is the pirate ship *Hyperion*. You will power down, unlock your doors, and welcome us on board." She paused, knowing from experience that her demands would be ignored.

Steyn's captain would be too afraid of his employer to

surrender without a fight. Herja had never had a ship concede to her demands at the first try, which was why she was surprised when the *Vector* powered down before she could issue a single threat.

She should have been elated. This situation had the potential to be over quickly, without risking any of her crew. Why, then, did every cell in her body go on high-alert?

The *Vector* couldn't fire without powering back up, and that would take a few minutes. In that time, the ship would be vulnerable. They had complied without any attempt to resist and so, she had to give them the benefit of the doubt. What else could she do?

"Why did they surrender so easily?" Treva asked, staring at the viewscreen like it displayed answers.

The boy. She had forgotten about him. Even he saw that it didn't make sense to comply so easily. The fact that he'd pointed it out took his standing up a notch.

Gosta came in at a run. "It has to be a trap."

Herja laughed, despite the adrenaline pumping through her body. The universe was screaming 'trap', so what were their options?

They could engage their independent jump drive and get away as far and as fast as possible, completely untraceable. It would damage their reputation, but that would be the sensible thing to do. The problem with that course of action is that she would have no choice but to sell the drugs sitting in their hold. Herja didn't want to put the stuff out there, despite the financial upside.

"We have to go ahead."

Gosta scowled. "Are you sure?"

He wouldn't usually question her in the middle of a raid, and especially not in front of others. Doing so in front of the boy demonstrated the depth of his concern.

She let it go. Gosta was the one person who'd earned the right to ask questions for the sake of their crew and their people.

She nodded once, even though it was a lie. The truth was, she *wasn't* sure. But, as the captain, she had no choice but to convince others that she knew what she was doing.

— — —

Treva hung back, hoping that he didn't have to board the *Vector* as he had with the raid of the *Shockwave*. The smell of burnt circuitry, shouts and screams, and rifle-fire had stayed with him. It was too real, and he couldn't shake the feeling that whatever happened, whoever it happened to, it was partly his fault.

Treva preferred to remain on the flight deck where it felt safe and he could know what was happening. It seemed that Herja had other ideas. So, Treva reluctantly trailed behind Gosta, yet again, as he was led into the depths of the *Hyperion*.

He wanted to ask what was happening, but he kept his mouth shut because Gosta's shoulders were bunched tighter than usual. The mood very different from Treva's last experience of piracy.

Treva had heard the exchange between Herja and Gosta, and he understood that the *Vector* had not behaved as expected; they had surrendered too quickly.

Aside from the vessel's odd response, it surprised him that Herja wanted to attack another ship so soon after their first interception. *Are they really that greedy?* Perhaps they were simply doing what pirates do, how would he know?

Currently, the lower decks of the *Hyperion* were full of activity, with people scurrying in every direction. A few were already suited up, but most were in the process of getting ready.

Treva waited for instructions to get into a suit. He felt relieved, and then guilty, when he overheard Gosta tell someone that he would remain on the *Hyperion* this time.

Treva counted eleven in the designated boarding party—more than half of the *Hyperion*'s complement. He didn't know how many would be on the *Vector*, but it was a big ship and must have a decent-sized crew. He worried that there wouldn't be enough pirates to take over the ship, and then a dissenting voice flipped his concerns to be that the pirates *would* succeed in taking over the ship. It was true that the pirates had deadly armaments like plasma rifles, but the *Vector*'s crew was likely similarly armed.

He scanned the faces of everyone in the boarding party as they checked their pressure-suits, dismayed to spot Kinder and Idra amongst them. His new friends' faces were set in determination.

Idra gave him a small smile, but it was strained. Treva nodded, wanting to tell her not to go; of course, he couldn't, and she didn't have any more choice than him. Again, he felt responsible for whatever was about to happen and hoped nobody would get hurt.

Gosta was too busy overseeing preparations to pay any attention to Treva, so he went to look out of one of the viewports. Space made his jaw fall open every single time. His mind struggled to accept that the vast expanse was real.

They crept closer to the *Vector*. The *Hyperion* maneuvered with incredible precision until the two ships were parallel, at which point, an umbilical was winched out and attached to the outer hatch of the other vessel.

"Secure," the computer announced.

All eleven pirates entered the flexible, fragile corridor one at a time. Treva locked eyes briefly with Kinder who gave him a salute, and then with Idra who looked too nervous to smile, as they passed by where he stood.

As the last pirate entered the umbilical, the *Hyperion*'s airlock hatch closed and there was a hiss as it sealed behind them. Treva gasped at the finality of the act.

Gosta appeared at his side. "A precaution, that's all."

Now it was too quiet. Gosta looked around, like he expected to find something, before setting off in a hurry. Treva supposed that he should follow.

They returned to the flight deck, where Herja was

braced against the console as she stared intently at the screen, muttering to herself. She went quiet as soon as she noticed their arrival.

Gosta stood stiffly. "Everything is going to plan."

Herja shook her head. "I don't like it. Everything is powered up, ready, but our people are too vulnerable over there."

As they neared the console, Treva heard static. It was an open channel to the boarding party. Herja would know as soon as anything went wrong.

Idra's soft voice came through, and his chest clenched, "Affirmative. On A-deck."

She sounded confident and professional, but he could tell by the space around her words that she was nervous. He strained to hear anything else, but there was only more static for a minute, followed by the odd word that made no sense to him. Idra didn't speak again.

Treva picked out Kinder's voice, sounding more serious than he'd ever heard him before, with none of his usual banter. It drove home the seriousness of the situation.

Treva focused on Gosta speaking to Herja, "I know you want to be with them, but we agreed not to do anything stupid. You are needed to make the decisions."

She grunted, looking unhappy. From what little Treva knew about her, he understood she wanted to be in the middle of the action, not safe here; Treva, on the other hand, was happy to be away from the thick of it.

Herja glanced at Gosta. "If there's any sign that the ship is powering up, we hit them with all we've got. I thought about doing it, anyway, but if I get the timing wrong, it'd only make matters worse." At his concerned expression, she said, "We have a solid plan, and I intend to stick to it."

Treva went to look out of the viewport again, but there wasn't much to see with the *Vector* so close; its smooth, silver-hued hull blocked the stars.

The comm crackled, and someone shouted, "We're

under attack!"

Treva didn't recognize the voice, but his heart picked up speed, knowing that Idra and Kinder were involved. He returned to stand next to Gosta.

Herja's knuckles were white where she gripped the console. His eyes flicked to the readings. Treva could see that the *Vector* was still powered-down.

Herja hit something on the console. "They can't do anything now the Catch-All is activated."

Gosta moved to stand beside her while Treva moved closer to the monitor, eager to watch the view from the pirates' head-cams. Pulse-fire zipped across the screen. It was difficult to see anything with movement coming from multiple viewpoints. The video was dark and confused. There were flashes of the bulkheads, overhead, and deck along with glimpses of people running.

Treva stared with wide eyes, trying to hold back and not touch the monitor. Idra might die to make Herja rich. It was messed up. He'd known that there were risks to boarding, but it was so much worse hearing and seeing the combat play out.

An alarm sounded, startling everyone.

Herja cursed. "Another ship is closing in. This is my fault. I knew everything felt wrong and decided to go through with it, anyway, because I didn't want to sell those foking drugs."

Herja didn't want to sell the drugs! So, that was why they had attacked this ship so soon after the last one. It wasn't out of greed. These were nothing like the pirates Treva had expected to deal with; they had an ethical code. All he wanted at that moment was for Idra and the others to get away safely.

It wasn't just Herja that felt guilty. If he hadn't given them the information, they wouldn't have been in the situation at all. As a kid, everyone expected Treva to make mistakes, but they should be minor ones that he could live with—drinking too much alcohol or dating the wrong girls—not the sort where people got killed.

Treva couldn't stand the thought of never seeing Idra and Kinder again. It was selfish, but they had been turning into proper friends. Not like Nash, with his lies and manipulation. He could barely breathe at the thought that they were going to die.

Treva remembered the locked hatch. "They can't get back, can they?"

The boarding party's comm crackled again. A weak sound came through, as if something was constricting it. "We're pinned down." Shouts and pulse-fire sounded in the background.

Treva looked at Herja, hoping that she'd know what to do, but she looked as stricken as he felt. Gosta held his head in his hands.

A voice came over the general comm. "This is Captain Vaughn of the *Vector*. You have thirty-two minutes to surrender or be blasted into pieces. Your crew now belong to me. They face questioning before being terminated." The communication ended as abruptly as it'd begun.

In the following silence, Treva was frozen. Herja had sent her crew across to the other ship, and was now in an impossible situation.

Should she abandon them to save the rest? Treva didn't envy her position.

"They won't really kill them, will they?" Treva looked at Gosta and then Herja. He knew his question was stupid, but Idra and Kinder were on that ship. He didn't want them to die. "We can't leave."

Herja glanced at him. "We don't normally abandon our people, but there are another ten people, as well as us, to consider here. More importantly, we can't afford to lose the *Hyperion*."

Treva scrunched his eyes shut. "There must be another way." As he said it, an idea sprang to mind.

He could save them. His father would want him back, no matter what he had done. Treva was certain of it. Marco had gone to a lot of trouble to find him in the first place, and then he'd taken action to get his mother out of the way.

Treva didn't know what his father would do to him once he got him back, but he suspected that his father had plans for him all along. Now, it didn't matter what they were; he could do something worthwhile and save Idra and the others.

He swallowed. Even if it killed him, he had to try. "Let me speak to the captain."

Herja stared at him, but there wasn't the slightest bit of surprise on her face. She moved aside so that he could get to the communications console. It was set to audio-only, but she switched over to video without asking and stepped out of range.

A high-pitched alarm sounded.

Gosta leaned over the console and silenced it. "Shite. The newcomer has weapons locked on us. Whatever you're going to do, hurry up."

The viewscreen cleared, revealing a man with black hair and grey-streaked black facial hair. "Are you willing to surrender?" he asked before blinking in surprise. Treva didn't know if his reaction was because of Treva's young age or whether he recognized him. Captain Vaughn frowned. "What is this?"

Treva's hands were shaking so badly that he tightened them into fists. He had to do this to save his friends. "Do you know who I am?" His voice came out steady, which was a small miracle because his insides had gone to mush.

The captain narrowed his gaze but remained silent, which made it clear that he knew who Treva was, else he would have terminated the comm link. For some reason, Captain Vaughn seemed unwilling to admit he recognized Treva.

Herja muted the transmission, murmuring from the side. "This might not work." She fiddled with the controls. "He might not want to give up his prize."

Gosta fixed Treva with a fierce stare. "Get rid of the

other ship, else none of us stand a chance."

"Are you recording this conversation?" Treva asked.

Herja smiled. "I am now." She must have activated something before she unmuted the comm link, nodding for Treva to continue.

"Captain Vaughn, it might help you make up your mind to know this conversation is being recorded. I have already sent a message to my father." The lie tripped off Treva's tongue far too easily.

Captain Vaughn glowered. "What do you want?"

"I will hand myself over to you on one condition: that you let everyone go. You can reunite me with my father. I imagine he will be pleased."

Herja was staring at him so hard that he felt the side of his face growing warm, threatening to break his composure. She could be thinking anything, from hating him to appreciating what he was doing for her.

"You give me no choice," Captain Vaughn stated. "Your father might not be pleased to discover where I found you."

Oh no, he's definitely not happy about the change of plan. Treva couldn't even begin to think about that. "I will come across to the *Vector* as soon as the other ship leaves."

The captain laughed. "I won't leave my ship open to attack. Since you've decided to be difficult, you now have *two* minutes until the *Gritter* opens fire—unless you can convince them that you are, in fact, Steyn's son."

They can't attack us! Treva knew he was deluding himself if he thought for a second that any of them were safe. Surely, he could convince them of his identity, but then what?

Captain Vaughn thought for a moment before continuing, "Let's compromise. The *Gritter* will hang back while we have a little heart-to-heart. Only once I have established who you are, for certain, will the individuals who so rudely invaded my ship be allowed to leave."

Treva hesitated, trying to decide how to respond. Of course, Captain Vaughn wouldn't leave his ship at the mercy of the pirates, but he didn't see how his terms were much of a compromise.

Herja stepped into view. "We will allow you to power up your weapons. The other ship goes, and you permit our crew to return to the *Hyperion*."

"Not before I have the boy."

Herja hesitated, but Treva could see that Captain Vaughn was not going to concede that point.

Treva stepped forward. "It's okay. I'll go." There was no choice now; the captain couldn't leave him on the *Hyperion* without having to answer to his father.

Herja stepped back, respecting his choice. Perhaps she thought that it was inevitable that Treva would return to his father.

Captain Vaughn nodded, still frowning. He turned away. Just before the comm link was severed, Treva heard him shouting orders to his crew.

Gosta looked at Herja. "The effectiveness of the Catch-All's command overrides was diminishing, anyway."

She nodded. "Yes, but he didn't need to know that."

Treva was hardly aware of the *Gritter* moving away, although its weapons remained locked on the *Hyperion*. Another alarm sounded as the *Vector* locked weapons on them, as well.

Treva turned toward Herja. "Won't they just close in as soon as I'm gone?"

She snorted. "As soon as you're safely across. We won't be waiting around, so don't worry about us. Just stay safe, and say 'hi' to your father for me." She winked.

Treva followed Gosta to the airlock hatch. There was no time before someone hustled him into the cold, quiet umbilical without even a pressure-suit to protect him. *The things we do for friends.*

CHAPTER 15

TREVA HAD NO choice but to go forward, but it was hard to take that first step in the low-gravity passageway between the ships. His legs felt heavier than ever before, despite almost floating, and the effort needed to lift one was almost more than he could find. If he could, he would have made a single moment stretch out until it stopped time, just so that he didn't have to take that second step into the umbilical connecting the *Hyperion* and *Vector*.

It could have been seconds, minutes, or days before he found the courage to move forward. Once he was moving, it was easier to pretend that everything would be okay.

Nobody had threatened him, and he didn't believe that his father would kill him, but in a way, he wished that he was dead. He had made a decision that meant giving up his right to choose, as well as any hope of finding his mother. Worse, part of him was relieved, and he was sure that made him a coward.

His breath misted the air, and it dawned on him that he might actually freeze in the makeshift corridor if he didn't hurry. The hatch at the other end was near to his head. Railings had been set into the outer hull of the ship for this sort of eventuality. Treva would have to climb them to get through the opening, but at the moment, the hatch was closed and locked from the other side. If they didn't open it soon, there was a chance he would die from hypothermia. Perhaps that had been someone's plan all along. Now, his earlier thought about wanting to be dead felt foolish.

Treva blew on his hands in a pathetic attempt to stop the tremor that had started. Then, he reached up and banged on the hatch. "Hey, open up!"

He had no idea if they could hear anything on the other side, but he had to try something. Could he go back? Just as he was about to turn around the way he'd come, the floor vibrated and there was a loud clang. The hatch swung open, revealing a figure wearing a complete EVA suit. There wasn't enough of the person visible to tell whether it was a man or woman.

Heart hammering so hard it might explode, Treva followed the person's gestures and climbed the railings as fast as he could, despite not knowing what waited beyond.

As soon as he was through the hatch, the figure swung the door closed and locked it with a finality that made Treva shiver inside. The gravity began to normalize, and he stood ridged, trying to hold himself together, not daring to speak.

The figure didn't say anything. He or she gestured for Treva to follow and went ahead.

Aren't they going to check me for weapons? Not that he had any, but he had anticipated being searched and it was a surprise to be ignored.

They exited the airlock into an interior corridor. The warm air that surrounded his body was starting to thaw him out. Although, it didn't affect his icy core where the cold had permeated deep during his time in the umbilical. Although Treva had no experience of being a hostage, it worried him that they weren't treating him as if he was valuable in any way. It was as if they didn't care if he died.

Something crashed against the hatch. An alarm sounded, but when Treva tried to turn back to see, his escort grabbed his arm and pulled him away. The alarm stopped as if it had never begun.

Treva tried to focus on anything to distract himself from his morbid thoughts. The ship was probably a standard model, but since Treva had so little experience with space travel, he couldn't say for sure.

"Hurry." The instructions came through a small speaker and distorted the sound enough that he still wasn't sure if the suited person was male or female.

Treva decided that he would be more comfortable with a woman who might be less likely to shoot him. He had no idea whether that was true or not, but he was happy to believe it for now.

Treva wondered if he could get her to talk to him. Perhaps get her name and try to get on her good side. That might be a bit ambitious for his first time as a captive, but he had nothing to lose at this stage.

He eyed the plasma gun strapped to her hip. It would be best to remember that she was armed and probably a lot more dangerous than she appeared. It couldn't hurt to initiate some conversation though, could it?

"I'm Treva."

She was three steps ahead, utterly unconcerned about having her back to him. Right, what was he going to do? Hit her over the head? She was wearing a helmet, and he wasn't a trained soldier.

It surprised him when she answered, "I know who you are—Marco Steyn's brat who thought that it'd be a good idea to play pirate. Well, don't get any ideas about getting a hero's welcome. You'll be passed over to your father as soon as we can. Until then, we have a comfortable holding cell with your name on it."

Treva's cheeks burned at the realization that everyone would think that he'd run off for an adventure with pirates like a child. He thought about trying to explain about his mother but she was too far ahead now. It was just as well; he could do without spilling his most painful secrets to a stranger who might just turn out to be an enemy. At least he'd found out that it was a woman.

She hadn't even waited for him. That was how little she viewed him as a threat. Sure, they might lock him up because they couldn't be bothered to deal with him, not because they thought that he might cause havoc if left free.

Well, we'll see about that.

Treva wasn't going to let them lock him in a holding cell without a fight. Whatever it took, he wouldn't become another victim for these people to use against his friends.

He was sure that the *Gritter* would attack the *Hyperion* as soon as they confirmed that he was no longer on board. Herja had to be planning something.

Mom is counting on me. Treva needed to tell her that he was sorry he hadn't believed her and explain how he'd walked into his father's trap. He refused to believe that she wasn't coming back.

As they continued down one corridor after another, Treva was starting to feel more angry than afraid. "Wait, what about the others? When are you going to let them go?"

The figure laughed. "They won't be going anywhere."

Vaughn lied. Of course, he lied.

Did Herja know that he would? Treva had sacrificed himself for nothing if his friends were going to die anyway. There was nothing he could do and nobody cared. This had been a mistake.

He jogged to keep up. A wide, dark corridor came into view on his left. It was like a dark hole, different to the bright white surrounding him. Feeling that there was nothing to lose, he plunged down it. His footsteps loud in the confined space as he ran.

Nothing feels real.

The stress must have gotten to him. He'd acted on a stupid impulse and this might lead to a dead-end. Except it didn't feel silly, it felt like an opportunity to take some control back. At the very least, he wasn't acting how they expected, else they would have kept a closer check on him.

It was strange that the corridor was so dark. It wasn't

pitch black, as it had seemed after the bright lights in the adjacent halls; rather, there was some illumination coming from higher up, but he couldn't see further than a meter in front of him.

Treva had taken the chance that the woman wouldn't shoot him in the back. He didn't think they would risk killing him.

What's the worst that could happen? Treva didn't want to discover the answer to that. He ran faster.

A sensible part of his brain suggested that he be careful and not make things more difficult than they already were, but he had a feeling it was too late.

I might as well embrace the reckless part of me.

"Hey!" The shout came from behind and was followed by a conversation at a lower volume, but Treva could only make out his captor say a few words. "He's run off."

"You should have had eyes on him at all times." A deeper voice drifted down the corridor. "Nobody's allowed down there."

That's right. Argue a bit longer and give me some more time.

Treva searched the walls and ceiling for an escape route. Not knowing anything about spaceships, he thought he might find a duct or a chute he could crawl into, but there was nothing. That left him with no choice except to follow the corridor.

He finally turned a corner just before hearing the dreaded sound of booted feet running behind him. His pursuers probably had technology that let them see in the dark, which put him at a major disadvantage.

Please let their suits weigh them down.

Treva was the fastest in his age group at school, plus running around with Nash had increased his endurance—not that he would give Nash credit for anything. Although, too much had happened to dwell on petty grudges.

Ahead, Treva could see that the corridor was fully lit. Once he reached it, he found that the light was soft, almost like it was designed with relaxation in mind.

There was a red sign on the deck underfoot in case someone missed the ones on both walls: 'Authorized Personnel Only'.

Ignoring it, Treva continued on, more cautious now and with an additional flutter in his stomach. Hazard warning signs appeared intermittently on both walls and deck, adding to his discomfort. Some said: 'Danger – Hazardous Lifeform'.

Treva didn't know what to make of the last one. Shouldn't it read 'materials' rather than 'lifeform'?

The footsteps behind faltered. "Of all places, why did he have to run down here?"

Treva wondered if they knew that he could hear their conversation as clearly as if they were next to him. Other than that first 'hey', they hadn't bothered to call out to him. Were they frightened of alerting someone, or something, else?

Further on, the number of warning signs were starting to make him consider turning back. The written statements were accompanied by symbols which clearly indicated death.

This can't be good.

There was no choice but to continue on the same route. A red sign read: 'Stop, by order of the Keeper'.

Stars! What's a Keeper?

Treva thought his eyes were playing tricks when he saw a man in the middle of the corridor. He almost tripped when he realized that the figure was real.

Small and dark, he wore what appeared to be a multicolored leather jacket sewn together like a patchwork. For some reason, his broad smile scared Treva as much as if he'd been pointing a weapon at him. He was too happy to see a stranger in a restricted zone.

What have I gotten myself into?

Treva hesitated, but the man's small stature and unusual dress made him seem like a safer option than his pursuers. Though, with wild eyes and dark hair curled tight to his head, he perhaps wasn't as good a prospect as Treva had hoped. As he got close, a strong floral scent emanated from the man that was bound to linger in Treva's nostrils for days.

The man tried to step forward, wobbled, and stumbled into Treva, who wasn't sure whether it was on purpose. When Treva continued to try to move past, the man kept pace, leaning into his side as if they were good friends or family.

"Stop, in the name of the Keeper."

At least, Treva thought that's what the man had said. The man's words were slurred and muddy, forcing Treva to concentrate.

"She doesn't like strangers. If you scare her, everyone will die." He grinned as if that would be a good thing.

Treva peered over the man's shoulder into the darkened room. All he could make out was subtle light cast from an active force field. Everything else was black.

Treva squinted, trying to let his eyes adjust. "What's in there?"

"I can't tell you." The man bumped against him again. "I'm not supposed to, but then why would I care about the rules? Pesta is very dangerous." He wagged a finger in Treva's face. "Don't upset her."

Treva wanted to ask why the door was wide open if the lifeform was so dangerous. Surely, they needed some basic safety protocols in place even if the *Vector* wasn't an official carrier of whatever it was. This was his father's ship after all. Then he remembered the signs on the floor and walls. Well, they wouldn't stop anyone, would they?

The man was rambling, and Treva caught the odd word. "Nobody ever comes to check... she... turned me into soup."

"That's what I'm here for," Treva interrupted, not knowing where the idea came from, but he went with it. "Captain Vaughn sent me to see if you were okay."

The man's eyes narrowed, and it was immediately clear

he didn't believe that Treva had come to check on him.

"It's true. I know I'm young, but..." he said the first thing that came into his head, "that's why they picked me. Because, most likely, Captain Vaughn wanted me out of the way."

The man tilted his head back until it faced the ceiling. He seemed to be listening. Treva checked, but there was nothing up there other than smooth metal.

In a last-ditch attempt, Treva said, "Why else would I be here?"

The man took in a long, audible breath, shuddering before returning his attention to Treva. "Well, that's the question, isn't it?"

They stared at each other in silence. Treva was unsure if opening his mouth would make things better or worse.

"I think you're in trouble."

Treva heard it then. Shouts from the corridor behind.

The man watched him. "Don't worry. They're too afraid to pass the first warning sign, regardless of their orders to pursue you."

There's nothing to be afraid of, is there? It isn't as if anyone is going to be killed now.

Since it was going to take a phenomenal amount of energy to sell his story, and Treva was too tired to carry on lying, he decided to tell the truth and see what happened. "Okay, honestly? I've escaped from the *Vector*'s soldiers and want to find my... friends." He was going to say 'crew', but that would lead to more questions. Besides, they *were* becoming his friends, even though he'd only known them for a short time.

The man stared at him for a few seconds, nodded, and turned away. He started to head into a room to the right— thankfully, not into the dark chamber with the dangerous creature.

Treva needed to know more. "What about the... what did you call it?"

The man chuckled. "Pesta. You can call *her* the destroyer

of planets."

Treva laughed. Was that supposed to be a joke? He must be exaggerating, but the man was already walking into the room. Treva followed, not knowing where they were going or whether he would turn Treva over to Vaughn.

"Wait." Treva ran to catch him up. "What are you doing?"

"Oh, I'm going to find your friends." The man led Treva into a small, cluttered room. "Now, that I know we share an enemy, I'm willing to help."

"What? Wait, why would you do that?"

"Let's just say, I need to protect Pesta from feeling threatened enough to destroy us all."

"Pesta is a type of weapon?"

The man frowned. "It's both her name and her description. She doesn't like the light. Thinks she's ugly, you see." He leaned forward to whisper in Treva's ear. "You won't be able to see her, but pretend that you can. It's a kindness."

Treva looked across as if he could see through the wall to the dark room, thinking that it was just as well he wasn't alone since he'd watched way too many horror films. Although, this man was creepy in his own way.

"What are you doing now?" Treva asked, paying attention to the piles of real paper stacked around them.

The man ignored the question, but it looked like he wasn't going to stop talking. "That's why I intercepted you. I don't want you to think I agree with what these barbarians are doing.

"I haven't had any choice until now, but that might change with you. I don't need to know your intentions. I just need you to cause chaos. You see, they let me stay with Pesta because I can control her, which reduces the risk of a misfire. She's one of a kind."

Treva listened to the flow of information, still unsure about whether the man was going to help, no matter what he claimed. But, whatever happened, it was better than being locked in a cell.

Inside the cabin, printed documents covered every surface. Treva touched one of the piles next to him, loving the texture of real paper. There were books and loose sheets in every size, with no order to anything. He'd never seen so much in one place.

The man grunted as he tossed pages left and right. Treva stayed well back, hovering in the doorway. There wasn't enough room for both of them with only one seat.

Eventually, after a grunt of what sounded like pleasure, the man returned, holding up a rolled sheet. It was larger than the others, and he looked around as if searching for somewhere to lay it out. Finally, he settled for the top of a storage container, which he cleared before smoothing out the paper. The man, whatever his name was, used one elbow to keep it from rolling closed.

He leaned over the sheet, and Treva went to peer over his shoulder. He had no idea what was going on and considered making a break for it, but where would he go? Nobody had come for him, but that didn't mean they weren't waiting, knowing that hunger or desperation would drive him out at some point.

The man traced something with the forefinger of his right hand. "This is it."

Treva stared at the squiggle. It meant nothing and certainly didn't warrant the triumph in the man's voice.

"This is a map of the ship—the only one I have on paper. You see, I made sure to get hold of it before Vaughn brought me. I knew they wouldn't want me to know how to get out. But nobody checked all my papers. Some people don't understand the value of hardcopies!"

Did he bring all this just to hide that one map? Treva had no idea how he had acquired a paper map of the ship in the first place, and he didn't care. He was just glad not to have to read it, because he couldn't make any sense of the lines and squiggles; he would have been lost in no time.

Treva's handheld might have been able to provide clear directions through the vessel, but he'd left it with Gosta on the *Hyperion*. At the time, it had seemed preferable to letting his father's people potentially get hold of it.

Since it looked like they'd be sticking together, it was time for introductions. "Hi, I'm Treva."

"Oh, yes, sorry. It's Macadema, but call me Mac."

They turned their palms upward to each other in greeting. Treva decided that he didn't have much to lose by trusting Mac for the time being.

"Once you free your friends, what are you going to do? Blow up the ship?"

Treva hadn't thought beyond remaining free, never mind rescuing anybody else. He shrugged, feeling way out of his depth.

Mac eyed him. "How old are you?"

Treva couldn't see any advantage in lying. "I'm fifteen."

"I thought so. You're a bit young to be a pirate, aren't you?"

How does he know about the pirate ship? Did they announce the boarding? Treva chose his words carefully. "I guess pirates come in all ages." Mac knew a lot about him, but the situation was still too complicated to even attempt to explain everything. "Are you going to help me or not?"

"I said so, didn't I?"

Treva needed any help he could get. If he could free the others, they might be able to do something. Although he didn't have any idea how he was going to free everyone, if there was a chance, he had to try.

Mac clutched the map in his hands. "Pesta cannot help us." He rummaged in a box before giving Treva a metal bracelet. "Here, put this on so the sensors won't be able to see you."

Treva slipped it on his wrist. "Where are we going?"

Mac set off and literally disappeared. One second he was walking ahead down the corridor, and the next he'd vanished.

Treva turned in a full circle, checking the entire area. He slowly approached the exact spot where he'd last seen Mac. There was nothing but a blank wall.

Macadema's head appeared, causing Treva to stumble backward as the little man laughed. "Hurry up." He disappeared again, but this time Treva could hear his laughter.

Treva approached the wall, there was... something... there. An opening, which was concealed by the angle of the wall. Once he knew where it was, it was obvious.

He stepped into a dark, narrow corridor. The walls were made out of metal and were shiny like mirrors, unlike anything that he'd seen so far. Treva thought that it might be some sort of route for the cleaning and repair bots to get around the ship, based on the track marks along the floor.

As he went in further, it became darker until it was pitch black. Treva could see a light ahead, which had to be Mac. He hurried to catch up, hoping that the floor was even because he couldn't see his feet.

A beam of red light shined from a flashlight in Macadema's hands; given how dark Pesta's holding chamber was, it made sense that he'd carry some form of illumination. As long as Treva stayed near to him, he could see their immediate surroundings.

"What about Pesta? Will she be okay without you?"

"She'll be fine for the short time it'll take me to find your friends." Mac used the flashlight to illuminate the map.

Treva was struck by the way he talked with such confidence. As if it was certain that they would free the others.

Despite not knowing Mac, Treva liked him. It wasn't just his willingness to help someone he'd just met, it was his commitment to care for a creature that could, supposedly, lay waste to a planet. Mac talked about Pesta with sensitivity and compassion—the way all sentient beings should be treated. Yet, others seemed determined to use and control this Pesta. Treva couldn't help but relate to the feeling of being manipulated by people for their own gain.

The corridor went on for a considerable distance, reminding Treva of the vast size of the ship. Occasionally, they encountered step-downs, some of which required Treva to slide over and dangle by his fingertips before his feet found the ground. It was a good indication that the corridor wasn't intended for people to navigate.

Mac didn't speak, but he hummed an unfamiliar tune under his breath.

Is he nervous?

A light caught Treva's attention and he let Mac move ahead while he went to examine it more closely. He found an illuminated sign: 'Storage Room'. Treva could barely make out a door in the gloom. He wondered if it was locked and what was kept in there. There might be something useful.

Mac grabbed Treva's arm, pulling him along for a couple of steps before letting go. "No time." He was panting hard. "Hurry."

"What?"

"I don't know when the last sweep happened."

Treva rubbed his arm to get rid of the feeling of Mac's fingers digging in. "Sweep?"

Mac look at his map. "Yes, to clear the corridor. That bracelet will keep you from setting off an alarm, but the sweep is an extra security precaution to prevent people from lingering in the areas where there aren't cameras."

"You mean, like *us* being in *here*?"

Mac didn't answer and, instead, set off at a jog.

"You didn't think to mention it?" Treva shouted as he ran after him, not wanting to find out about what the 'sweep' entailed.

They must have gone nearly half a kilometer before Treva saw a light that could indicate an exit. Mac grabbed his arm again, and Treva yanked it free.

I'm going to end up with a lot of bruises at this rate.

"This is as far as I go," Mac whispered in Treva's ear. "The cells are through there."

He meant the shaft of light ahead, shining through a grate that presumably separated the maintenance corridor from the habitable areas of the ship. It was good that they were so close, but Treva couldn't help feeling that if he walked through there, he'd effectively be delivering himself to the place Captain Vaughn had wanted him in the first place. The bracelet may prevent sensors from flagging him, but it wouldn't matter if he found himself face-to-face with a guard.

Treva tried to control the rising panic constricting his chest. "Really? Don't you want to see this through?"

Mac shook his head. "No, absolutely not. Just make sure you cause enough havoc to delay our arrival and buy me some time."

Treva didn't know how causing chaos would help Mac or Pesta, but he nodded. "I'll try."

He couldn't ask Mac to do more than he already had. His friends might only be a few meters away, which was a bonus. Treva needed to take full advantage of the opportunity.

"Thank you," Treva said, shaking Mac's hand.

Mac stared at their clasped hands for a long moment. "Oh, fok it. I can't leave you to do this alone."

Treva ignored the obligation he felt to let Mac off the hook. He was in no position to turn down assistance, especially from someone knowledgeable about the ship and his opponents. "Thank you."

"Wait here." Mac ran the remaining length of the maintenance corridor and dove through the grate.

"No, wait!" Treva grasped at empty air too late to stop the man.

The moment Mac cleared the exit, a clang reverberated along the walls. The hinged grate slammed shut and the louvers tilted closed, followed by what sounded like the hiss of air released from a valve.

A low tone sounded, and the temperature began to rise.

Oh, no. The sweep!

CHAPTER 16

I HAVE TO get out.

The temperature was rising fast, and Treva was blind in the dark corridor. He felt his way toward the grate—not caring that Mac had told him to stay—but found that it was now locked. He wasn't sure whether Mac's exit had triggered the sweep or if it was coincidental timing, but Treva knew he was in trouble.

With no way forward, he headed back the way they'd come, feeling his way through the blackness with his hands along the wall. As the heat intensified, Treva soon couldn't touch the walls without being burned. Sweat beaded his forehead and his shirt stuck to his back. He stumbled onward, sure he was going to die if he didn't get out.

His eyes found a tiny light, which might have been his brain tricking him. As he propelled his way toward it, he realized that it was one of the storage rooms. If he could reach it before his clothes caught fire, there was a chance he'd live.

Treva ran with arms outstretched, and his left shoulder hit the wall. He yelled and jerked away as agonizing pain seared his flesh. He kept moving, knowing that if he fell, he'd die.

He'd almost reached the light, barely able to keep

moving forward. It felt like his body was going to combust at any second. His burnt arm stung and hot air scorched the inside of his nostrils, making each inhalation torturous.

The hissing noise had become louder. Like in a dream, he fought to take every step.

Finally, he made it to the door where he pulled his sleeve over his hand before yanking on the handle. *Ahhh!* He pulled away as heat seared his flesh. He would die if he didn't get the door open. Praying to the stars that it would be unlocked, he grabbed the handle again. For a second, it wouldn't budge. Then, it flew open.

He staggered inside. A wall of hot air blew past the spot where he'd stood just as the door slammed shut behind him, cutting off the worst of the heat.

Each breath Treva took was slow and steady. Part of him was convinced that he hadn't made it and he was still outside that door. He didn't dare move for an inordinate length of time. The storage space was no lighter than outside, and he couldn't see his burned hand in front of his face.

If I stay here, life will be short.

He shuffled forward with both hands outstretched, trying to discover something about the environment. Perhaps activated by his movement, a light flickered on above, momentarily blinding him.

Treva blinked at rows upon rows of robots. Some stood, and some were in a heap of limbs and circuitry. Various shapes and sizes, ranging from Taran android forms to more utilitarian machines, were arranged throughout the vast space.

What are these machines doing here?

Treva's arm throbbed. It was more painful now than it had been when he'd injured it. Groaning in pain as he pulled his arm out of his shirt, he found the skin a deep shade of red with one large blister in the center. He had the sense that it was going to get worse. Tears pricked his eyes as he slid his arm back into his clothes, unable to do anything else.

Aware that he had to get medical help quickly, Treva moved closer to the robots. Each one was either damaged or missing a part. When he reached out to touch the nearest, it crashed to the floor.

Treva froze. The noise was too loud to have gone unnoticed. He wasn't sure if he was more afraid that someone might come to investigate or that a robot might spring to life and throttle him.

When nothing happened, he allowed himself a couple of breaths, trying to calm down. The first thing was to find out if there was another way out from the storage room that didn't involve going through the Corridor of Death.

He spotted a narrow pathway between the jumble of limbs, torsos, and heads. He was careful not to bump into any more of the robots for fear of drawing further attention to his presence.

As he passed by the robots, his unhelpful imagination pictured them waking and tearing him limb-from-limb. But, even that might be a better fate than what would happen if the ship's captain caught him after this stunt.

He shook himself. There was no time to mess around; he had to stay focused to have a chance of getting out alive. He needed to free the others, then they could rescue themselves the rest of the way. After all, they were the seasoned pirates, not him.

Cold metal touched his arm. Treva jerked away and shrieked before clamping a hand over his mouth.

A robot hand had reached out where his arm was a second before, though it was now motionless. They weren't all inactive like he'd thought.

When nothing else happened, his brain started to work again. There was no reason for any of them to attack him. It was an irrational fear, that was all.

Treva hurried to the other side of the room without encountering any more grasping hands. As he approached the wall, he heard a beep and the sound of the door. As it started to open, voices carried inside. He dropped to the floor.

"The sweep has only just finished. Can't you feel the heat? How could anyone get inside?"

"The lights are on."

"Come on, everything in here is faulty. Why not the lights as well as the sensor?"

"Yeah, but they're usually off, not on."

Treva was on his hands and knees, crawling between the forest of legs. It was impossible not to touch them, but he did his best not to knock the robots over. If any of them reached for him, he was unaware.

"I hate it in here. It's foking creepy."

"They're only robots."

"It's like a foking army after a massacre."

"Let's get this over with."

"I have a better idea. Just lock the door and increase the security clearance required to open it. If anyone is in here, they can stay."

On hearing that, Treva thought about letting them know where he was. The thought of being locked in with half-dead robots and no food or drink was less desirable than being captured.

What about Mac?

He clamped his jaw. They were trying to scare him into revealing himself.

There was a pause before the door hissed closed and the lights went out. Treva remained in the same spot for a long minute. It could be worse, although he wasn't sure how.

Backing out the way he'd come, Treva hoped to find the clear channel again. He felt his way to the space without anything cold grabbing him and could have kissed the metal top of a robot when he triggered the lights to come back on.

Treva found his face next to a pink-skinned kneecap. He flailed backward, knocking over something metal. It fell with a loud clang.

Kneecap! What robot has a fleshy kneecap?

Without thinking, he whispered, "Sorry."

There was a whir. Treva felt the air displaced. Something had moved, and he was sure it was the robot.

"Do you require assistance?"

Treva fell entirely onto his butt. It took his brain a second to work out what had happened. An android had followed him through the metal forest.

He looked up at a naked man. Except it was evident that he was synthetic. There were no sexual organs, just smooth skin. It was nothing like the small unnoticeable bots that busied around in the background most places.

"Do you require assistance?" The volume had increased.

"No." Then, worried that the noise might trigger sensors, Treva added, "Actually, yes. But can you be quieter?"

"I can." The volume had reduced, but it was still too loud. "How can I assist?"

"Talk quieter." If anybody bothered to investigate, he didn't want to draw more attention than he already had. "Whisper, like me."

"What would you like me to say?" the android asked, altering his voice to mimic Treva.

"No, I mean..." There was nothing to lose. "I need to find a way out of this room."

The android started toward the door that Treva had come in through.

"Not that way, or the front door." Treva tried to control the panic that tinged his voice. "I need another way out."

The android whirred and immediately crashed into a pile of metal, sending it skittering across the floor.

"Seriously, you need to be quiet. Do you understand?"

The machine stopped and seemed to consider. "Of course."

"Good. Now, be careful."

Treva was beginning to think that it had been a mistake to recruit the machine's help. So far, it had increased the chance of him getting caught.

The android wandered to the corner of the room, where it suddenly punched through a metal panel.

"Hey! What are you..." Treva faded out when he realized that the damage was already done. If someone was going to hear them, that would have done it. Besides, there was probably no way to manufacture an exit without making a noise.

The android continued to pound the wall panel, creating a racket so loud that Treva's eardrums vibrated.

He kept his eyes on the door in case anyone came to investigate. His stomach lurched when the door did, indeed, slide open. The pair who had been in earlier ran inside. Metal went flying as they crashed through the middle of the rows.

Shite. I have to go now.

Treva didn't think they would shoot, but he'd rather not take the chance. The hole the android was diligently creating for him was barely the width of his torso, but when the android paused, Treva took a chance and forced his body through. His shirt caught on a jagged edge of metal, ripping the cloth.

Metal sliced through the skin of his burnt arm, adding to the agony. The adrenaline pumping through his system numbed the worst of the pain. He didn't have time to both check the injury and escape.

It was dark beyond the hole. Treva slid for a short distance before coming to a stop with his feet against a panel. He was surprised when the android clattered down behind him, only stopping a couple of centimeters from his head. He hadn't expected it to fit through the gap or follow him.

Treva rolled out of the way, crying out with the pressure on his arm. He couldn't see which direction was best, and with no time to assess the situation, he said, "Help me get away."

He couldn't see the machine but heard a whirring sound as it moved. His feet landed in a narrow channel, which was only big enough for him to put one foot in front of the other. It did nothing to help his balance and was like walking on a tight rope without the drop—well, no drop that he could see.

Without illumination, there was only a small red dot marking the android's position. Treva's eyes remained fixed on it as he followed, trying to ignore the sound of pursuit.

A bright light suddenly created shadows on the wall behind, but they must have gone around a corner because the light didn't find them.

"Do you have a stealth mode? "

"I do not understand."

Treva had little experience with machines of any description. His mother hadn't been rich enough to have any synthetic assistants at home. He suspected that there was no such thing as stealth mode, but he thought it was wise to check.

Ahead, the android punched another wall.

Stars, it's going to pummel our way to freedom.

With the noise it made, Treva wouldn't have been surprised to discover the entire crew waiting for him to emerge with weapons drawn.

As soon as the hole was big enough, the android stepped back and Treva climbed through. To his relief, nobody was waiting to apprehend him. He looked down both sides of the nondescript corridor, seeing no indication of where he might be.

No time to waste. He ran down the corridor without bothering to check whether the android was with him. He doubted the machine would fight, since it wasn't armored. Someone had probably designed it to carry heavy loads, but he couldn't fault its capacity to punch through the interior walls of a ship.

Since his emergence no doubt drew attention, Treva decided that it was best to get as far away, as fast, as possible.

It felt good to run again. His legs pumped hard, and he slipped and slid around the bends. His arm hurt, but while someone might be chasing him, he pushed it to the back of his mind.

Treva had no idea where he was or in what direction he was running. Ahead, a door blocked his way. Without any other corridors to either side, Treva slowed and peered through the reinforced grill in the top part of the door. His view was limited, but it looked as if he'd come full circle to the cells.

This is it. My chance to free the pirate crew.

He tried the door-release, but nothing happened. There might be a way back into the system of tunnels he'd just escaped. He shuddered, and his arm throbbed at the thought of arriving in time for another Sweep. Even if he found a route, he might end up running in circles again until he was caught.

Footsteps sounded from behind. Trapped against the door, Treva swung around to see the naked android turn a corner. Treva sagged in relief at the strange sight that probably wouldn't be much better if it was clothed.

"Can you open this door?"

Is it upset that I left it behind? What a stupid idea; it was a machine. Of course, it didn't suffer from emotion.

The android pushed him aside as if he was a piece of debris and inserted something into a slot. There was a loud whirring noise, and Treva had to hold himself back from telling it to be quiet. He didn't know who was on the other side, but there was no way to work silently.

The door slid open with a hiss, revealing a control console in the center of the room. Individual cells, barely large enough to lie down in, lined the perimeter of the space. It looked as though the prison might have originally been a storage area.

It was only when Treva reached the middle of the room that he spotted Idra. Why hadn't she called out? There was Zinder in the cell next door and the others. They were still alive. He'd reached them in time.

Then, he noticed that Idra's mouth was moving, but he couldn't hear what she was saying. There must be a dampener that prevented sound from penetrating the force fields active behind the physical bars securing the cells.

Idra gestured frantically, and he moved toward her, trying to read her lips, but it was useless. She shook her head, putting her hands up. Other members of the *Hyperion's* crew also came forward in their cells, motioning for him to stay back.

Red light surrounded him in a flash, and an alarm blared. The bracelet on Treva's wrist began flashing red. An electric charge passed through him, freezing him in place. His attempts to pull free were powerless against whatever invisible force was holding him in place.

A figure appeared from the back of the room. Treva tensed, ready to fight despite his present inability to move. He'd gone through too much to give up.

Upon closer inspection, there was something familiar about the person. "Mac?" Treva managed to say through the heaviness in his chest.

The little man smiled, lifting his head from fiddling with one of the panels at the central console. "Somewhere... Ah, there."

The alarm stopped, and the red light went off. Treva could move freely again, and his bracelet had stopped blinking.

"What are you doing here?" he asked the older man. "Why did you run off like that?"

"Didn't I explain?"

Treva was starting to think that Mac was absentminded. "No."

Idra said, "Uh, is he with you?"

"Oh, thank the stars! I can hear you now." Treva ran to her cell.

"You can? Good thing I didn't call you any names."

"What the fok are you doing here?" Kinder asked, stepping forward as far as he could. The force field had been deactivated at the same time as the red light went out, but the metal bars were still firmly in place.

Treva beamed. "Rescuing you, of course."

Idra eyed the naked android and Mac. "And they are...?"

"Helping to get you out of here, so you're welcome," Mac muttered. He kept fiddling with the controls until all the cells popped open. "It is now safe to go."

Nobody moved. It seemed that they weren't ready to trust Mac's assurance.

"He's a bit crazy, but you can trust him, I think," Treva whispered to Idra. He suspected that Mac's tampering would have been noticed by now, which was all the more reason to move quickly. He opened her cell door the rest of the way. "Come on, there isn't much time."

Idra followed his lead and stepped out. When nothing bad happened, the other pirates exited.

They seemed eager to be free from the small spaces, which didn't even have bedding or other furnishings to make a prisoner comfortable. It suggested that Captain Vaughn hadn't planned to keep them there for long. No doubt, this was where Treva would have ended up, himself, if he hadn't made a run for it when he'd first arrived.

With dark realization, Treva wondered what made Pesta so special that she needed her own containment zone on the ship rather than being kept in this area. Thankfully, that wasn't anything to worry about right now.

Kinder slapped him on the shoulder. A bolt of pain shot through Treva's arm, and he almost jumped in the air.

"I've missed you, too, Kinder. Just watch the injuries."

Kinder peered at Treva's burn. "Ah, it's only a flesh wound. We'll fix you up when we get back on the *Hyperion*."

"Speaking of which, what now?" It was one of the

female crewmembers Treva wasn't acquainted with.

Treva didn't want to tell her that he had no idea, so he said, "We get out of here."

Idra started to laugh. "It's that easy?"

"Well, nothing's been easy so far, if I'm honest. But we don't exactly have a choice."

She was staring at Treva. "I don't even know why you're on this ship."

"That's a long story." The last thing Treva wanted to do was to explain who his father was and what had happened. "We should try to get back to the *Hyperion*."

Idra frowned. "Obviously. But if Herja has any sense, she'll be far away from here by now."

Kinder shook his head. "I wouldn't be so sure. Knowing her, I doubt she did the logical thing if it meant leaving people behind."

"Regardless," Idra replied, "we need to get as far from this ship as we can."

Something occurred to Treva, and he turned his attention to Mac. "How did you know how to override the system?"

Mac smiled. "They don't know what a powerful enemy they made when they took us. I was waiting for an opportunity, and you provided it." His eyes slid away. "I might have had a little help from some of the *Vector's* crew. Not everybody believes it's right to use intelligent lifeforms as a weapon for their own ends. It was Vaughn's mistake not to take that into account when they captured us."

Treva had a distinct impression that if he had not come along to disrupt things, the *Vector* would have been in trouble, anyway.

Without warning, the ship shook violently. Treva fell to the deck, where he skidded until crashing into a wall. His ribs took the brunt of the impact, and he struggled to draw air into his lungs. Fortunately, he hadn't landed on his injured arm this time.

A few of the pirates had stayed on their feet, but most

were also sprawled across the floor.

"What in the stars was that?" an unknown crewmember exclaimed.

"I think we've just been hit by weapons fire," Idra responded from where she lay, almost back in the cell she'd just escaped.

"Not just any weapon," Kinder said, his eyes bright. "Disrupting the artificial gravity and stabilizer's like that? Told you Herja wouldn't abandon us!"

Treva didn't know much about the Catch-All, but it went without saying that this was as good of a diversion as they would ever get to cover their escape. "Come on! We need to find a shuttle—"

He cut off when he saw Mac rushing toward the door.

"Not without her," the Keeper said.

From the way the man had spoken earlier, it'd been a big risk to leave Pesta unattended. Now, with this attack to agitate her, they were all in danger.

Treva turned to his pirate friends. "Change of plan; we have to make a detour. Try to keep up."

Mac shouted something over his shoulder, but Treva didn't catch it. He looked at Idra.

She shrugged. "No idea, but we should head for the escape shuttles. Surely, he'll meet us there if he can."

Treva bounced on his feet, ready to move but not knowing in which direction to run. Sweat beaded on his scalp. Why was he more nervous now than before? Understanding came all at once: he had more to lose. It would be worse to have achieved the impossible and rescued the crew, only to fail at the last moment.

Kinder was trying to access the *Vector*'s systems, but if his language was any indication, he wasn't having much luck. He slapped a hand down hard, not caring what he smashed or set off in the process.

Treva had an idea. Turning to the android, he said, "Take us to the emergency shuttles."

There was a short delay that caused Treva's blood

pressure to spike, and then the android ambled off down the corridor. "Come on," Treva shouted when the others didn't immediately move. Turning back to follow the android, he called to it, "Stay stealthy."

All at once, everyone piled after him, and they ran down a familiar corridor for a short distance. Shouts sounded in the distance, but they didn't see a soul. The android stopped suddenly, and Treva thought he understood why. He didn't ask, remembering that the machine was too loud. Instead, he held his hand up to stop the others as he proceeded quietly. On reaching the corner, he heard voices.

Shite. Of course, they would protect the shuttles.

He didn't think that anyone would stand much chance against armed personnel. They didn't have a weapon between them.

Well, they did have *one* tool that could follow orders. He would send the android as a distraction and then slide down the corridor, taking both guards down with nothing more than surprise, sheer guts, and a whole lot of luck. And... *No, that's insane.*

The moment's pause made him realize that one of the voices sounded familiar. Not wanting to waste any more time, Treva stepped into full view.

"Mac! I thought it sounded like you."

Mac stood next to a control panel set into the wall, scowling. "Hurry."

"Where's Pesta?" Treva asked, running toward him.

"She escaped her confines and came to meet me. Everyone I've seen has run in the opposite direction, apart from you."

He could now see a patch of darkness where a hatch stood open. Mac had done something to the controls so that the shuttle was accessible.

Multiple footsteps came from behind, followed by a shout and gunfire.

Oh no, please, not when we are so close.

"Move it," Mac shouted and shoved Treva toward the shuttle.

He started to go as the others raced past and then looked at the android. His heart lurched, knowing what he had to do.

CHAPTER 17

HERJA SAT IN her seat on the flight deck of the *Hyperion*, watching the *Vector* for signs of damage.

There really were advantages to every situation. Neither Vaughn nor the captain of the *Gritter* had recognized the difficulties of targeting the *Hyperion* while she was in close proximity to the *Vector*. They hadn't considered how a clever captain might use it to her advantage by positioning her ship on the opposite side of the *Vector*, away from the *Gritter*.

Gosta was still upset about losing the umbilical, not to mention the damage to the *Hyperion's* outer hatch. It was also true that she hadn't been one hundred percent sure that the boy was on the other ship when she'd pulled away, but the way the *Gritter* had changed course suggested that he was safe and they were coming for them.

She nodded in satisfaction as the *Vector* listed to its port side from the impact of her latest volley. As usual, her timing had been uncanny. Gosta called it her gift, and she supposed he was right since it happened too many times to be coincidence. She didn't want to examine the phenomenon too carefully for fear that if she identified the cause it would ruin things.

Partial shields hadn't been enough to protect the *Vector*

against the first and second missiles. It was clear they had struck something vital. She couldn't work out why they hadn't retaliated.

It didn't surprise her that Vaughn had written her off as a threat. He'd seen what he'd wanted to see—Herja trying to save herself after handing over the boy. Perhaps he'd never dealt with a pirate ship before, but she wasn't in the habit of surrendering even when everything was against her.

"Gosta, I'm *not* afraid to die."

"Fok," his head shot up from the viewscreen, "it's not what I'd choose to do today either." He thought about it for a second, "Is this because you believe in an afterlife?"

"Nope," Herja couldn't say why she didn't fear death, "doing it once will be enough."

She stared at the *Vector*. It couldn't have occurred to Vaughn to watch his back. He was too much like Steyn—both confident in their power. He believed she would comply because he held hostages, except he'd already told her what would happen to her crew regardless of what she did.

Gosta had argued that they needed to get away as far and fast as possible, but Herja wouldn't leave her people to be tortured and killed like animals.

"Compassion is a weakness," she told him.

"What?" Gosta looked mystified as he leaned against the console with a frown on his grizzled face. "It was me that said, 'let's go'."

She sighed, having told him to sit four or five times in the past half-an-hour, but he remained standing, nonetheless. "You should listen to your captain—enough is enough. You can take your chances."

Gosta raised his eyebrows. "We're attacking while our crew members are still on that ship. What are you planning to do, blow a hole in their side to get our people out?"

"I don't care." She scowled. "Vaughn is going to kill them, anyway." She turned her attention to the *Vector*.

"This is what they would want. It's what I would want in their position. What about you?"

He answered without any hesitation, "I want to die in battle. I will die a hero."

"Then you are arguing with me for the sake of it. We are in agreement."

Gosta grumbled under his breath, "Tell me again, why this is better than attacking straight out before we sent the kid over there?"

"It's a matter of tactics. Not something you'd understand, old man."

The truth was, Herja hadn't wanted things to unfold this way. Even so, they *should* have finished off the *Vector* when they'd captured it the first time around—but, having more than half her crew taken prisoner had changed Herja's priorities. Fortunately, they'd caught the *Vector* by surprise when the *Hyperion* had turned on the offensive after handing over Treva. The command overrides and control that the Catch-All enabled were temporary, but for that limited time it was quite effective. Sadly, their haphazard tactics meant that the *Hyperion* now only had a few minutes to destroy the significantly larger ship and its companion.

The lack of planning wasn't lost on Gosta. "I don't like this. Our people are going to die."

"You don't like anything." She waved off his critique.

"Attacking them now is madness."

Herja ignored him. She wasn't planning on saving anyone. With rescue out of the question, the best she could do was make sure that no one could disclose anything under torture; she didn't want word to get out that anyone had gotten the better of her. No survivors, no one to talk.

The *Vector* had not returned fire yet. They were probably scrambling to locate them with their sensors scrambled by the Catch-All.

Then, Herja spotted something on the viewscreen. The tiny dot had her full attention. "There." She pointed at the object, which had broken away from the main ship. "Zoom in."

Her heart picked up speed. It couldn't be... could it? But why else would anyone launch a shuttle at such a critical time, when it was liable to be blown into a million pieces?

Someone was trying to escape. Herja's pessimistic mind refused to allow her to believe the possibility that more than one person was on board; it would be too much to hope for it to be everyone.

"Don't fire."

Herja felt Gosta's glare, insulted that she would even suggest that he'd act without a command from her. He knew her well enough to take any command she gave seriously, no matter how crazy it sounded.

An alarm blared. It seemed that the *Vector* had managed a targeting lock on the *Hyperion* and the weapons were hot.

The communication system pinged. Herja nodded for Gosta to open the connection.

Chatter filled the *Hyperion*'s flight deck. "We're in the shuttle. Can you see us? Please don't shoot us. Do you hear me?" The voice was familiar.

"I do not fire on unarmed shuttles." Herja was trying to pick out individual voices. "Idra, is that you?"

"It's everyone," a male voice said.

Someone started to sing, and Herja blinked a couple of times. Her crew hung in space between two waring ships. They weren't out of danger yet.

"Gosta, make sure you keep the *Vector* busy!"

He stared at her with his mouth open for a heartbeat before turning his attention to the controls. Mumbling, he fiddled with the controls.

Satisfied that he would do everything he could, Herja turned her attention back to the shuttle. "What about the boy?" They might not know he'd gone over later with noble ideas about trying to help. "What about Treva?"

"He's here."

"Found them, Captain." Treva's voice was faint, but it was definitely him.

Herja grinned at Gosta. "Told you. It's going to work out fine."

"You said we were going to go down in a blaze of glory. Is that still the plan? Because, if not, we've got to get out of here." Gosta grumbled some more, but she couldn't understand what he was saying. "We're too far away. They're going to get blasted."

Herja ignored his complaining and maneuvered toward the shuttle. There was no way she would allow that to happen. The universe could not be so cruel as to dangle such hope in front of her, only to snatch it away. Except, she knew better.

Intercept in fifteen seconds. Another alarm went off— warning of incoming missile fire.

Undeterred, Herja spoke to the shuttle. "Let's pick you up so we can party."

A cheer sounded, and Herja grinned.

The flight deck shuddered as a missile detonated against their rapidly failing shields. Stars, they really were too far away to intervene, and their only hope lay in distracting the *Vector* to the point where the shuttle became insignificant.

Another plasma beam lanced out from the *Vector*, not near them this time, and Herja's heart was in her mouth. She watched, helplessly as the shuttle's starboard maneuvering thrusters were destroyed. The tiny vessel spun out of control, causing a follow-up blast to miss by a hairsbreadth.

Herja took manual control of the *Hyperion*, already correcting for the change in trajectory. She had to get between the shuttle and the *Vector*. It was the only chance they had. She knew they wouldn't make it when a fresh burst of weapon's fire skimmed over the shuttle's hull.

"Do you have any shields on that thing?" Herja shouted into the comm unit.

Still hanging onto the console by his fingertips, Gosta returned fire. The computer system compensated for their changing position. Two missiles hit the *Vector* in quick succession, causing zero damage. The *Vector*'s shields were back at full strength, the Catch-All's control broken.

"Another shot like that is likely to take out the entire shuttle and all of this will have been for nothing," Herja shouted at Gosta, not expecting him to have any answers but wanting him to feel her frustration.

Treva's voice crackled over the comm. "We have something on board... a weapon that could wipe out all of these ships if we're hit. They call it Pesta. Supposedly, it can destroy an entire planet."

Herja wondered if she'd heard correctly. *Destroy a planet?* She'd heard about such powerful tools used during the past war, but those had only ever been in the hands of the military. A weapon of that power in criminal hands... If it was true, they should be flying away from, not toward, the shuttle. Still, she couldn't leave her people, even if they were acting crazy.

This wasn't the time to question the accuracy of Treva's statement. She would try to use it, to see if the assertion spoke for itself. If Vaughn laughed at her, she'd have her answer.

Herja put a call through to Captain Vaughn while at the same time banking to port, narrowly avoiding another missile.

The comm hissed and spat out Vaughn's voice, "You want to talk in the middle of a skirmish?" His face appeared on-screen, calm and collected.

Herja knew that she didn't look composed, but she smiled to herself. He wouldn't have answered if he didn't want to talk. "We have your Pesta, so I suggest you stop firing on the shuttle."

His face drained of color. "How are we still alive?"

Although she was happy to have some leverage, his response chilled her. It was true, then. Without looking at him, she transferred manual control of the ship over to Gosta. They were close enough to the shuttle now.

Vaughn cleared his throat. "Rather, I should say, it would be illegal to own such a rare and dangerous creature. I'm not admitting to anything."

Creature?! What kind of weapon is this 'Pesta'? Herja understood why he would want to be careful not to incriminate himself. "Okay, then."

Gosta maneuvered the *Hyperion* between the shuttle and the *Vector*. Herja let out a breath. She was uncertain how long their shields would last against a bombardment, but she was betting that it wouldn't come to that.

The comm went silent. Vaughn had ended the call; that didn't bode particularly well, but she was determined to hope for the best.

The next few minutes were tense as the shuttle docked with the *Vector*'s airlock hatch. Once everyone was safely on board, they cut the shuttle loose, much to Gosta's disgust. He was such a scavenger, but there really wasn't time to check it for trackers.

Herja waited on the flight deck for news of the crew as they prepared to enter subspace. They had to get out while they still had a chance. Not wanting to celebrate prematurely, Herja only allowed herself to relax a little. She couldn't believe that her crew had made it back.

The *Vector* hadn't moved. It hung there, too close for comfort, and she was worried that at any moment, it would fire. *What are they waiting for?*

The *Gritter* was still out of action but not for long. Despite that, Herja was mindful that it might not be far away and it wouldn't know about the Pesta.

Gosta went to deal with any injuries. Herja was surprised when he came back quickly.

"No dead or seriously injured. Treva had a scratch and a burn to his arm, which were easily treated," he reported. "But, we need to talk about Pesta once we are somewhere safe."

The nav course was plotted, and she was ready to engage the jump drive. Hands shaking, she initiated the command.

Hyperion slipped into subspace just as the alarm sounded, accompanying a flash of weapon's fire from the *Gritter*. They'd made it out just in time.

Once safe amongst blue and green swirls, Herja laughed. They had achieved the impossible and escaped. For now.

She shared a look with Gosta, both knowing that the *Vector* was sure to come after them. Their course would be impossible to track with the independent jump drive, but someone would spot and report them sooner or later. Vaughn had to track them down, if he wanted to retrieve his weapon cargo that had the potential to be worth a fortune.

Now, Herja had to deal with transporting the most dangerous weapon she'd ever heard of, as well as Marco Steyn's only child.

"We are still alive." Herja's words had become a ritual whenever things got tough, and they had never felt more appropriate. Her hands had barely stopped shaking. "Okay, I'm ready."

—

With the ship on its course through subspace, Herja left Gosta on the flight deck and headed down to the galley. She needed to see everyone for herself.

There were hugs and congratulations. Nobody had expected to escape. Treva was dirty but whole, and it appeared that he had acted like the hero. She'd been half afraid of that when she'd sent him across.

"This is Mac," Treva introduced a small, dark-haired man with a vacant grin. "He's Pesta's handler."

A wariness crossed the man's face, but he nodded. "Keeper, yes."

Herja liked this situation less and less the more she heard. "So, Pesta, the weapon... What is it, exactly?"

"She. It's a she," Mac stated.

Everyone had gone quiet. The crew listened intently, no doubt wondering what Herja was going to do next. The truth was, she didn't know herself.

"Is *she* somewhere safe?"

The Keeper remained on edged. "She's in the hold, amongst your cargo."

Herja didn't miss the note of judgment in his tone, though she wasn't sure if it was because of the drugs they carried or because Pesta was being treated like a commodity.

"All right, we'll leave *her* there for now, but I want to know everything there is to know about her. Okay?"

Mac shifted on his feet. After a moment, he nodded.

She could understand his reluctance, but he was on her ship now. Herja locked eyes with him. "What is Pesta?"

"She is alive, although we cannot see her," the Keeper explained. "I am bonded as her handler."

"Get to the point."

Mac jumped a little at her sharp tone and began wringing his hands. "Pesta was created in the laboratory where I worked. I had access to the research, but it didn't make a lot of sense. I'm not a scientist, you see." He rubbed his forehead. "They wanted a biological weapon—"

Herja tried to keep her anger in check. "And, that didn't worry you?"

"By the time I found out what they were doing, it was too late. I was in too deep to walk away. SPEAR Tec doesn't take chances when it comes to their secrets."

Something else occurred to Herja. "Pesta isn't like other biological weapons, is she? Vaughn was afraid of Pesta even though he was sitting in a sealed ship across the vacuum of space."

"She's unique." At Herja's glare, Mac continued, "SPEAR Tec wanted to make a biological agent that could replicate itself with any organic material—create a chain reaction. In an isolated area, it would effectively wipe out any life."

"And what about a *not* so isolated area?"

Mac looked down at the deck. "This is why she has a Keeper, to control her."

Herja didn't like the implications one bit. She knew all too well of the devastation that a traditional biological weapon could cause, and Pesta clearly had the potential to be magnitudes more dangerous.

"They engineered her to be their tool." He paused. "Except, she can do things that shouldn't be possible."

Everyone was listening intently as Herja asked, "How do you know?"

"Apart from seeing the results of tests," Mac licked his lips, "she told me."

Herja was aware that she was staring. "She *told* you?"

"I'm pretty sure she wasn't supposed to be sentient. It was a side-effect." Mac took a deep breath and rubbed his head again as if he had a headache.

It was a side-effect. Herja repeated it in her head to see if it sounded any more plausible. It didn't. It sounded like a nightmare.

"The real danger is if she detonates herself," Mac went on, sounding reluctant to share Pesta's shocking truth. "When placed under extreme duress, she could give up her life, releasing all of her destructive potential in one blast. Within the atmosphere of a planet, it was a world-killing event."

" 'Was'?" Herja didn't want to know, but her sense of responsibility wouldn't let her off the hook.

Mac's voice went quiet. "It happened before, with another Pesta. That was before they discovered that a bonded Keeper like me could act as a stabilizing factor."

"How is it possible that a planet's destruction wasn't all over the news?" Herja could guess, and the explanation concerned her even more than Pesta.

"They are powerful people, with the sort of

resources—"

Herja finished his sentence for him, "That can cover up the obliteration of a planet."

"I'm sure they chose the target carefully."

It would be difficult to believe, if not for what happened to her own people. Herja would have steered clear of the *Vector* if she'd known the nature of their cargo. Pesta must be immensely valuable, but it wasn't the kind of cargo Herja ever wanted to deal in. It was on her ship now, so she would need to decide what to do next.

"Don't speak of this to anyone," Herja instructed her crew. They nodded, and she trusted them. "Please, treat Mac as an honored guest. We owe him our lives." She smiled and patted him on the shoulder.

The small man gave her an awkward smile.

The chatter started up again as most people tried to forget what manner of creature shared close quarters with them. Eventually, the conversation turned to an account of the crew's harrowing escape from the *Vector*.

Herja half-listened while Treva told about an android punching through walls; she was glad to discover that at least that machine had remained behind on the enemy ship with instructions to cause as much trouble as possible; she wouldn't have wanted one of Steyn's androids on her ship, no matter how it was programmed. However, it might explain why the *Vector* had delayed attacking them.

"They won't be coming after us right away," Treva said when he neared the end of his tale.

Herja frowned. "What makes you say that?"

"Mac did something to the engines before we boarded the shuttle. It will take them a while to repair the damage, which gives us a good head start to wherever we're going."

"We'll use the lead to our advantage," Herja said.

Even the kid knew that the *Vector* would be coming after them at some point. He was too wise for one so young. Herja couldn't forget that he had sacrificed himself for her crew and done his best to free them once he was on board.

He either had talent or a lot of luck—both of which could be useful in the right circumstances. She supposed that she might like to keep Steyn's boy around, after all.

"Thank you for your hospitality. Excuse me, but I must go check on Pesta." Mac shuffled of the galley and headed in the direction of the cargo hold.

"Where *are* we going next?" Treva asked.

Herja didn't know, but when she opened her mouth, she found herself saying, "I thought we'd take a trip to Red Ghost, if everyone agrees."

"Really?" Treva's whole face lit up, and Herja felt as though she'd made the right decision.

"Let's have a vote. Who thinks we should go to Red Ghost to look for Treva's mother?" A cheer rattled the drinks glasses on the galley's table. "I'll take that as 'yes'."

Idra grinned, looking at Treva. "I think we owe it to you after everything you've done."

He looked away. "Does it bother you, knowing who my father is?"

Everyone had gone quiet again. The boy sure knew how to put a damper on a party.

They were waiting for her to respond. Herja smiled. "No. Although, I don't know what to think of the trouble you've brought along with you."

"Oh." He looked sheepish. "Well, we couldn't leave her there. They were going to use her as a weapon, or sell her to the highest bidder. That wouldn't have been right—not after Mac risked everything to save us." Treva grinned. "Besides, Mac managed to sabotage the ship and everything. They didn't dare shoot him because they didn't want to risk angering Pesta."

"Yes, well, I need to assess the situation."

"But you won't hurt her." It wasn't a question, Treva had acquired some ridiculous ideas about his level of authority while he'd been on the *Vector*.

"I better change course for Red Ghost." She was regretting the decision already. "I'm not sure what we'll find there, since it's the one place most pirates avoid."

Treva gulped, and there were tears in the corners of his eyes. "Thank you, everyone. I just need to make sure that my mother isn't there, and if she is, get her away."

Herja nodded, feeling uncomfortable with the intense emotion flying around. "That's enough touchy-feely stuff for one day. Get some sleep—everyone who doesn't have duties."

Herja returned to the flight deck to tell Gosta the news.

After she'd given the order to alter their course, he stared at her. "When did you get so soft?"

"Don't start. I'm already regretting the decision, and we're not there yet."

"Why would we go to one of the most dangerous planets in the sector to help a boy look for his mother? I can guarantee that there will be no profit in it."

For once, she couldn't tell how much was teasing. It didn't matter, since they were already on their way.

"Do you need any help programming the coordinates?" she asked.

Gosta huffed and walked off without answering.

She couldn't help wondering what they'd gotten involved in. Not even Gosta had ever gotten them into this much trouble before. *A planet-killing weapon, for fok's sake!*

CHAPTER 18

KALI HATED FEELING trapped. Even though she wasn't physically confined at the moment, she knew that they were one bad performance—or an unpleasant conversation—away from being treated like the full-on prisoners of Diamond-Boy and his goons.

Most of the band members seemed oblivious to their dangerous predicament on Red Ghost. Caryanne was, of course, off in her own little world, while Vaira, Honk, and Owen just seemed happy to have a genuinely appreciative audience to watch them perform.

Mika, meanwhile, had maintained a singular focus since the moment they landed to find the hidden facility, or whatever it may be, that Tregaren had used for his clandestine business. Though Kali appreciated his determination, and his goals aligned with hers, they needed to be working as a unified front rather than being at odds with each other over petty differences of opinion. His stubbornness had made him reckless, and that had gotten him caught.

Their 'hosts' had been suspicious since the *Sepiantia* arrived on Red Ghost, but Mika's most recent snooping had crossed a line. Diamond-Boy's remaining patience would no doubt be exhausted in short order. His 'holding' of Mika was meant to send a message, and Kali had received it loud and clear.

Kali hadn't wanted to press the issue of speaking with Mika. Since Diamond-Boy had said the band needed to be on good behavior, she'd made a point of ensuring everyone kept their heads down. Look compliant, and Diamond-Boy might be more willing to negotiate.

As Kali shared an evening meal with her bandmates the day after Mika was apprehended, it was clear that the others didn't understand they were in the middle of a delicate power-play.

"Why haven't you demanded to speak with Mika?" Owen asked as he chewed his meal of synthetic meat and a slightly sour-tasting tuber vegetable.

Kali checked around them to make sure no one was openly watching their conversation. There was enough background music that she felt reasonably comfortable they could converse without unwanted ears tuning in, provided no one was close by. It looked clear for now.

"I wanted to give Diamond-Boy time to see that we're willing to play his game," she replied. "We'll be good little performers, just like they want us to be."

"How is a band supposed to get by without its manager?" Honk took a gulp of his drink; Kali was pretty sure it was his third of the still-young night.

"Bookkeeping and tour scheduling aren't the priority right now," Kali said. "We know how to put on a good show, and that's exactly what we're going to do."

"Well, *we* know how to perform," Vaira stated. "You're still..." she frowned at Kali, "well, you're doing a fine job of holding the bass and staying upright on the stage."

Kali's cheeks burned. "I'm working on it, okay? The bass is deceptively difficult."

"All you need to do is find the beat." Honk drummed a riff on the edge of the metal tabletop with his fingers.

"I know, I know. I'll get it eventually." She was eager to bring the subject back around to the important issues. "I will talk to Diamond-Boy, but it's important we treat these people with respect. They've earned that much from us." The lies sounded hollow to her, but she figured that if there was a hidden recording device, a nuanced tone would be less important than the words themselves.

Owen, at least, appeared to pick up on her intention. "Kali's right. We were hired to put on a good show, and the Bruisers never disappoint."

"How much are we getting paid for this gig, anyway?" Vaira asked.

Kali actually had no idea. "I'm sure Mika can answer that question as soon as he's back from his time off."

Honk raised his eyebrow and took another gulp of his drink.

"Since when has it been about the money?" Owen said. "A hearty cheer is payment enough for me."

"Might not say that too loudly, or they might stiff us," Vaira advised.

Kali kept her mouth shut on the matter, fearing that the privilege of staying alive might be all of the compensation they could expect to receive.

"We'll play our best, and the rest will follow," Owen said.

Kali nodded. *Right now, that's all we've got.*

—

Like the previous night, the crowd rewarded the Bruisers' performance with thunderous applause. After the band had completed a second encore—which Kali was beginning to think would be obligatory each night—they exited the stage to find Diamond-Boy waiting for them, yet again.

Kali motioned for the other band members to see themselves out for the night. Owen tried to hang back, but a reassuring nod from Kali saw him on his way.

"Very entertaining. You're the best band I've seen all

day," Diamond-Boy said.

His tone was just flat enough that Kali wasn't sure it was a compliment. "We aim to please."

"Yes, trying quite hard to be on your best behavior." He looked her over. "Don't you miss your band manager?"

"Mika didn't respect your right to privacy. A little time to think about what he did wrong would do him some good."

"How long is long enough?" Diamond-Boy tilted his head.

"You're more experienced in personnel discipline matters than me, I'm sure. But, from a purely selfish perspective, we could use his opinion about what to play for our next performance. Assuming we're going to be sticking around here for a while, we need to plan out new material."

"How long do you think you can keep this up?"

"Pardon?"

"Pretending like you're just a band here to play a gig."

"It's not pretending when that's exactly what we are," Kali replied as innocently as possible.

He eyed her. "I don't buy it. Maybe some of them, but you... you're not like the rest of the group."

She shrugged. "I am a new addition, I can't lie. My aspirations for adventure got a little ahead of my skill-level for playing my instrument, but when I saw the Bruisers perform on my world, I knew I had to be a part of spreading their joy for music." Stars, she was making herself sick from all the sweet words.

Diamond-Boy remained quiet for too long. He kept his gaze intently focused on Kali, and she didn't dare move beyond plastering a friendly smile on her lips.

"Stay in line and we won't have any problems," he said, at last.

"Absolutely." She bowed her head and smiled wider. *Lies. All lies!*

Diamond-Boy snapped his fingers, and two of the men

who'd been flanking him left down the hallway. They returned a minute later, prodding a sulking Mika in front of them.

Kali breathed a sigh of relief when she saw that he was unharmed. The dark under his eyes and mussed hair suggested that he'd had a sleepless night, but she'd count the lack of bruises or blood as a win.

"Keep this one out of trouble," Diamond-Boy advised. He bumped his shoulder into Mika as he passed by through the hallway, followed by his men.

Kali waited until they were well out of sight before she spoke. "Are you okay?"

"Been through a lot worse," Mika responded, his voice tight.

"You shouldn't have gone off alone."

"I had to do *something*."

"The only thing you *have* to do is make sure that this band delivers on our fans' expectations." She motioned for him to follow her. "Come on, let's get you back to your room."

"Do you think they're listening?" His voice floated into her mind while they walked.

"I can't be sure. I'd rather exercise an abundance of caution."

He fell into step next to her. *"These are bad people, Kali. They're up to something... I just don't know what."*

"Successful criminals do tend to be good at hiding their criminal enterprises."

"There's some sort of underground factory, but I didn't sense any prisoners down there. It was more like a manufacturing operation. They caught me before I could discover more, but I saw something weird while they were bringing me back here."

That got Kali's attention. She glanced at him, but his gaze was straight ahead. *"What was it?"* she asked.

"They held me at the docking station. This whole time on Red Ghost, I was focused on trying to find something

underground. But while I was there, I noticed a surface-to-station shuttle. What if we've been looking in the wrong place?"

"There isn't a space station on this planet."

"Exactly."

Kali had to admit, Mika might be onto something. Such shuttles were small and typically designed to only go short distances. While they could be retrofitted with jump drives, it wasn't practical to use such a compact craft for meaningful travel. Its presence suggested that there was something nearby that warranted visiting. And, considering that they hadn't noticed any structures on the way in, the location was probably hidden.

I hadn't given these people enough credit to think they'd have a secret space station, but maybe I underestimated them. Kali gave Mika a mental nod. *"It's worth looking into."*

"How? We can't leave the planet."

That was going to be a complicating factor, no matter what they tried to do. For now, they needed alternative eyes to gather as much information as they could. *"Give it a day or two, and then go to the* Sepiantia *to run a scan."*

Mika stood up a little straighter at that suggestion. *"Will they let me on the ship?"*

"They have it physically locked down. Make up an excuse for why you need to be there."

"You make it sound so easy." The sarcasm came through in his mental tone, but there was also an edge of excitement. They had a plan they could both get behind, and they always worked better as a team.

"What about you?" he asked.

"I'll keep eyes and ears on the streets to see if there are any other 'guests' Diamond-Boy is keeping around."

"Hopefully you'll have more luck than in the last place."

"That investigation led us here, didn't it?"

He glanced over at her. *"Yeah, I guess it did."*

"We'll get to the bottom of this mystery, Mika. I promise."

CHAPTER 19

TREVA SAT IN the *Hyperion*'s galley, trying to imagine what he would say to his mother. How was he going to explain arriving with a bunch of pirates?

He'd woken from a short sleep, convinced that she'd spoken to him. The words dissolved as soon as he opened his eyes, and he was left with the memory of being together. One of the rare times they'd gone to a restaurant and so it must have been his birthday. She'd conspired with the stuffy waiter for dessert to take home. It was the first time he'd noticed how likable she was.

The ship dropped out of subspace, and he rushed to look out the galley's large viewport—too excited to sit still. Since there wasn't anything for him to actually do, he would make it his mission to help. He grinned, still in disbelief that he was going to set foot on Red Ghost. The goal had seemed impossible only a few days ago.

Idra, who was in the process of dispensing food, shook her head. "They won't let you go onto the planet."

Treva was puzzled. "Why not?" When she didn't answer, he said, "I've got to go, else how will they recognize her?"

She shrugged. "It's too dangerous."

There was no point arguing the matter with her, so he

ran to the flight deck. Arriving slightly breathless and with a tight throat, he requested entry using the comm panel outside the sealed bulkhead. The door slid open to reveal a frowning Gosta.

This was such a bad idea, but he couldn't come this close only to fail. "I just..."

"Let him in," Herja's voice came from somewhere behind Gosta's frame. "You might as well, since he's going to annoy us no matter what we do."

Treva didn't wait; he squeezed past and ran over to look out the forward viewport. A red planet with a yellow ring framing the outer edge dominated the view. Based on the size, they must be close to the planet's atmosphere.

Is she here? He felt nothing, but that didn't mean anything. He'd never been conscious of the connection with his mother when she was there every day, but he'd been sure that he'd know when she was near. He refused to acknowledge the doubt at the back of his mind, or the fear that rose from time to time that she might be dead.

"Stay quiet, else you're out of here," When he didn't respond, Herja said, "Answer me."

"Yes." Treva tried to soak in the planet's beauty before turning to grin at her. "It's magnificent."

Herja sighed, rolling her eyes to Gosta. "I believe he thinks that we're going to step off the ship and his mother will be waiting with open arms."

Gosta checked the readings. "He has no foking idea. We have to dock first, and it's never easy in this part of space. Too many wrong-doers."

Treva blinked. *Wrong-doers—what are pirates?*

He hadn't thought beyond getting to Red Ghost. It had seemed such an impossible task to start with, and it would have been stupid to consider all the extra hurdles. Now that he was here, it was different. Still, how hard could it be compared to getting this far? He resolved not to let anything stand in his way.

Treva turned back to stare at the planet. "How long

until we get there?"

Gosta let out a short laugh but didn't say anything. Treva didn't like that laugh, but he waited because Gosta wasn't the one in charge. Though she was faced away from him, Treva could see Herja's reflection in the glass, looking contemplative.

Finally, she said, "You won't be going with us."

Treva swung around to face her. "Why not? That's why we're here—looking for my mother. I *have* to come. You don't know what she looks like, and you won't know where to look."

"All true, but you have no idea how dangerous these people can be."

"I'm Marco Steyn's son." Treva wasn't about to tell them the truth about his limited experience with his father's associates. "I know how these people behave. Besides, I escaped from the *Vector* with the crew." He waited for her to tell him how lucky he'd been in finding Mac to help.

Herja met his gaze. "And, that is another reason. They might recognize you like Vaughn did."

Treva didn't have an answer for that, but he maintained eye contact. "Please, I have to go. If she is near, I will know."

Silence stretched until the comm beeped.

With a sigh, Herja said, "Don't make me regret it."

Gosta snorted in disgust.

"Thank you." Treva grinned. Everything was going to work out. He stared at the view of the planet, hoping that he would go unnoticed enough that he could listen in to the conversation. That tactic had worked before.

Gosta looked at him. "Wrap up warm. It will be night on the planet, which means cold."

Herja looked at the comm console's display to evaluate the incoming call. "Audio only contact from the planet." Herja opened a channel. "This is the captain of the *Hyperion*."

A male voice laughed. "Shouldn't it be the pirate ship

Hyperion?" The voice became more serious. "You will hand over control of your vessel to our helpful navigator."

Treva turned to look at Herja in alarm. She was never going to do that, especially not to someone who sounded so casual.

"I'm curious, do pirate ships normally hand over their ships when you demand?" Herja sounded bored.

"They do if they don't want to be blasted out of orbit. We have a lock on your position."

"We would be out of here before they had time to detonate."

"True, but keep coming closer, little girl, and I'll let you get acquainted with my missile."

Treva cringed. He couldn't imagine the man saying such things if he was closer to the captain.

Herja laughed. "It's been a long time since I was a 'little girl', and we'll see how big your missile is when we get there. We will land on your lovely planet regardless of whether you welcome us or not."

The voice stiffened. "I don't care who you think you are. If you expect to land, then you will submit to your ship being locked down like everyone else."

Treva swallowed. *This might not be as easy as I'd hoped.*

— — —

Herja usually enjoyed the challenge involved in obtaining permission for a known pirate ship to dock on a planet. Sometimes it involved assurances, sometimes threats, and even on occasions, bribery. Fortunately, there was always a way, it was just a case of finding it. The joy came from outwitting the planetary authorities who often wielded too much power.

"We're different from your other visitors." Herja was calm while she analyzed their options. "For a start, the *Hyperion* has a reputation to uphold." A reputation that Herja had cultivated and used as a tool whenever she needed.

She waited, hoping the lack of response meant someone was checking out the stories surrounding her ship. There was no way she'd hand control of the ship over to anybody. Besides, she'd only just got her crew back, there was no need to make them vulnerable so soon.

"Continue along your current trajectory and you will soon be in range of our missiles."

She settled on what she needed to do. It was a calculated risk, but spoken negotiations seemed to have hit an impasse.

As she leaned over the comm console, she caught Gosta's eyes. He mouthed, 'Are you sure?'

She gave him a nod. "You will make an exception for us because we have a delicate cargo." There was silence, but Herja could almost feel ears listening. "We are carrying a weapon that can wipe out your planet."

There was an audible intake of breath from the other end before the sound of laughter coming through the comm unit filled the flight deck. "Oh, that is a good one."

Well, at least she'd introduced the idea. That was a start. Herja was well aware that they would need some sort of proof and she doubted that Pesta would supply it. What she did have was a theory.

"We took it from the starship *Vector*." Herja was counting on them knowing something of the *Vector*. After all, the ship had been destined for Red Ghost when they had intercepted it. It was obvious that the planet and Steyn's ships were inextricably connected, but to what extent, she didn't know. "Since the detonation of such a weapon will wipe out your planet, I will give you a moment to check."

She muted outgoing communication. "Gosta, make sure our shields are raised."

The planetary weapons could destroy them with or without shields, but there was no sense in making it easy for them. A warning alarm sounded; they hadn't been lying about the missiles.

Gosta silenced the alarm. He didn't look happy, and she

couldn't blame him. There was so much that could go wrong, but Herja had learned a long time ago that risks were necessary in her line of work.

The same voice came over the comm again, more subdued now. "We are satisfied that you are telling the truth. You have clearance to enter the planetary shield."

She wondered if they had spoken to Vaughn directly. Either way, it was only a matter of time before the *Vector* came to reclaim Pesta. It wasn't the best outcome she had ever achieved—they would gain access to the planet and keep their ship but only by giving up vital information that would make them a target.

"I need a little more time to identify our next course of action." The voice sounded more professional this time, and Herja wondered if it was the same man.

"Don't be gone too long." She smiled grimly. "We might get impatient and turn Red Ghost into Red Mist." She ended the communication before he could say anything further.

She let out a breath. This could well be a case of winning the battle but losing the war.

Pesta's destructive potential would no doubt prove a massive temptation for anyone who thought that they had a chance of controlling her for their own ends. Not to mention that she was delivering Pesta to where she had been destined for in the first place. Even now, they would be trying to work out how they could get their hands on the weapon.

"They don't sound very friendly," Treva said from over by the viewport, where he'd blended into the background.

Herja had forgotten he was there. "We'll be fine." Now, if only she believed it. "It's normal to have to negotiate landing rights out here."

The comm pinged, Herja shared a look with Gosta before he opened a channel without speaking.

An older man whom they hadn't spoken to before asked, "What business do you have on Red Ghost?"

"It's personal."

"Recognize when you have won. I have almost decided to agree to your request but first, I repeat, what business do you have?"

Herja huffed. She was going to have to compromise if she wanted to speed things up. "I'm looking for someone. If she is not on the planet, we will leave, and if she is, we need some of her time."

There was an extended period of silence. Herja guessed that there was a discussion going on in the background. As it wasn't her first time dealing with the criminal gangs that acted as planetary authorities, Herja knew better than to give them too much time.

She muted the comm. "Take us in to dock."

They were close to the planet's surface now—too close for the authorities to use missiles without a risk of damaging their own infrastructure. However, Red Ghost didn't strike her as the sort of planet that would be short on other weapons that would be effective in those very circumstances.

Gosta only stared for a second before moving to initiate the landing sequence. He guided the ship smoothly toward the surface port on the outskirts of the planet's primary settlement.

An urgent message came through. She ignored it. Perhaps they were having second thoughts about providing accommodation for Pesta. If so, it would be better to act now and ask permission later.

Only when the landing gear was extended, did she turn on the comm. The link spluttered to life with the sound of outraged voices. There were too many for her to understand.

Herja asked cheerfully, "Where would you like us to dock?"

"You cannot. We haven't agreed."

"I needed to speed up things before we all died of old age. Where do you want us to dock, and can I have the helpful guy back, please?"

The silence was shorter this time, possibly because they didn't want to leave a ship the size of *Hyperion* hovering above their only docking station for too long.

Gosta checked the sensors. He would be looking for anything suspicious.

So far, everything was going as expected, but Herja had a bad feeling about this planet and its over-the-top commitment to keep everyone away. Vaughn would be on his way, which ramped up the danger. The crew and Pesta would remain on board, where they would be relatively safe.

Herja found herself curious to find out what secrets were hidden on the mysterious Red Ghost.

At last, the statement she'd been waiting for came over the comm. "You are free to land."

— — —

Idra refused to look at Treva as he passed her, which wasn't fair because if it were up to him, she would be going with them. As it was, it was hardly his fault that Herja thought that it was too dangerous for the rest of the crew to leave the ship. Idra knew how desperate he'd been to be included in the landing party, and couldn't she see that he didn't have any choice?

Mac was standing near the hatch as they went to leave. "Why did you have to bring us here?" He didn't give anyone a chance to answer. "This is where they wanted us all along! I saw it when I broke into their ship's systems. They aren't going to let us leave without a fight."

"This was the *Vector*'s destination?" That was news to Treva. Based on Herja's expression, no one else on the *Hyperion* had been aware of that fact, either.

Herja stared at Mac intently. "Why do they want Pesta so desperately?"

"I don't really know, only that this was where we were heading. They've been trying for months to create one that they can control, and she's probably the only one that has bonded with a handler. That is why she's so unique."

Herja took a deep breath. "Stay on the ship, and under no circumstances set foot on the planet. Kinder has instructions in case there's any attempt to interfere with the ship or in the event we don't return." She continued to the door and paused, turning to look at Mac. "When I get back, we need to have a long talk about you and your Pesta."

Treva thought that Herja should have let the authorities dock the ship and lock it down, if that's what they needed to do. Was it because they were pirates that they couldn't just cooperate? All this was taking up too much time. He wanted to get on with things and find his mother.

It was Treva's first time on another world, and he was excited, even though he wasn't there as a tourist. Growing up, his mother had never had enough credits for them to travel. If there'd been more time, he would have tried to explain that to Idra, as well, but Herja wanted to get off the ship immediately.

Gosta exited first, followed by Herja.

Treva's heart skipped as he stepped through the outer hatch into a deafening roaring and blinding light; the bright floodlights must have been intentionally aimed at the hatch to disorientate them. It took him a few seconds to get his bearings.

They were standing on a metal walkway, with a lot of steps down to the ground. The brilliant light didn't give off any warmth, and he could only make out dark shapes until his eyesight adjusted. As he stepped away from the ship, he realized that the wind was the source of the noise. A strong gust whipped his clothes and battered his body.

Six rough-looking men waited for them below. All held large weapons, which were thankfully not pointed in their direction. Treva realized that he had no idea if Herja or Gosta were armed. If they were, their guns were well concealed.

"Treva, be careful what you say." Herja's eyes slid to him. "You're good at keeping secrets, so don't start spewing everything you know now, and don't mention your mother."

Treva felt his face grow warm. "How will we find her if I can't talk about her?"

"Leave that to me."

Herja was treating him like a child. He had earned more respect than for her to speak to him like that. Was she going to help him find his mother or were they here for another reason?

Treva followed Herja down the slippery metal steps, with Gosta bringing up the rear. He was still irritated by the time they reached the ground. He scuffed his shoe in the dirt. If he'd held some fantasy that it would be warmer and more scenic, he was mistaken.

When Gosta stepped up to stand next to Herja, Treva slunk back, feeling like a spare part. He'd thought that they needed him to find his mother, but they were ignoring him, as usual.

The wind whipped away Herja's words before he caught them. Forget keeping a respectful distance; he could at least get close enough to listen. Before he could move, a hand landed on his shoulder.

Treva missed a breath as he looked up into the face of a man so covered in red hair that he wondered if he was part animal.

"You look mighty familiar," the man said in a deep voice.

Treva gulped. Even though Herja had said it was a danger, he hadn't really expected anyone to know who he was out here. He glanced toward Herja, who was in the middle of a heated conversation with one particular man. The others stood around with bored expressions.

"Ah, don't bother them. I ain't gonna hurt you." His eyes crinkled, and Treva supposed that if he could see his mouth, he would be smiling. "Didn't mean to frighten you with me question. I was just curious whether you are Steyn's boy."

Treva remembered Herja's warning, but the man already knew. There was nothing he could say to make things better or worse.

Treva let out a dramatic sigh. "Marco Steyn is my father."

The man held out a dirty, calloused hand. "I knew it. My name is Paulo."

Treva shook his hand. "Please to meet you, Paulo. It's Treva." Paulo wasn't so bad, just a bit intimidating on a first meeting.

"Want to do something fun?" Paulo asked.

Treva shook his head, gesturing at Herja and Gosta. "I better not."

"Okay."

Paulo didn't seem upset that Treva had turned down his offer. Relieved, Treva turned back to the conversation. He would have to stand right behind them to hear anything.

"What you here for?"

"I'm looking for someone," Treva tried to hear what was being said.

Paulo laughed and became excited. "If they are anywhere on this planet, I can find them. It's my specialty."

Treva returned his attention to the man. "Are there women on the planet?" What could it hurt to put out feelers?

Paulo got even more excited. "Women? There are so many women. If that's what you're into, I could get you a woman, or someone your age."

"Ewww, no thank you."

Paulo frowned. "I thought you said you were looking for someone?"

"I am... never mind. I shouldn't have said anything."

Treva risked a glance at Herja, but she hadn't noticed him talking to Paulo. Well, she wouldn't; he was invisible to her most of the time. Perhaps, he should see what he could find out on his own. The *Hyperion* was only ever supposed to get him this far.

Paulo didn't seem to notice the others. All his attention was on Treva.

It might be the wrong decision, but it was his choice, after all. "I'm looking for my mother."

Paulo nodded.

When he didn't say anything further, Treva asked, "Can you help me find her?"

"Yes, I can find anyone." Paulo looked in the direction of a single-story building complex a short distance away. "I will show you."

Treva looked back at Herja and Gosta. He should tell them where he was going, but Paulo was already half-way to the building and they might try to stop him. If he missed this chance, he might regret it.

What was the worst that could happen, anyway? Paulo might hand him over to his father. At this stage, Treva decided that wouldn't be so bad. He needed to take the risk.

CHAPTER 20

THE ACCOMMODATIONS WERE basic but clean. Herja and Gosta had certainly stayed in worse places, and so she wasn't about to complain. She checked the room a second time for recording devices. There didn't appear to be anything, but she didn't trust that was the case. It would have been less suspicious if they'd uncovered a couple.

Herja moved to the side of the window and peered out. "I still can't believe that Treva disappeared before we even reached the hotel." She really hoped that he hadn't gone looking for his mother, but what else would he be doing? "I knew he was getting impatient, but I thought he was mature enough to recognize that things take time."

"He's fifteen. What do you expect?"

Gosta wore a familiar expression she interpreted to mean 'I told you so'. Since there was no need to encourage him to be more annoying than he already was, she didn't ask for his opinion. Unfortunately, he didn't wait to be asked. "You're expecting too much of the lad."

She didn't respond because he was right. Although, it was very suspicious that neither Diamond-Boy nor any of his entourage had asked where Treva had gone. They didn't care that Herja suspected them of abducting him, and there was nothing she could do about it.

"I'm going to look for him." She let the door bang shut as she stepped out into the cold.

The room was on the ground floor of the hotel with direct access to the grounds. Three surveillance cameras swiveled to follow her every move. Perhaps Diamond-Boy wasn't bothered about what happened inside, only where they went when they stepped outside.

A bitter wind cut through her clothing. Ice had formed on the ground, and she almost slipped on the path. Darkness had come quickly since the *Hyperion* touched down, but lights mounted on the buildings made it appear as bright as day in the center of the settlement.

There were few people out on the streets, which wasn't much of a surprise given the cold. It did make her stand out as an outsider. Nobody followed her, except for Gosta. She didn't plan to let him know that she was aware of his presence. That way, she didn't have to talk to him.

Herja was trying to work out how she was going to find anything within the culture of secrecy that surrounded this planet. Part of her was curious to discover what they were up to, but it was probably more grief than it was worth.

The inhabited area was tiny, and so it wasn't long before she reached the outskirts. The wider streets made for easy walking, thankfully, because there were far fewer lights on the buildings. The large, red moon offered just enough illumination to see where she was going but not much more.

Where would Treva have gone? She had no idea, so allowed herself to wander and trust in her uncanny ability to find people. It was a skill that only worked if she didn't try too hard.

She cursed herself for not anticipating that Treva would set off alone or be coerced away. But, in her defense, they had only just arrived. The truth was, she had no idea why she wasn't celebrating his disappearance. They should have taken the opportunity to get out of there and leave him. After all, she had kept her part of the bargain.

Herja shoved her hands deep into her pockets. She was glad for the woolly coat that she'd bought at the hotel. Somehow, synthetic fabrics didn't keep out the wind in the same way. She supposed it made sense for the local animals to have coats that protected them from their environmental challenges, not that she'd seen any animals.

She paused at a point between two buildings—there was no path. Left, she decided, following her gut. She could just make out strange-shapes. In the dark, they appeared to be upside-down buildings, narrow at the base and heavy at the top.

Herja trudged onward, pushing her hands even further into the large pockets. She lowered her head and appeared for all the world to not be paying any attention to her surroundings. Even so, she felt, rather than heard, the commotion ahead.

Picking up speed, she made her way toward the end of the street, where she saw a figure up ahead. Even though she was too far away to tell for sure, she knew it was Treva, and he was in trouble. A large handgun was pointed at his head. She started to run, knowing that she wouldn't get there in time.

A female figure stepped out from the shadow of an abandoned building closer to Treva than her. Herja expected her to scream and run when she saw what was going on, but she didn't.

Herja raced flat-out toward the unknown man with the large weapon. Later, she would question her sanity.

The weapon was suddenly whipped from the attacker's hand, as if snatched by the wind, and went skidding down the dark street. Herja slowed, not entirely sure what she had seen. Had the woman done something?

She knew of people with abilities—the Gifted, some called them. Those trained by the TSS would certainly be capable of taking a weapon and throwing it like that, not that an Agent would have any reason to be on a backwater world like this at the fringe of the Taran Empire. And, why would they be interested in what happened to Treva? There had to be some other explanation.

Treva wasn't out of danger yet. The attacker's head swiveled around, trying to work out what had happened. He saw Herja and ran in the opposite direction, probably still confused. She had to grab Treva and they needed to get away before he returned with reinforcements. It wasn't clear what the woman wanted.

Treva waved at Herja as if nothing had happened. Herja shook her head in exasperation. *The young have no sense of survival.*

The woman walked up to him, and they began talking as Herja jogged over. She wasn't sure about any of what had happened and was breathing heavily when she finally reached them. The woman watched her, with a look that was more curious than cautious.

Herja wondered if she was the one who'd thrown the gun away. It was the only explanation, unless she had imagined it.

Treva said, "This is my friend, Herja."

The woman didn't smile. "I'm Kali. What did that man want?"

Herja interrupted, "We need to get out of here before he comes back."

Kali scanned the street. "I agree."

There wasn't much of her visible under the pile of garments. She moved quickly and quietly into the shelter of the building. Treva followed.

Herja sighed. It seemed that he hadn't learned his lesson and would follow any stranger. She joined him and they stayed in the shadow of the numerous abandoned buildings. It would have made sense to split up, but nobody suggested it. Herja supposed they were all too curious about each other to go their separate ways.

Kali must be as much a visitor to the planet as they were. She didn't fit with any of the people they'd met so far. But, if that was the case, what was she doing on Red Ghost where they didn't welcome strangers, and if she truly had disarmed that man, it meant she had to be TSS. From what Herja had seen so far, it seemed impossible that the TSS would have a presence on Red Ghost.

The last thing Herja needed was any attention from the TSS. It was her greatest fear. If she had any sense, she'd stay well clear of Kali, just in case. Unfortunately, Herja's sense had jettisoned when she set a course for a dangerous planet to find the missing mother of someone she had just met. Since Herja and her crew had outstayed their welcome before they arrived, they did not have long to find Treva's mother. They needed any help they could get.

Herja walked next to Treva, finding herself annoyed by his casual attitude despite what had just happened. "You disappeared!" It slipped out, sounding like the accusation it was.

Treva dropped his head. "I'm sorry. Paulo said he could help, and I was worried you weren't going to look for her."

Herja shook her head in exasperation. Somehow she managed to hold back from asking if his mother had ever taught him not to go off with strangers.

"Who are you looking for?" Kali asked.

"My mother."

Herja groaned. So much for her order not to tell anyone why they were here. It wasn't something she wanted to deal with now and was more curious as to whether Kali really had saved Treva and why.

Kali might be able to help them if she was not TSS. Herja wondered again at her own priorities—she should be concentrating on acquiring resources for her people, not helping one boy find his mother. Yet she couldn't walk away. If she'd had any doubt about the danger to Treva, that was dispelled by the shooter. It would be a death sentence for him, despite who his father was—or, perhaps, because of him.

Herja held out her open palm to Kali in greeting. "Look, I don't know what you want but thank you."

Kali returned the gesture. "I was too far away to help." She frowned, staring at Herja for a long moment, and then did an excellent job of looking confused.

"If that's the way you want it, I'll pretend that you didn't do anything."

"We're staying at a place called Red Rock." Herja grimaced at the unimaginative name. "I'll buy you a drink to say thank you for... helping." She needed to learn more about Kali and what she was doing on Red Ghost if they were going to be here for any length of time. Besides, she just had to find out about things, even when they were none of her business.

"Will the man following us be joining us?"

"Oh Gosta, I forgot about him. I'm not supposed to know that he's there, but probably."

Kali hesitated, and Herja understood her caution. She was already likely to get into trouble for interfering with the attack on Treva. With so few strangers on the planet, the attacker would know who prevented him from killing Treva.

Eventually, Kali said, "Okay. We might be able to help each other. For now, I think we should get off the street. I'll find you later." She disappeared between the buildings.

— — —

Kali didn't want to ask Mika to come with her to Red Rock, but it would be stupid to go alone. Not only that, but the woman—Herja—was Gifted in some way. It wasn't strong, and it wasn't like anything Kali had felt before, but it made the situation more dangerous.

Mika wasn't quite right, and she couldn't work out what was going on with him. He'd been quiet since Diamond-Boy had released him, but perhaps doing something might help.

Kali had explained about her encounter on the street. "The boy seems innocent enough, but Herja looks far from harmless, and she has ability potential."

"This is becoming a habit." At her puzzled look, he added, "You playing the hero."

"It's my job to help people. Anyway, are you saying that you wouldn't have done anything?"

He was silent for a long time. "I don't know. That's the trouble."

"Mika," she put a hand on his arm, "if you want to talk—"

He pulled away. "Not now. It's not productive to wallow in self-pity." He did his best to give her a reassuring smile. "Tell me, why are you going at all, if you're worried?"

Kali sighed; they were rapidly running out of time. "We're not getting anywhere, and I can't see Diamond-Boy letting us have the ship back anytime soon. I don't think they intend to ever let us go. Plus, the man who was about to shoot the boy will have run straight to Diamond-Boy to tell him what I did. Who knows when they're going to come knocking on our door."

"Perhaps you should tell them you're TSS."

Kali snorted. "That'd be a sure way to get us all killed."

"They must be suspicious if he knows that you used telekinesis."

"He could have been mistaken, and even if he is sure, Diamond-Boy might not believe him."

Mika headed to the door. "Well, let's get on with it."

Outside was even colder than earlier and they couldn't speak for the rush of the wind in their faces. With her telepathic sense on high alert, she felt a group of men coming in their direction.

Mika turned wide eyes to her. "They're heading this way."

"Let's hurry. They'll go to our rooms and find we're not there, and then they'll go looking. We won't have long."

Each step was a battle to get to the Red Rock Hotel on the other side of the city. Kali didn't think that it was a coincidence that they had been placed as far away as possible from the settlement's central amenities. Fortunately, nowhere was too far away in the inhabited sector.

The single-story building was in slightly better condition than their own accommodation. As they approached, the man who had followed Herja earlier stepped out from a doorway.

"It could be a trap," Mika said.

"Too late, now."

Kali felt they'd said all they needed to on the subject. She pushed her reservations aside; they had made their decision. Without speaking, she followed the man into a small room.

Herja and the boy were lounging in front of a compact heater. They both stood as Kali and Mika entered. The wind whistled outside and made the building feel as if it was shaking, although that could have been her imagination.

They stood in a semi-circle sizing each other up for a long moment before Herja gestured to a low chair. "We've checked the place for surveillance a number of times and haven't found anything."

"That was the same in our hotel. I don't think they are overly concerned with what we do. Their secrets are elsewhere on the planet." Kali reached out with her mind. "Still, it won't be long before we have company." She had no qualms about reminding Herja of what she could do now they were in danger. It might keep them safe.

Herja didn't look bothered. "Since I invited you, I will start. As you know, my name is Herja. This is Gosta, and this is Treva."

Kali nodded. "I'm Kali and this is Mika."

"You are TSS?"

Kali didn't answer. Once she'd confirmed Herja's suspicions about who she was, there would be no going back. Instead, she asked, "How long have you been here?"

"Two days." Herja looked at Treva. "It's up to you, how much you want to tell them."

The boy was younger than Kali had first thought outside in the street. He couldn't be more than sixteen, and he was different from the other two. His skin was a rich brown, and his eyes black in the artificial light.

Treva spoke to Herja. "She saved my life and put her own at risk. I think that we should trust them."

Kali bowed her head, acknowledging the vote of confidence. She was grateful that she wasn't the one to have to take the chance, even though she didn't sense any animosity from anyone in the room.

She evaluated Treva. "I'm sorry, but you need to hurry. Diamond-Boy's men were heading to our hotel when we slipped out, and then I imagine they'll soon be on their way over here."

Treva swallowed. "I'm searching for my mother and thought she might be here because... well, that bit is complicated. Herja and Gosta helped me get to Red Ghost."

Kali raised an eyebrow. "Why?" She directed the question at Herja.

"Later. It would take too long to explain." Herja didn't appear to have taken any offense at the question.

It was time to take a risk. Kali took a deep breath. "You are right about our connection to the TSS. I'm here as part of an investigation into missing women."

Treva sat up straighter but didn't interrupt. She didn't like the hope in his face that her words had sparked.

She looked Treva in the eyes. "We haven't found any sign that they are on this planet." She glanced at Mika. "There's also no indication that they are still alive, but while there is any chance, we will continue to search."

Treva said, "There are so many buildings and possible places underground."

"Yes, but if I'm close enough, I will sense them, and whatever is happening on this planet, there are no signs of activity outside of this small area and..." She didn't know how much to say about what Mika had seen.

Herja didn't appear to notice her hesitation. "Do they

know who you are?"

"Stars, no. We wouldn't be alive if they suspected."

Herja frowned. "What do they think you're doing here?"

"Playing music. While we're being truthful, what abilities do you have?"

Herja laughed and then seemed to realize that Kali wasn't joking. "I'm sorry to disappoint you, but I'm not Gifted."

Kali shook her head. "I'm not so sure."

Mika nudged her in warning, but she had already sensed the group Diamond-Boy's men heading toward the hotel.

"They're coming. We have to go." Kali had an idea. "Come and see the band play tonight. We can meet up afterward and plan our next move."

"If we're not put under armed guard first," Mika muttered.

Not daring to stay any longer, they slipped out of the door and headed around the back of the building. Kali could just hear Herja's loud, raucous laughter before it faded away behind them. She had a feeling that the woman would delay their pursuers long enough for them to get away.

CHAPTER 21

MIKA WAS ALONE on the flight deck of the *Sepiantia*, just the way he liked it. He frowned. Just the way he *used* to like it. Now, he preferred it when Kali was around.

It would be a better view if his ship wasn't shackled to the planet's surface. With the propulsion, weapons, and communication systems locked down, there wasn't much he could do, even though everything else functioned okay.

The full lockdown was no doubt why Diamond-Boy's men had allowed Mika to board the vessel alone. He'd fed them a flimsy story about needing to cycle the antimatter generator to keep the batteries from losing their charge. It was nonsense, but he'd correctly gambled that the sort of criminals who were put on guard duty weren't educated in mechanical engineering.

With his cover story in place, Mika was free to power up the *Sepiantia's* scanners without concern of drawing unwanted attention from the port authorities.

He needed to get to the bottom of his observation about the out-of-place shuttles. At six meters long, the vessels couldn't be going far, but why would they have such a craft when there was nowhere for it to go? There were no ships in orbit, let alone a station. A plausible explanation might exist, but Mika had a feeling that he was onto something.

The situation reminded him of Tregaren hiding behind the asteroid, and made him wonder what else might be out there. They hadn't picked up any anomalous readings on their arrival, and he'd been on the lookout for any sign of a hidden ship. Was it possible that he had missed something?

He reran the scans. Nothing. There was only one place that a ship could hide—a small, unnamed and uninhabited moon they had passed by on their arrival. The moon was visible with the naked eye as a dark shadow during the day and a light disk at night. There were possible places further away, but in the opposite direction from where the shuttle had been heading.

He focused the scan more tightly in the suspicious area. There was nothing except for an unexplained increase in radiation, which could have been generated by the moon itself.

He tracked the path of the shuttle and decided that it warranted an investigation, regardless. If only he could free the *Sepiantia*...

An alarm sounded, which made his heart kick up a notch until he remembered he had set the sensors to let him know if any new ships entered orbit.

Mika identified the ship—the *Vector*—and it looked like it was in a hurry. Mika had a bad feeling.

He checked the time. The band should be coming offstage about now. They had agreed to keep each set short so that the locals didn't get bored too quickly.

He sent an alert through to Kali's handheld, which had been restricted to local communications with all long-range and subspace messaging capabilities blocked.

Kali answered, "What is it?" Her voice was tense.

"A ship called *Vector* is coming in fast. Check with Herja, because it isn't one we've encountered before. It might not have anything to do with us, though I have a feeling we're not that lucky."

"Shite, I hate your bad feelings."

Despite the tension, Mika couldn't help but smile. He

could tell from her voice that the gig had gone well. She would be full of adrenaline and ready to do it all again, not that she would admit it.

Kali continued, "We'll meet you on the *Sepiantia.* Diamond-Boy wants a word, probably about what happened earlier. I'll try to avoid him."

Mika didn't like the sound of that. They had concocted a cover story about needing to find somewhere to practice, but it was unlikely to convince anyone. If Diamond-Boy chose to believe his man, there was nothing they could do. Mika ended the transmission and resumed his calculations, needing to be sure of his suspicions. If they could get off the ground, they needed to go and check out that moon.

Ten minutes later, there was a commotion at the hatch and the sound of running footsteps as people entered the ship in a hurry.

Mika jumped up. "What's going on?"

Kali appeared in the entranceway. "The *Vector* is here for Herja." She waved her hand as Mika tried to speak. "Their ship is not locked down like ours—we can leave."

Vaira and Caryanne stood in the hatchway, each with an instrument case over their shoulder. They were deep in conversation and seemed oblivious to everything going on around them.

Honk leaned against the wall before sliding down onto his ass. He didn't seem to know where he was or what was going on. Nobody was surprised or bothered to help him up. Herja and Gosta stepped over him as they entered, neither sparing him a second glance.

Mika stared at Kali, trying to work out what she was saying. "You want me to leave the *Sepiantia*?"

"You could stay with the ship and lock yourself in." She was already shaking her head. "No, I don't think they love our music that much. They would blow you up along with half the port."

Herja went to study the main holodisplay. "That is the *Vector.* I thought they would take longer to get here."

Mika looked at her in alarm. "Yes, it's coming at us fast."

"I'm sorry, but we have to leave before they arrive."

Treva shouted, "No, you can't. I won't go. I have to find my mom." There were tears in his eyes.

Mika pointed at the screen and spoke to Herja, "A short-range shuttle took off in that direction, and we need to find out where it's going. There's nothing there, and yet it hasn't—"

"First you have to listen," Herja interrupted. "I have a long story, but I'll keep it short."

Mika's mouth dropped open as Herja explained how they'd had a dangerous weapon on board and it had enabled them to escape. There was one aspect of her story that interested Mika. "How did you get them to open their doors and let you in?"

"That is top secret."

"Whatever it is, can you use it to release us from the planet?"

Herja stared off into the distance before slowly nodding. "Yes. It should work."

"I have an idea," Kali said. "You release us to go and investigate the moon, while you lead the *Vector* on a tour of the system."

"I will come with you. Gosta can fly the *Hyperion*," Herja stated.

"Could he take everyone, except us?" Kali asked. "I'd rather the others be someplace safer than where we're going."

"Not me," Treva said immediately. "I'm coming with you, too."

Herja snorted. "It isn't going to be safe with that," she pointed at the *Vector* on-screen, "on our tail."

The ship was rapidly descending through the atmosphere. Herja kept her eyes on the screen, no doubt working out how long they had.

"I bet they don't have the same problems with planetary authorities as we did," Mika grumbled.

"Okay, let's do this. I will speak to my ship."

Mika gave Herja control of the comm so that she could explain the plan directly to Kinder. She looked uncertain, and Mika guessed that she wasn't comfortable teaming up with the TSS, no matter the situation.

Kali must have seen it, as well, because she said, "Timing is going to be everything. We have to trust each other, which is a big ask considering that we have only just met."

Mika pointed at an image of the moon. "I'm willing to risk everything on one shuttle without a destination. I can't stand a mystery, so why not?"

Herja looked at Gosta. "Okay, let's get on with it. Lead these people to our ship." She waved her hand at Honk on the floor.

He made no effort to leave. "I don't like being separated."

"I love you, too. Now, move it!"

— — —

Herja felt her anxiety rising as the *Vector* got nearer and nearer. It was chaos on the flight deck of the *Sepiantia*. She itched to take control, but the ship was weird, its controls unlike anything she'd seen on other vessels.

Kali scowled. "Where the fok is Owen?"

"He stayed to take one for the team," one of the women said with half a smile on her pretty face.

Herja raised an eyebrow because Owen was pretty. She should have been paying more attention.

"What do you mean, Vaira?" Kali snapped.

"He stayed to do whatever Owen does with women— said he was going to try to get some information so we could get off this rock." Vaira picked at a nail as if there was nothing else to do. "Don't expect me to do anything like that; it's disgusting."

Herja saw the other woman—Caryanne—smile. She

glanced at Treva to see if he was following the conversation, but he was staring out of the viewport.

Oh, no... She'd thought her lot were bad, but she wouldn't fancy trying to control this bunch. The older one had passed out on the floor, forcing people to step over his prone body. Nobody acted as if it was anything out of the ordinary.

"We'll have to leave him," Kali said, although she looked like it was the last thing she wanted to do. "There's no choice."

Nobody argued. Herja managed to resist the urge to shout and issue orders, although that was going to change if they didn't move faster.

At least Gosta was finally ready. He gave her a last look as if she might change her mind. She patted his hand and smiled. His head drooped as he led the mismatched group through the hatch.

Kali stared after them. "I hope they'll be alright."

"Don't waste your energy worrying about them. Tell me how you fly this thing." Herja looked around with a critical eye. It wasn't so bad once she got used to the garish color scheme. Still, there was no way that she was sitting down in one of those strange blob-seats—she avoided any furniture that looked like it would swallow her.

"You need a neural link for this ship to be able to operate some of the controls," Mika explained.

"Well, you'd better patch me in quick. I'm not a passenger." Herja wasn't at all sure that she wanted anyone messing with her neural pathways, but there was no time for second thoughts. "Does it hurt?"

Kali shook her head. "No, but—"

Mika looked up from the console. "It doesn't matter; because I won't do it. I made an exception for you, Kali, but nobody else gets to fly her." With that, he got up and left the flight deck through an internal door.

He'd better be doing something useful at a time like this. Kali glanced up and frowned, no doubt thinking the same.

Herja gestured toward the door. "Shouldn't he be on the *Hyperion*?"

Kali stared at her for a second. "He has abilities, like me."

Herja had not expected that. He didn't look TSS, with his overgrown hair and way of speaking.

"He's not formally trained, but he'll be useful," Kali said.

"Okay, I'll take your word for it. We have officially run out of time." Herja activated the comm link to the *Hyperion*. "Kinder hit the Catch-All. Keep it aimed at the station." Then she added, "Gosta is on his way."

Kinder's voice was faint. "Activating now."

"You'd better get us out of here," Herja said to Kali.

The Agent prepared to launch the ship as soon as the docking clamps were free.

Mika careened through the door. "I'm here! Just had to make some alterations in engineering."

Herja stayed out of the way, knowing that the lack of familiarity with the *Sepiantia* would be a hindrance. She watched the activity with interest, trying not to dwell on her need to be in control.

The flight deck seemed eerily quiet now that most of the band members had left. Mika sank into one of the blobs and it changed shape, molding into a chair.

Kali looked at Herja. "You need to sit as well."

Herja was about to refuse when she remembered Gosta's idiocy and decided to be more sensible than him. She sunk into the cool goo. It molded to her shape and was surprisingly comfortable. As soon as she worked the release a couple of times, just to be sure she could get out, she was happy with her seat.

From her position, she watched the main display panel as the *Vector* drew closer. She was disturbed by the way it rapidly closed the distance.

She leaned over and hit the comm, ignoring Mika's glare. "Gosta, get out of there now!"

Gosta's red face appeared over the video feed. "Our ship was further away than I thought in the dock, but we're here now." He gasped for breath.

"Did you leave the women behind?"

"Of course not."

"They ran with heavy instruments and still beat you, didn't they?"

She could see his flush, even with his already red face. "We're leaving now. I'm busy."

Mika grabbed Kali's arm. "What about Owen?"

"We'll have to come back for him."

The *Sepiantia* shuddered, and it sounded like every alarm was going off at once.

"That's it." Herja looked at Mika. "Take control now and get us out of here."

Kinder had probably needed Gosta's help to operate the Catch-All; it was a complicated tool, especially when it needed to be directed toward a specific target. She should have thought of that, but it was done now.

The *Sepiantia* thrust away from the docking clamps. They were too close to the port for the authorities to attack them with missiles, but it was touch and go whether they would use a plasma beam.

Herja was equally concerned about the *Hyperion* getting away safely. She could see it out of the front viewport as it also pulled away from the port. She didn't think Diamond-Boy would risk hitting it with Pesta on board, but she held her breath until the *Hyperion* was clear.

The *Sepiantia* shuddered as her tail hit the control tower. Herja was about to complain about clumsy flying when she realized that Mika had done it on purpose. Now, the authorities would be more concerned about putting out fires in their port rather than shooting them out of the sky.

The comm flashed with multiple requests. Diamond-Boy wanted to talk. She ignored him, since she could guess what he wanted. Besides, he needed to believe she was on the other ship.

Herja opened a comm channel with Gosta. "Is everyone okay?"

"Fine, but Diamond-Boy is threatening to attack."

"You haven't spoken to him, have you?"

"Of course not. He would want to speak to you, and what would I say? I'm not stupid."

She breathed out with relief. "I don't think Diamond-Boy will attack because of Pesta. Not so close to the planet, anyway, but as soon as you're far enough out, he'll try something."

"What's far enough for Pesta?"

"Who knows, but be safe. I'll speak to you soon."

"You take care of yourself, and remember you aren't indestructible." Gosta smiled and ended the call.

She stared at the blank viewscreen for a long moment before Diamond-Boy's face appeared. "Answer, else we will fire on your ship."

Kali had stopped what she was doing. "What's a Pesta?"

"Nothing you need to worry about right now." Herja hadn't forgotten that Kali was TSS.

Kali's eyes narrowed, but she went back to the console. There was too much to do if they were going to get away in one piece. If Vaughn found out where she was, the *Vector* would come after them and leave the *Hyperion* alone. It was the real reason that Herja had agreed so readily to join this mission. Even now, it was tempting to answer Diamond-Boy's hail. As a last resort, she'd do it to save the others.

Mika was concentrating hard on the thrusters and didn't seem aware of anything around him. Herja didn't know what to think now she was aware he had abilities. As long as he didn't try to use them on her, she'd be fine about it. At least he wasn't a foking TSS Agent. Having one on board was too many.

Herja called to Kali, "Hey, can you deflect one of those missiles?" Kali didn't even look up this time, so Herja added, "I'm a lot easier to have along if I have a job to do, and you could do with an extra pair of hands. I mean, if you didn't trust me, you wouldn't have sent your people on my ship, would you?"

"Bomax!" Mika shouted. "I'll sort the neural link as soon as we're out of immediate danger."

"Thank you." Herja grinned. "You won't regret it. I'm the best pilot you've ever seen."

The communication channel spit out something, but she'd tuned it out as unimportant. If she couldn't play a part in the conversation, she wasn't going to suffer listening to Diamond-Boy.

"Are the weapons working?" she asked.

"I think so." Mika was up and moving around the console.

At one point, she was sure that he used telekinesis to alter their course. She shuddered. It wasn't natural.

Diamond-Boy's voice came over the comm, "Warning. Power down your engines, or else I will be forced to fire."

Herja glared at Kali, who shrugged. "I've left it on one-way. Better to know what he's thinking."

"How's that working out for you?"

Kali ignored her and spoke to Mika, "Is the jump drive online?" She sounded calm, but the tension in her shoulders was visible. "I don't understand why they haven't fired on us."

Herja studied the readings. "There's no weapons lock on the ship. The Catch-All shouldn't have disabled all of the station's weapons, but perhaps you did some damage when you left." She looked at Mika.

They were pulling away rapidly. Mika had the ship on manual control, and he took them through a set of maneuvers, spinning and changing course in an attempt to stop any weapons getting a lock on them. Herja was thankful for her seat.

She smiled. This was good fun, especially as her crew were safely out of the way on the *Hyperion*. She prayed to her ancestors to give the *Vector* engine trouble.

The *Sepiantia* shot into space, moving up and away from Red Ghost. Mika corrected their course, heading toward the moon.

"What's the plan if there is no hidden ship?" Herja was studying the controls, which weren't so different now that she'd seen them in use.

Nobody answered her. Herja's gut told her that they would find something, even if it wasn't related to the disappearance of Treva's mother. She could turn anything to her advantage.

Mika said, "Jumping now."

Kali let out a long breath. "Let's hope that this has not been for nothing."

The *Sepiantia* slipped seamlessly into subspace, taking them away from the possibility of weapon's fire. Swirls of blue, green were visible through the front viewport.

"We will be there soon," Mika said.

Herja gasped, realizing that only one kind of nav system would have permitted such a short in-system hop. "You have an independent jump drive?" She hadn't forgotten that Kali was TSS and so didn't mention the *Hyperion*'s own drive.

"Needed to avoid those missiles," Mika said. "We're about to find out if this trip has been worth the risk."

CHAPTER 22

TREVA COULDN'T TAKE his gaze off the front viewport. The beautiful lights of subspace captivated him while he thought about everything that had happened.

He felt something in his chest and dared to hope that meant he was getting closer to his mother. Even if they did find her, he couldn't quite bring himself to think about a happy ending yet—not after the disappointment of not finding her on Red Ghost. It felt too much like tempting fate.

An alert flashed on the navigation console.

Mika muttered something inaudible, then he stiffened. "Hey, we're changing course!"

Kali jumped to high alert. "What?"

"We're... This doesn't make sense. We're no longer moving through subspace along the predicted route. It's not a huge change, but we're definitely drifting."

"Drop us out!" Kali ordered

"No." Mika's attention was glued to the readouts. "I think this is what we've been looking for.

"I don't see anything." She pointed out the front viewport at the endless swirling light. "What could possibly be in subspace?"

"There's some kind of bizarre energy field. It can't be a coincidence."

Treva's heart skipped a beat. *No coincidences...*

"I guess your instincts were right about there being something odd out here," Kali acknowledged.

Mika frowned. "I wouldn't celebrate yet. I've never seen readings like this."

"Is it dangerous?"

"We're about to find out. Whatever it is, the epicenter is up ahead."

At first, Treva thought he was seeing things and that the feeling in his chest was nothing more than wishful thinking. But, no, something was outside, and it was solid. A giant structure hung amongst the swirling colors of subspace.

He blinked a few times to make sure that what he was seeing was real. Indeed, it was a spherical space station. Lights flashed along its circumference.

"What the fok?" Mika straightened in his chair. "Of course! The secret base is hidden in subspace!"

Herja joined Treva at the front viewport, admiring the impressive structure. "I had not expected this."

Mika's hands flew over the controls. "I'm trying to alter course to intercept it, but maneuvering thrusters aren't working—no surprise there."

"How did they get this here?" Wonder filled Kali's voice.

"No idea, but the motivation behind the secrecy is obvious now!" Mika shook his head. "This explains why all of that traffic from Red Ghost seemed to go nowhere."

Kali looked thoughtful. "The perfect hiding place. Only a ship with an independent jump drive would be able to execute such a precision jump to access the facility. And they aren't likely to get accidental visitors, since it's crazy for most ships to jump so close to a planet."

Herja raised an eyebrow. "Indeed, who would be so reckless?"

Mika flashed her an annoyed look before returning his attention to piloting. "Gah! Even if you do find the bomaxed thing, it's not designed for easy docking. How are you supposed to get to it when you can't use maneuvering thrusters?"

"There's probably an automated docking assistant station-side. At least, if you have an invitation." Kali gnawed on her lower lip. "Can you figure out a way to access it?"

After several seconds, Mika groaned. "Simply put, we can't get there from here."

Kali frowned. "Why not?"

"I'm not messing with you. Look." He brought up an active scan of the station and its vicinity on the front viewscreen. "I won't pretend to understand anything about the underlying tech, because I have no foking idea, but look at the energy readings coming off of this thing!"

Kali scrunched up her nose as she took it in.

Treva crossed his arms while he tried to make sense of it, as well. The graphical depiction on the scan looked almost like the magnetic field coming off of a planet, with lines arcing out from the spherical station. The energy seemed to be most concentrated at the structure's poles in narrow columns, and it rapidly dissipated as it moved outward. However, the furthest reaches of the field had created a subspace eddy in the surrounding area. The *Sepiantia* appeared to presently be coasting the outskirts of that disruption.

"For the sake of analogy," Mika explained, "this thing looks like it's making its own weather in subspace. We're still traveling to our designated exit point for the jump, but this field is deflecting us along the outer edges of its current, swinging us around to our destination rather than allowing us to travel in a straight line."

Herja tapped her fingers against her elbow. "So, our plotted course happened to take us close enough to see the station, but now there's no way to break through the outer edge of the field to access the station?"

Mika screwed up his face. "Maybe? Everything I've said is an educated guess. With that said, it looks like there's a narrow column within the field at the station's poles that might be passable, but I can't get us there as things stand."

"Could we get into that zone from another angle, then?" Treva asked, surprising himself even more than the adults in the room.

"Maybe that's how they do it. A specific approach vector." Mika shrugged.

"I don't know of any tech strong enough to manipulate the flow of subspace like this," Kali said, her calm Agent demeanor cracking at the edges.

"What about TSS Headquarters? Didn't that used to be in a fixed subspace position?" Herja asked.

Kali's brow furrowed and she cast the pirate a suspicious glance. Treva got the impression that wasn't common knowledge. "Not quite like this, but I guess there's precedent. I wonder if this is an old Aesir facility?"

"Could be," Mika agreed. "Tregaren was ex-Priesthood, after all, so he'd know about the location of abandoned facilities better than almost anyone else."

Treva swallowed hard. He didn't like how that had made the TSS Agent look even more nervous. The Priesthood had fallen from power when he was too young to understand its significance, but he knew they were corrupt and evil. *Was my father somehow involved with them?*

Kali was studying the readouts. "I'll pinpoint this structure's exact position. We can exit subspace, plot a proper intercept course, and then hopefully find a way inside."

Herja turned to the others. "We need to be cautious. Assuming this is run by the same people as Red Ghost, they're bound to be armed. And I doubt they'll welcome us."

As they dropped out of subspace, the colors disappeared, changing to a dark starscape. Treva tried to assess where the space station was relative to their location in normal space, but there was no sign of the hidden structure.

Kali pointed at something on the scan. "There. A tether beacon. It's so small, we would never have found it if we didn't know where to look."

Herja joined her at the control panel. "What now?"

"It'll be impossible to break in through that containment shell around the facility." Kali paused in thought for a moment. "We're going to have to go in through the front door."

Just as she said the words, the communications console lit up, and a voice message played for all on the flight deck to hear. "You are in controlled territory. Please leave. If you do not vacate the area in the next two minutes and thirty seconds, you will force us to take drastic action."

"Shite, what now?" Kali's hand hovered over the console.

Herja beckoned Treva over. He looked around, checking that she meant him. She smiled. "We'll never be able to break in. Tell them who you are. Get them to let us on board."

He gulped. "What do I say?"

"Tell them the truth. Well, except for the bit about looking for your mother." Her eyes brightened. "I know, tell them that you are looking for your father. Hurry, we don't have long."

Kali had been listening in, and she seemed to approve of the plan. She pointed Treva to the comm. "Here, I'll help you." She opened the response channel.

"Hi, I'm Treva Steyn." His voice sounded small and uncertain to his own ears. "I'm looking for my father."

There was silence before the voice said, "We will get back to you."

Kali muted the comm while they waited for a response.

Mika started muttering to himself again. "We're a sitting target out here, hanging around for Diamond-Boy to send a ship to pick us off."

Nobody said anything, because it was true. But what

could they do? Treva watched Herja try to find the *Hyperion* on any of the scans, but there was no sign of them.

Kali initiated a new call while everyone listened. It took a few seconds to connect. Kali bit her nails until an image appeared on-screen.

Treva held in a gasp when he saw the glowing eyes of an Agent staring back.

"Andy." Kali's voice contained so much relief that the man at the other end sat forward in his seat.

"What's wrong?"

"I need you—"

The comm pinged with a notification from the station.

"I'm sending you our location," Kali said. "The facility is in subspace." She switched back over to the station's channel.

Treva guessed that it wouldn't go down well if they got caught communicating with the TSS. He met Herja's eyes. "They are just going to tell us to go away."

Unexpectedly, the voice said, "Transferring jump coordinates now. Proceed to the dock."

Treva's eyes widened in surprised, and Herja smiled. Surely, they hadn't had time to check out who he was? Not that quickly. Go with the flow. They had achieved the impossible—an invitation to board the hidden station.

Treva felt even more nervous now. "They aren't going to let me look around, are they? It's more likely that they will lock me up."

"Lock us all up, you mean," Mika mumbled.

If that was meant to make him feel any better, it hadn't worked.

Mika initiated the precision jump that placed them in docking position with the structure hovering in subspace, aligned to enter at the northern pole.

"The ship's not handling like in normal space, but I do seem to have a measure of maneuvering control within this column," Mika observed as soon as they'd completed the transition to subspace.

"What happens when we power down the ship?" Kali asked. "Normally, the spatial disruption generated by the jump drive is the only thing holding us in subspace."

"Good question."

"We have a lock on your vessel," the docking attendant announced over the comm.

"How do we handle—" Mika started to ask regarding Kali's point.

It would seem the dock workers had encountered similar concerns before, because they anticipated what he was going to ask. "The station generates its own spatial disruption to remain suspended in subspace. So long as your vessel is within the field, it will remain stable. Hand over your navigation controls and power down your jump drive."

Mika clenched his hands into fists. "Haven't we only just lived through this nightmare?"

Treva thought that he was going to refuse, but Kali put a hand on his arm, and he complied. Sure enough, the ship remained in subspace, even after the jump drive was deactivated.

The *Sepiantia* began smoothly gliding toward the docking facility on the upper side of the station. There were three shuttles already tethered, and one of the open berths was clearly designed for larger vessels. Their ship smoothly glided toward the open slot.

"What can you feel?" Herja asked Kali.

"There are lots of men and women. I can't tell if they are being held against their will. There is no single mind that is crying out. It might be nothing to do with the kidnappings and everything to do with some other type of criminal activity." She looked at Mika. "We have to check it out."

Treva wanted to make sure that his mother wasn't here, but he wasn't comfortable with the way they were willing to allow him on board.

"No weapons," Kali said looking at Herja. "They will

only take them as soon as we are on board. We should try to act innocent."

"I haven't been innocent since I was a child," she replied with no regard about who she was talking to.

"Well, think back to that time and fake it."

Mika looked at Herja. "Let's sort out that neural link."

"Now?"

"I don't know what's going to happen. I may stay—call it a feeling. If that happens, you need to get the boy and Kali out."

"I can get myself out," Kali said.

Herja went with Mika without speaking.

Treva was still staring out the viewport when she went past him. He turned to face her, nerves twisting his stomach. They were about to go into the belly of a beast.

— — —

It occurred to Marco that he could not have been in a worse place to hear news of his son's arrival. He was sure that the bright light hanging over the table in the oversized Command Center highlighted every line of tension in his face. He tried to empty his mind, which proved impossible.

Marco couldn't recall a time when a meeting with his older brother, the Commander of the station had ever been interrupted. Although, it wasn't beyond his brother to play games.

The messenger had entered the room and said that Marco's son had requested permission to come onto the Space Station Spadrosi. It took Marco too long to interpret the information, afflicting him with a rare paralysis of his mind. He put it down to the fact that Treva's arrival was so unexpected, and although he was desperate to find him, it wasn't exactly welcome at this precise moment.

His inability to think clearly might have been for the best, since his brother had some telepathic ability—though nobody knew how much. Ability ran in the family line, but

Andrei was the only one that had gone away to be trained by the TSS.

How had Treva found Spadrosi? That was the one question that rocketed to the top of the list. Marco didn't want Treva anywhere near this place, and yet at the same time, there was no way he could turn him away.

Marco had better respond before news of his meltdown spread through the station. "Allow him to board, but make sure all security measures are in place. I will see him as soon as possible—"

The Commander interrupted, "Marco, you should have cleared this with me first."

"You're right." Marco lowered his head. He had no intention of disclosing that he hadn't expected Treva. Not when the Commander could stop him from seeing his son on a whim.

"It might not be him," his brother said, echoing Marco's fear and hope.

"If it is, I will deal with any trouble. And if not, they already know our location. We need to take action to contain any threat."

Privately, Marco was sure that it was Treva. The thought made him uncharacteristically nervous. It didn't matter that the boy had stolen vital information, and, the last he'd heard, was running around with pirates. So, why was he nervous that he might mishandle their reunion?

Marco wondered if his brother knew he'd issued a reward for information relating to his son. He hadn't said anything, but then he often sat on knowledge until he could wield it with maximum devastation, no matter how he had acquired it.

Perhaps it would have been better to wait until Treva had shown up on his own, but Marco had panicked. He'd already spent years searching for the boy, and he hated the thought of losing him again.

Okay, so the two of them had some issues to sort out. He might need to come up with an explanation for what had happened to Treva's mother. Proof might be necessary. With the resources available to him, he was sure that he could supply something. Although, it was no coincidence that Treva had discovered the station. It suggested that he'd found out more about what they were doing, but Marco would have to deal with that as it happened. The biggest threat to Treva was his uncle.

Marco didn't know what had happened with the *Vector*. Word had reached him that Treva had contributed to the ship's difficulties. At present, the *Vector* was missing, while the captain of the *Gritter* claimed not to know anything.

Too much had happened in a short space of time, and just when things were at their most critical on the station. First, Marco needed to make sure that Treva was safe and take him under his protection.

Marco waited until the young messenger had been dismissed to address his brother. "This is a family matter, Commander." He hated calling Andrei 'Commander', but his brother insisted on it whenever anyone was present. He did it now in an attempt to gain favor. As far as Marco knew, there was no such rank in the TSS, aside from someone currently in command of a ship, but Andrei wanted everyone to believe that he had been an important leader in the TSS. "I would be grateful for a little time to work it out."

"As long as it does not impact the security of the station, I can give you that. But I need your assurance that you will inform me of any potential risk."

Marco nodded curtly. It was the best that he could ask for, and he knew that he should be grateful, but the two of them would never like each other. Still, they had to work together.

Marco was grateful to be dismissed soon after. He hurried toward the boarding area, where he anticipated that Treva would have an escort. He tried to compose himself as he marched the length of the corridor. It would not do to show any weakness. Treva may only have used his name to get access to the station and might not have anticipated that his father would actually be present.

One of his brother's trusted personal security guards was a few paces behind. So, he was not going to be given as much leeway as he'd hoped.

Marco arrived in time to see the boy escorted by an armed man. He had to resist the urge to race up to Treva and check that he was okay. The Commander would no doubt be collecting information about their reunion. It wouldn't be a good idea to let him know how vital Treva was to him.

Treva had not arrived alone. That nuisance Herja was with him, as well as two other people that Marco had never seen before. The others didn't look like pirates, and Marco could only imagine what might have happened to lead the boy into the company of this bunch of misfits.

Marco stopped at the same time as Treva, and they stared at each other. Marco became aware of the number of ears listening to whatever he said next. Treva was too young and didn't have enough knowledge to recognize the dangerousness of the situation.

"I'll take it from here," Marco said to the security guard.

The guard paused and looked uncertainly at the Commander's man, who was standing behind Marco. The man must have permitted it because in the next second, the guard moved away.

"Hello, Treva."

The boy had the good grace to look down. After all, he had stolen sensitive information and put Marco in an awkward position.

"We need to talk in private." Marco scanned everyone in the holding room.

Herja stepped forward. "I don't think so."

Anger rose in Marco. The woman had been involved in several attacks on his ships and had run off with his child. It was about time that he dealt with her once and for all. But one look at the wariness in Treva's face made him realize that now was not the time. He remembered where he was and acknowledged that anything they said would not be private.

"Okay, let's calm things down. I bet you're all hungry. Let me take you to the mess hall to get some food. Everything will be better with a full stomach."

Herja didn't look convinced, but Marco didn't give a shite about what she thought. At least, she had the sense to keep her mouth shut.

They went as a group with the security guard trailing behind. Marco tried to think of a way to lose him, but it would be difficult on the station when he had access to the surveillance. The Commander had clearly given orders for Marco to be watched at all times. The worst thing was that he didn't blame him—not with the sensitivity of the current operation.

Marco let the others walk ahead, even though they didn't know where they were going. He wanted to check whether there was any way to convince the security guard to give them a little privacy.

"I can watch them. There's no need for you to come, too. There's more than enough security. It's unnecessary."

The man just nodded but continued to stride along behind. His plasma gun was pointed at the ground. Marco sighed. The rest of the station would presume that he was acting as Marco's security. There was nothing for it. He would just have to be careful about what he said. It wasn't like he was planning to tell Treva the truth, anyway.

The young woman in the lead followed the signs to the mess hall, turning off the corridor at the correct point. She was a little too confident in this environment and she didn't look much like a pirate. *Who is she?*

That reminded him that the Commander didn't know who Herja was yet. It was wrong that Marco was amused at the thought of his reaction when he discovered that he had a known pirate in his most secret base. Marco was going to be in so much trouble.

Nobody spoke until they'd all sat down with the lunchtime special of synthetic meat protein in a vegetable sauce and a helping of spongy bread. Their security guard chose not to eat.

Marco thought that he'd better start, in the hope of controlling the direction of the conversation. "What are you doing here?"

Treva looked up for the first time since they'd sat down together. "Looking for mom."

Marco thought that he did an excellent job of managing his reaction, considering that it was the response he'd been dreading. He didn't believe that Treva would accept the truth—that he'd been afraid of losing his son for a second time. It would be ironic if he'd lost him because of that decision. Perhaps he should have thought more about the impact on Treva of losing his mother.

"Is she here?" Treva asked, eyes narrowed.

Marco considered being honest, but with the guard present, that would have been too dangerous. "Of course not."

Treva shook his head. As expected, he hadn't believed him. Perhaps the boy had some of his mother's dormant ability. Treva didn't speak for the rest of the meal.

Marco was careful not to speak to Herja. He wasn't entirely sure that he could stop himself from throttling her if they started a conversation.

"Who are you?" Marco directed the question at both strangers.

The woman was the one who spoke, "I'm Kali and this is Mika. We are in a band called the Bruisers," she said, as if it was an explanation. "We are very popular."

Marco stared at them for a long moment. Treva had some explaining to do once they were alone.

After they'd eaten, Marco decided he'd best identify somewhere for everyone to sleep. He had the feeling that Treva was going to refuse to bunk with him and took some comfort from his skill to determine how much freedom the boy would be allowed. It would be best if they were all kept together in one place. That would make it easier to keep an eye on everyone—Herja in particular.

It was clear that Treva didn't trust anything that he said, and he wasn't the only one. Despite being family, the Commander didn't trust Marco, either.

If he'd been thinking clearly, Marco would not have taken the visitors past the restricted area, but he was tired and too busy worrying about what he was going to tell Treva. It was the quietest route, but by the time they turned onto the corridor and he'd realized where they were, it was too late.

Marco wasn't sure what triggered Treva's reaction— whether he'd sensed something or it was the large sign spelling out, 'Restricted Zone' in large, black letters. The only warning he got was when Treva gave him a furious glare before running straight toward the forbidden area.

For a couple of seconds, there was only the sound of Treva's feet slapping against the hard resin floor.

The guard shouted, "Stop!" At the same time, he drew his plasma gun and trained it on Treva's back.

Marco didn't know for sure if the man planned to pull the trigger and shoot his son in the back, but he couldn't take the chance. Before he'd thought about what he was doing, he'd drawn his pulse gun.

Marco felt the moment the guard squeezed the trigger with every fiber of his being. He cried out—a wordless shout of anguish. His eyes blurred as he brought up his weapon, the device cool and inert in his sweaty palm.

Impossibly, the guard tripped. His shot went wide, marring the overhead with dark singe-marks.

Marco didn't hesitate. The overwhelming loss was too fresh in his head to chance it becoming real. Marco shot the guard in the head with the pulse gun on a lethal setting. He felt nothing for the man who had almost taken his son's life.

Marco froze for the second time that day. It couldn't become a habit.

Treva had stopped and was staring back at the scene. Marco would rather that Treva hadn't had to see the man die, but there was nothing he could do about it.

With the guard out of the way, Marco pointed the gun at Kali. Her eyes were steady as she met his. There was no doubt or confusion; she looked prepared to attack. He'd seen telekinesis used before, and it had taken him a few seconds to recognize what he'd witnessed. The highly trained guard hadn't stumbled or fired a warning shot. She had forced him to miss.

"What instrument do you play?" he asked.

"Bass."

Marco's mind was working furiously. For Kali to have deflected a shot like that in subspace, where abilities were dampened, she must be quite powerful. Moreover, there were cameras everywhere, and it was only a matter of time before someone came for them.

Herja went to Treva's side. "It's okay."

It was apparent that nothing was okay, and they were in a great deal of trouble. Marco still didn't regret killing the guard; he had got what he deserved. Treva would never had made it through the security into the chamber. There had been no danger—no need to pull a fatal gun on a child, not with a pulse handgun on his hip that could have stunned him instead. But that did not change the consequences.

It was unlikely that Marco would be able to talk his way out of this one with his brother. That left them with limited time. It was then he realized that there was only one person who he trusted to care for Treva—his mother.

Marco lowered his handgun. "I can help you get back to your ship."

Treva averted his eyes from the dead guard. "She's in there, isn't she? I can feel her calling me."

It was past the time for lies, and it was obvious that Treva wasn't going to leave voluntarily. Marco nodded stiffly. He didn't want to destroy what was left of the relationship with his son, if it wasn't already too late.

"It wasn't your fault," Herja said to Treva as if she had any right to comfort the boy. "He didn't need to fire the weapon."

It was Marco's job to make him feel better. Just because he'd been a crap father so far, it didn't mean that he was totally incapable. His priority now was to get Treva to safety.

"I need her." Treva's soft words cut through Marco's panic. "She's my mom, and it's my fault you took her away. If only I had listened to her..."

"No. She shouldn't have taken you in the first place. I knew she'd do it again." Marco blinked. "She would do anything to protect you. That's why she left, because she saw what would happen if you had grown up with me. I didn't have a choice."

"You have a choice now," Kali said quietly.

Marco let out a bitter laugh. "Is that what you think?" He had to make them understand. "You need to get out of here. These aren't the sort of people you want to upset. Their reach goes farther than you can ever imagine, with plans that will shake the Taran Empire. They won't let anyone as insignificant as us stand in their way."

"She's there, isn't she?" Treva pointed in the direction of the restricted zone.

"Yes, and it was all my doing. I'm sorry. I just didn't want to lose you again."

Marco looked at Treva, taking in his determination. There was no way he would walk away from this, no matter what arguments Marco came up with. And even if he did, he wouldn't be safe. There was only one option.

Marco headed toward the secure area. "We don't have much time. Let's go."

"What about him?" Herja indicated the body sprawled across the corridor.

"It's a miracle that nobody has discovered us already. Come on."

Treva didn't speak or look at his father as he followed him. The others were close behind, except for Herja, who lingered.

Marco glanced back to see her dragging the body. It was a waste of energy, but it might buy them a few minutes. Mika ran back to help her while Kali stayed with Treva.

Part of Marco was horrified at what he was doing, while another part celebrated. It was the first time he had disobeyed orders, and it felt good.

CHAPTER 23

TREVA FOUND THE restricted zone a bit of a disappointment, since it looked exactly the same as the rest of the station. His mind grasped at all the little things—bits that didn't matter, so he wouldn't have to think about what had just happened. There was a danger that he might be responsible for that man dying, as well as for his mother going missing, and the crews on those two ships.

If he hadn't run… no, he didn't want to think about how he had almost died. He would think about how close he was to finding his mother. He wouldn't fail.

What would she have done if she'd found out he'd died, meters away from where she was waiting for rescue? He frowned.

That didn't sound like his mother. She wouldn't wait for rescue. What had they done to her? What if she was dead? Did his father even know what was happening in the restricted zone?

He looked over at Marco's profile. He could be lying. It wouldn't be the first time, but what did he have to gain from it? He had killed that man to save him. Treva couldn't make that fit with everything else he knew.

There was a door ahead. It was the same as any other door, except for another warning sign plastered across the middle.

Marco placed a palm against the biometric scanner, and there was a beep. Nothing happened for a few seconds. It was enough time for Treva to become convinced that someone had discovered the dead guard.

He hopped from foot to foot, unable to stand still. When the door slid open, Treva bolted through into another grey corridor, convinced they were about to be captured. The others were close behind.

Herja hurried to catch up with Treva. "I don't know what we are going to find, but I want you to stay with me."

He nodded, grateful for her interest even though it should be his father. Except, he couldn't trust Marco. Perhaps, if his mother was alright, he might be able to forgive him. But until he knew for sure, it was impossible.

Treva saw the way that Marco looked at Herja, and he remembered their confrontation in the Blue Pixie. That felt like a lifetime ago. He wanted to say something to let her know how grateful he was, but he couldn't find the words.

"Not another door," Treva groaned when he saw an identical door ahead of them.

It represented yet another obstacle, and it made him doubt that he would ever reach the end of his search. They had been fortunate so far. They hadn't encountered any personnel, but he worried that their luck could not last and that would mean more killing.

Sure enough, when the door slid open, a man stood up from behind a desk. Treva barely noticed because the chamber beyond demanded his attention. His mouth dropped open.

Gigantic tubes of glass rose up to a transparent domed ceiling. A shock of white light ran along the outside of the tubes every few seconds, illuminating the entire spider-like structure. Along a center aisle were rows upon rows of cubicles. The interior lighting was subdued, as if to compensate for the bright flashes. There was a bluish cast to everything. In some ways, it reminded Treva of one of the many museums on his home planet.

Treva stepped onto the glass floor. He heard his father explaining that he was conducting a tour of the facility for his son and friends. Whoever Marco was in the organization, he ranked high enough that the guard didn't question his right to be there.

Treva was compelled to go down the center aisle. It was as if something was pulling him. Unable and unwilling to stop, he carried on, no longer able to hear what was said behind and no longer caring.

He drew level with the first cubicle, and his heart leaped when he saw a woman inside. Preserved in fluid, she was either dead or in suspended animation.

This woman was tall and blonde, where his mother was dark. Treva was even more certain that his mother was somewhere in the chamber.

He raced along the row. He was vaguely aware of Herja following close behind. A distant part of his brain heard her sharp intake of breath as she reached the first cubicle.

Treva looked back to see his father smiling at the guard. It made him shiver to know that Marco wouldn't think twice about shooting the man.

He averted his eyes from the women who stood in silent stillness. He ran along the row until he reached the final one.

Treva looked up at the faceplate. His lungs were full as he prepared to see her face. Condensation on the glass obscured the features of the woman inside. Her outline was clear, but it could have been anyone.

Swallowing, Treva tried to wipe the glass, only to discover that the problem was on the inside. It was too much.

He smashed at the glass with his fist. She had to wake up and come home with him. For a couple of seconds, he felt nothing, and then pain blasted up his arm.

Perhaps Marco was explaining to the guard that his son had something wrong with his brain, but Treva no longer cared. He'd had enough. It was his mother, and she had to come back now because he had managed the impossible by getting this far. There was no way that she could be dead in an upright coffin.

Herja took his arm. "It's okay. We'll get her out of there. Just hold it together for a little bit longer."

The guard was walking toward them with Marco following a couple of steps behind. Treva watched, disconnected from the world as his father pulled out his pulse gun and aimed it at the guard's head.

Rooted to the spot, Treva did nothing, said nothing, as Marco pulled the trigger. The man dropped to the floor without making a sound. Marco straddled him and shot him again in the head, as if he executed people all the time. His mother had been right—Marco Steyn was a dangerous man.

Kali skidded around the corner to confront Marco. "Was that really necessary?"

Marco didn't bother to answer. The pulse gun disappeared into his suit, and he strolled toward a bank of electronics. "Does anyone know how to operate this if I authorize clearance?"

Kali stared at him, seemingly considering how to respond. "How senior are you in this organization?"

"Near the top, but not enough to save any of us when they catch up to us. I suggest we get on with this and get out of here. We have been ridiculously lucky so far, but that isn't going to last for much longer."

— — —

Mika studied the ancient interface. "These women must have been kept in stasis. I have no idea how long they've been here."

Treva had left the containment chamber to investigate the operating panel when Mika noticed him frown and felt a sudden surge of anger. "Ask your father why they did this."

Mika returned his attention to the electronic system as Treva glared in his father's direction. Mika felt guilty for the outburst. It wasn't the boy's fault, but there was nothing he could do about it now. Better to concentrate on finding a way to bring the women out of stasis without causing irreparable harm, rather than causing strife.

The truth was that he couldn't look. He was afraid to know if his mother was in one of the rows that stretched out into the darkness. He was also afraid to recognize any of the faces trapped behind the glass. What he did to free them was vital, and yet, he didn't know what he was doing. Knowing for sure that she was one of them wouldn't help.

"We don't have long," Steyn said.

Mika concentrated on the readouts. Some of these figures must be temperature readings. He tapped a digital number that might have something to do with how they titrated a cocktail of drugs before pumping it into the system. They would need something to make the women compliant and facilitate stasis. What would happen if Mika turned it off at the wrong time and they woke, trapped inside glass tubes?

It was right that the responsibility to free them fell to him. He couldn't ask anyone else to do it but he would, if there had been someone more qualified. Still, facilitating their freedom was the only action that could help him begin to make amends for all his wrongdoing.

Mika looked at the next bank of machinery. Each chamber had an individual reading relating to brain activity and other bodily functions. A number was the only identifying factor, which was a blessing. It meant that he wasn't confronted by any details.

"I'm not a foking doctor," he muttered to Kali. "I don't think we can do this quickly. If I try, I might well kill them." His mouth had gone too dry to speak, and it took a second before he could continue. "Essentially, they've put them in extended hibernation. It looks like it will take at least two hours to run the wake-up procedure, and if they are going to survive, they'll then need time to acclimatize before we attempt to move them."

Kali stared at the screen. "There are too many of them. Even if we could wake them, I can't see a way to get them all out safely." She paused. "And, at the moment, I can't see a way to get *us* out unharmed, either."

Mika checked. "There are forty-four women." He was surprised when the words came out without any emotion, even as his hands shook. "Here goes." He hesitated. "I don't know what I'm doing."

"We have to try. I think they would want a chance to escape this place." Kali's voice was gentle.

Mika locked eyes with her. "Are you sure?" It was cowardly to have her make the decision, but at her firm nod, he turned off the supply of chemicals and activated a self-evident program called 'wake-up procedure'. "I hope this works," he whispered so that only Kali—his conscience—would hear.

"Do your best. I'm going to see if there's any way to get the boy out of here." She patted Mika's arm before leaving.

He sighed. He hadn't bothered to ask if she would consider leaving any of the women behind because he already knew her answer. No, this was where he needed to make up for all the suffering he'd caused. He regretted dragging Kali into this mess. He had to save her, just as much as he needed to save as many of the women as possible.

He tried and failed to tune out the raised voices to his left. Treva and his father were arguing. Mika felt guilty again for taking his anger out on the boy when it was Steyn he was angry with.

"This is the first time I've been in this part of the station," Steyn said. "I told you that your mother betrayed me by running off with you, and I couldn't be sure that she wouldn't do it again."

"It didn't matter to you that she *is* my mother?" Treva's fists clenched at his sides. Something told Mika that he would take a swing at Steyn if the man didn't back off. "Did you think at all about how I would feel?"

"I was afraid that she was going to hide you away like she did when you were a baby. You didn't seem that bothered when she disappeared at first."

"That was because I thought she'd gone off to teach me a lesson. I didn't know that she was in real danger, or else I would never—"

Mika felt for the boy. He understood as well as anyone what it was like to have a piece of shite for a father. He'd discovered firsthand the difficulties of trying to build a life afterward. It was better if Treva didn't discover that just now.

A clang reverberated through the chamber, causing everyone to stop what they were doing and look at Mika. "It's fine. I'm sure it's fine."

The readings were stable. There'd been a spike in the heart rate and blood pressure across all the chambers, as would be expected if they were waking. There was no need to worry.

Mika didn't know which reading belonged to Treva's mother or his own, if she was here. He supposed that it didn't matter, since he was trying to ensure that they all survived. As far as he could tell, the system was a combination of modern and ancient. Based on the tech, it looked like it had been put together from whatever the engineers could get their hands on. If that was the case, there was no guarantee that any of these women would survive the wake-up procedure.

"They were due to be shipped somewhere else," Steyn was saying, but even Mika, who didn't know him, could tell that he was not telling the whole truth.

"You should consider using telepathy on Steyn," he said to Kali.

"On what grounds?" she sent back. *"He's helping—I checked that much. He wants us to get out of here."*

"It doesn't hurt to bend the rules sometimes."

She didn't respond, but he felt her irritation.

An alarm sounded on the equipment. The readings showed the heart rate and blood pressure in chamber fourteen dropping rapidly.

"Kali!" Mika shouted.

She was beside him, looking over the readings. "Can you do anything?"

"I don't know." His hands moved, but every attempt did nothing. "Pod fourteen is in trouble."

Kali was gone, racing down the rows. Everyone watched in silence, and Kali's footsteps thudded as she frantically tried to locate number fourteen. Then, she stopped moving, and there was the whoosh of a breached seal. Unable to do anything to help from the control center, Mika ran toward her.

Silhouetted against the pulsing lights, Kali held a body in her arms. She turned to him, her eyes glistened in the low light, reflecting the tear tracks that streak her face. She made no attempt to resuscitate the woman. Mika couldn't see why until he reached her.

The woman wore a cut-off rubberized suit that failed to hide the large wound in her side. Kali's hands were bloodstained even though nothing leaked from the woman's body.

"What happened?" He couldn't say the words out aloud despite Kali being the only one who would hear him.

"She must have carried the injury before they put her into stasis."

"Kali, I want you to leave with the others," Mika urged. "I can continue the wake-up process and you can go for help."

She gave him a blank look.

He touched her arm. "I want you to live. It's important."

"We *all* need to live."

"Some more than others. It's okay. I deserve..." it was hard to say the words, "to die, protecting the women I helped Tregaren to capture. After everything that happened—"

"No." She glared at him with such fury, he almost fell back. "It wasn't your fault. You didn't have any control over what you did."

He looked at the ground, speaking as if she hadn't interrupted. "It was partly my fault. This is the only way to keep you safe and make amends."

"Why me? You didn't do anything to me."

She really doesn't see it.

Another alarm sounded. It was too much. Mika didn't feel able to deal with any more right now, but after another look at Kali, he raced back to the bank of equipment. Once there, he realized his mistake. The sound was coming from above. Someone had discovered them.

CHAPTER 24

HERJA STARED AT Kali, not quite believing what she was hearing. "You want me to leave?"

What is her agenda? There was no way Herja was about to confess that she'd been thinking of leaving anyway. As far as she was concerned, this whole scenario was a lose-lose situation. The best she could hope for was being locked up by the TSS for life after they'd been saved from certain death.

"Take Treva and go." Kali paused before adding, "I just need you to do one more thing."

Here it comes. The real reason she's asking me to run.

"As soon as you can, I need you to get a message out and let my contact at the TSS know that we're trapped and need rescue. He knows where we disappeared, but he might need direction about how to access this subspace location."

Herja raised an eyebrow. "Why don't we all make a break for it?"

"I can't leave the captives, and we won't be able to move them for a few hours." Kali glanced in Treva's direction. "I'm going to try to persuade him to go."

Herja wasn't above running, as she'd already decided that it was the best option. It wasn't entirely selfish; she had people relying on her.

There were, however, significant problems with Kali's plan. She went for the second most obvious first. "Treva won't go."

Kali looked over at him. There was a frown on his face as he watched them. It was almost as if he could hear their conversation, even though that was impossible across the distance that separated them.

"We have to try."

Herja sighed, now forced to point out the other glaringly obvious difficulty and the reason she hadn't already gone. "The time for sneaking out is over. Everyone and their ancestors know that we're here."

"Leave that bit to me." Kali sounded too confident. "Will you do it?"

"Yes. I will leave with or without the boy." She met Kali's eyes. "I've done all I can and never intended to die for him." She shook her head. "To be honest, I have no idea how I ended up in this situation. While it would be glorious to die in battle, there are people outside who need me."

Kali frowned. "Who?"

Herja smiled. She had no intention of answering the TSS. "When do you want me to make a run for it?"

Kali paused.

Herja snapped, "Don't be peering in my head."

"As if we have time for me to sort through that jumble." Kali scanned the chamber. "You'll have to go now before I destroy the locks. After that, nobody is getting in or out."

They both knew that such an action would only buy them a short amount of time, and so Herja stayed quiet. She was willing to go along with whatever fantasy got her out of this bomaxed nightmare. These people were going to die if they were lucky.

She watched as Kali tried to convince Treva to leave. Even his good-for-nothing father weighed in, trying to persuade the boy that his mother would want him to go. When that didn't work, Steyn told him that she was dead and all of this would be for nothing if he died as well.

Treva wasn't as gullible as he looked; she had discovered that in their time traveling together. While she wished he had a bit more sense and would come with her, she'd known that he wouldn't. What did they expect? He'd fought hard to find his mother, and he was hardly going to abandon her before they could have a conversation.

As Herja listened to them argue back and forth, she wondered why they were wasting time. How could she know the boy better than any of them when they'd spent such a short amount of time together?

If she was going to go, it had to be now. She strolled over to the small group. Treva looked up with wary eyes, while Kali and Steyn went quiet.

She smiled and grasped his arm. "I have to go, but it's been good knowing you."

His shoulders relaxed a little, but the tension in his face stopped him from returning her smile. "Thank you."

"It was good to know you." He was too young to die, but the world did not care about such things. "If you survive and fancy a life of adventure, come and find me." That last was said for Steyn's benefit and it had the desired effect.

He spluttered.

She laughed, knowing that his disapproval was one way to guarantee that Treva would seek her out.

Treva nodded. "Thank you for helping me when you didn't have to."

Herja didn't dare look in Steyn's direction. He radiated irritation, which was satisfying enough. She had no idea how they had ended up on the same side, but she didn't like it. Time for her to go.

"If you do make it out of here," because it looked unlikely, and Herja didn't shy away from such truths, "be on the lookout for any strange messages. That will be me."

Herja released Treva's arm and turned her attention to Kali. "We must be about out of time."

Kali looked over at Treva once more. She must finally

have seen the determination that had been obvious to Herja from the start. Kali threw her arms in the air and marched toward the only entrance and exit.

Steyn trailed behind. "When I secured the door, I changed the codes. They'll override it in time."

It was weirdly quiet. Herja suspected that nobody wanted to contend with the damage that a breaching charge would make or any other method of forcing their way through a meter of metal. Certainly, the precarious subspace position was working to their advantage, in that regard. Finding a key to open the door was a much safer approach, even if it did take a bit of time.

Herja wasn't going without a weapon. "Where's that guard's rifle?" She could see it hooked over Steyn's shoulder.

Kali stared at Steyn. "She will need it."

He narrowed his eyes and she thought that he was going to argue, but then he sighed and handed it to her. "Anything else? I guess you've already taken my son." Steyn's laughter had a hysterical edge to it.

Kali looked for Mika. He was still across the other side of the chamber, but their eyes locked and she smiled. Herja felt something pass between them.

Herja shook her head. *I'm losing it.*

When Kali looked back at her, Herja took a deep breath. It was good that their luck had held, but since experience told her there was only a finite amount of the stuff, that might mean that it would run out just when she needed it the most.

Steyn was paler than she'd ever seen him. She wondered if he was concerned about the damage they were about to cause or if he'd realized there was no way back.

Kali nodded to Steyn. "Open it."

He didn't move. "This is a mad plan."

"She's the only chance we've got. You know better than anyone that there's no way anyone is going to find us in time." Kali gestured to Herja. "You can leave with her."

Herja did not like the idea of being stuck with Steyn. She didn't trust him, and they would be lucky not to kill each other before they got off the station.

Steyn glanced at Treva, who stood next to Mika and shook his head. "I can't."

Steyn turned his attention to the door control and tapped in a code. It slid open so quickly that Herja wasn't ready, but neither were the six armed figures in the corridor. They must have been told to hang back, because none were close to the opening. By the time, they'd raised their weapons, a sphere of pure glowing energy had emerged from between Kali's hands. It grew rapidly.

Kali glanced at Herja, before bowling the fireball straight into the corridor.

"A warning next time," Herja shouted as she ran into the unknown.

CHAPTER 25

KALI WAS AWARE that things didn't look good for them and yet, there was no way that she could leave Mika alone to take care of the awakening captives. It was her responsibility to keep people safe, but he had made her consider ways of getting someone out.

She patted Mika's arm and couldn't help smiling. "Thank you." When she'd asked him to link with her, he hadn't hesitated. "Had you done anything like that before?"

"Never."

"Neither had I."

That meant that nobody had known what they were doing. The nearest that Kali had ever come was the time that she'd helped Tanya's boyfriend Rabin contain his grief. It was impressive that Mika had opened himself up so readily and allowed their abilities to merge and create the most spectacular ball of energy she'd ever seen in a dampened subspace environment.

In that first moment of joining, something alive had moved between them. It felt as if they shared a heartbeat and was both exhilarating and terrifying. Kali felt an overwhelming sense of gratitude to Mika.

Herja had gone. Kali didn't expect her to stick to her promise to contact Andy, but it offered a fragile hope that she wouldn't be without. They were trapped and were going to have to fight until... she refused to think about how unlikely it was that help would arrive in time. It had been a gamble to try to get someone out, and Herja was the only one who would leave and was capable of flying the *Sepiantia.* Mika had made it clear that he wouldn't abandon the mission because of some warped sense of responsibility.

She detected the arrival of more people in the corridor outside, and it reaffirmed their current danger. It was inevitable that the station's leaders would send backup, but she'd hoped for more time, especially since the energy ball had worked better than expected. The effort had drained her, but not as much as she'd imagined.

Kali wanted time to rest but feared that wasn't going to be possible. She didn't want to ask Mika for help again because one of them needed to be left standing to help the women as they woke.

Steyn was at the viewscreen. He had discovered a way to monitor the corridor outside. Kali supposed that it was a good thing that they could prepare for what was coming, but she didn't like the frown on his face.

"They won't need to override the doors if they use those breaching charges," he said.

"Why didn't they use them earlier?"

"Perhaps, they didn't want to risk the structural integrity. There's no guarantee there won't be further damage, and some of the stasis pods are likely to be destroyed in the process."

"We can't allow that to happen."

He gave her a look and she didn't need to read his mind to know that he thought she was being naïve. "We will do what we can."

Kali saw the opportunity to get more information. "You think that they want to protect the women?"

Steyn nodded. "They represent immortality."

"But only if they can get the technology to work, right?"

Kali looked at the antiquated controls for the stasis pods. "The setup isn't awe-inspiring."

"This isn't it. The laboratory..." He trailed off and then chuckled. "I don't know why I'm trying to keep secrets now." He met her eyes. "You smell of TSS, but I can't figure out why you would keep the company of pirates."

"It's a long story and we don't have time."

He let out another laugh. "Sorry." With a deep breath, he appeared to get himself under control. "I was just imagining my brother's face when he found out that, despite his extensive security, there was a TSS Agent on his precious space station."

Kali didn't smile, her patience stretched thin. "I need to know what you were going to tell me."

"Of course. SPEAR Tec has laboratories, but I don't know where. I was in charge of the Steyn family's transport systems. Only Andrei, my brother, has an overview of the family empire."

"Empire?" Kali had never heard of them.

He shrugged. "I don't know the extent of their resources, but it was enough to attract an ex-Priest with dreams of immortality."

Inside, Kali shuddered. They'd had enough resources for a secret space station hidden in subspace and forty-four victims, waiting to be moved to a secret laboratory. She'd say that their resources were extensive. And, as far as she knew, the Steyn family wasn't known to the TSS.

"The women were put into stasis when the ex-Priest died." Steyn pointed at the viewscreen. "Do you think we can get hold of that?" he asked, referencing a breaching charge held by one of the guards.

Kali wanted to ask more about the women, the Steyn family, and SPEAR Tec, but their safety was the more immediate concern. She considered his question about getting the device. "How? We'd have to open the door again."

"Use your magic powers."

Magic! Right. Kali thought he was joking, but when she looked at his face, saw that he was serious. "I'm still recovering from what I did before—"

"Yeah, that was an impressive party trick, but can you do anything useful?"

Kali felt the hot sensation she associated with her temper and took a deep breath. "I could take control of a mind." He stepped back, and she added, "Just to be clear, Agent code forbids violating someone's mind unless there's a dire need." Before he could point out that they were in deep trouble, she added, "So, in this case, I could, but it means opening that door again."

In a cheerful voice, Steyn said, "It went well enough last time. If we get the breaching charge, it means they can't use it."

Kali was suspicious, so scanned the surface of his mind. There was nothing treacherous, just a deep-rooted fear for Treva.

She nodded. "Okay, let's do it. I'm going to focus on her," she pointed to a woman carrying two blasting charges in their direction. "When you open the door, shoot at the ceiling or something, and I'll make sure she delivers those charges to us."

Steyn met her eyes and nodded once. "After three."

Kali felt for the woman whose mind she invaded. She was young and nervous. This was nothing like her short, intense training, and she wondered if she'd get to see someone named James again. Kali grasped her mind, ready to take full control.

"Three, two, one."

Steyn activated the door release.

The woman tried to slip out of Kali's power. She wasn't trained in protecting herself and didn't have any shields, but some part of her must have recognized the danger and acted to break free. The dampening effect of subspace on Kali's abilities didn't help, but she held on tight, reminding the woman that she had been coming toward them and so needed to continue.

Steyn fired pulse blasts, unconcerned with who or what he might hit. The shots rippled the air down the corridor. Someone screamed, which hurt Kali's ears.

She was suddenly terrified that their woman was going to be hit and drop the charges. She wanted to yell at Steyn but didn't have the energy.

The woman—Kali didn't want to know her name—stumbled through the door. Her eyes were glazed. The blasting charges slipped from lax arms, rolling to the floor in a heart-stopping clatter.

Kali released her mind but not before she felt a tremor go through her body. With eyes huge and wide, the woman appeared disorientated for a second. Then, to Kali's relief, she ran back the way she'd come.

A blast sent Kali reeling to the deck. When she pushed herself up, she saw the woman lying in the middle of the corridor, unmoving. In the split second before she tore her gaze away, Kali saw that her eyes were wide open. A streak of blood marked her pale, smooth face and her legs were twisted at an impossible angle.

Despite the danger, Kali closed her eyes briefly. When she opened them, she reminded herself that her priority was still to protect the people inside the chamber. For them to live, others would die.

Someone continued to fire, but nothing came close to hitting them. At a guess, they were firing blind.

Steyn had stopped shooting and was staring at the charges. Without any warning, he grabbed the bag and ran out into the corridor toward the enemy. Kali surged to her feet but she was out of energy and without a weapon, she couldn't do much. Steyn rapidly placed charges on the walls outside the door.

Stars, what's he doing?

Plasma bursts narrowly missed his head, leaving long scorch marks along one wall. Kali had to do something.

She reached out, trying to deflect the fire using her

telekinesis, but she was exhausted and hardly affected the trajectory. She stumbled to the door, not sure what she was planning to do. More attackers arrived, some wearing the same dark-blue uniform as the guy that Steyn had killed.

"Come on!" she shouted.

Steyn didn't seem to hear her. Without thinking, she ran to grab his arm.

He thrust her away. "Go back."

"Dad!" Treva's terrified voice came from behind them.

Kali turned to see three people in blue raise weapons. She dove for Treva, connecting with his upper body. They both went to the ground in a tangle of limbs.

Something slammed into her from behind as a blast deafened her. Heat scoured the air. As soon as she could, she rolled off Treva, trying to process what had happened or identify the most immediate threat. She was relieved to see that Treva was unhurt.

Steyn had the door half-closed. The fabric of his suit was burned away from the left side and across his back. Blood coated the bare flesh of his arm and shoulder. As the lock automatically clicked into place, it muted the sound of more pulse-fire with the occasional plasma blast.

Steyn turned, his face contorted in pain before he crumpled to the floor.

Stars, he must have taken the full impact of the detonation. He must have been what hit her in the back, also diving to protect Treva.

Kali scrabbled to get to Steyn before Treva saw too much, but it was hopeless. The boy was already on his feet and ahead of her. He had one hand over his mouth as if he was trying to hold in a scream.

Kali was barely aware of the nonsense coming out of her mouth, "It's okay. We can get help." As if there was anyone or anywhere to get help.

Treva reached his father. Another explosion shook the floor and sent them both flying. The blasting charges that Steyn had laid on the wall must have gone off.

It felt like the whole station would be shaken apart. Kali had an image of their chamber separated from the rest of the station and drifting in subspace for eternity. She understood that Steyn had been trying to buy them time.

When Kali pushed up from the floor, pain flared through her left arm. She flexed the fingers of the same hand. They responded as they should, but her arm still throbbed. She rolled to her feet and saw that Treva was at his father's side.

Kali felt for Steyn with her mind. He was alive, and his consciousness flared in response to her touch. She heard him speak with her mind as well as with her ears.

"Read me. I need you to tell Treva what's in there."

"Don't speak, Dad. You're wasting your energy."

"I'm dying. There's nothing anyone can do about it, but I want you to know the truth."

Each word was an effort. Kali felt his determination, his desperation that his son should understand and not think too badly of him.

"I know that I shouldn't be asking you to do this. There are more important things to do but—"

"I'll do it," she agreed.

Sinking through the layers of his mind, she absorbed all the images and feelings that she could. Kali tried to remember everything for Treva.

Steyn's thoughts were all over the place, and she caught glimpses of events and incidents out of order. So much of it didn't make any sense, but she felt the love that he held for Treva and how much he'd wanted to get to know his son better.

She saw him give up the details of Treva's mother, knowing what would happen to her. He felt bad that he hadn't considered how it would affect Treva. He planned to fill the gap she left. It was fading, and she felt everything drain away.

She'd started to withdraw because it would be dangerous to stay. She didn't want to be there when Steyn died. The color was leaking away, leaving grey behind but something bothered her. There was a splash of vivid red. A conversation between Steyn and a man she couldn't see. Something told her it was important. She went closer to the memory.

"SPEAR will start by attacking key cities in the outer colonies. Once there's enough fear, they will all look to us for protection and we can make sure that the TSS and Guard never get a foothold here again."

Steyn was thinking about his first meeting with Treva. Kali commanded him to show her the memory.

"Everything will be in place by..."

No, it couldn't end now. She needed to know more.

Marco's voice was everywhere, *"Thank you. Tell him, please."*

"I will." What more could she say? He was dying.

Kali opened her eyes to find that Steyn had stopped breathing. Treva's small hand was pressed to the side of his father's face. Her mind was a whirl with everything she had found out, but she had to concentrate. Treva was the most important at that moment.

"He loved you."

"He loved the idea of having a son."

"No. It might have been like that until he met you, but then it became about you."

Treva shook his head. "I betrayed him. That's why he's dead."

Kali grabbed him, forcing him to look at her. "It really mattered to him that you knew the truth." She understood now why it had been so important. "He regretted what he did to your mother, but it was too late by the time he understood the effect of losing her on you. That's the reason we're here, not because of the choices you made."

Tears ran down Treva's face. He didn't even seem to realize. Kali didn't have time for this, but she couldn't leave him, either.

She searched for something that he could cling to. "We

have to help your mother."

It was the only thing that might cut through the loss, and it worked. Treva's eyes came into focus, and he looked to where Mika was still at the control panel. Kali only hoped that they could save her, because if they didn't, Treva was going to lose his mind. Then, she wanted to laugh hysterically at the thought, since it was highly likely that they were all going to die.

CHAPTER 26

HERJA HAD RUN down the narrow channel that Kali had left
on one side of the corridor. Her right shoulder had brushed
the wall. If that energy-thing had grown any bigger, she
would have fried.

Herja had reached a junction. The ball of energy had
been shrinking rapidly, and she hadn't had much time until
she was visible to the entire corridor. She'd flattened
herself against the wall and peered around the corner.

She'd made it past the danger zone and nobody had
followed her. They might not even have seen her, they'd
been so busy diving for cover.

Remind me never to upset the TSS.

Where was the rifle-fire? It was too quiet, and she
didn't like it. Give her predictability, anytime, even if it
meant that someone was shooting at her.

She kept her rifle pointed ahead. All thoughts of
unfinished business were gone. She didn't think of Gosta or
the *Hyperion. Why isn't anyone trying to kill me?*

Within a couple of seconds, she reached the end of the
corridor and still hadn't been shot at once. There was
nobody there! She realized that they had all run.

It's a good day to be alive.

Despite being sure that she had used up every drop of

luck, and she still had to get across an entire hostile station, Herja chuckled. Her enemies had weapons, but they couldn't have been trained much in combat. Perhaps they were scientists called off their jobs to attack a bunch of intruders.

When the action heated up, they hadn't been able to run far or fast enough to get away from whatever the stars Kali had thrown at them. She had no idea whether any of her guesswork was true but she wouldn't lose any sleep over it.

Herja slung the pulse rifle over her shoulder and forced herself to walk briskly, not run, as if she had every right to be there. Nobody knew what she looked like and they wouldn't be expecting her. Now, if only she knew how to get to where she was going.

There were colored lines on the walls. The problem was that Herja didn't know what they meant. She turned left. A couple of people strode toward her. They were deep in conversation and didn't even glance her way as they walked past.

She paused and considered asking for directions to the docking airlock but she wasn't desperate enough to risk their attention. Still, she didn't have time to waste wandering around in circles.

There were a few more people around her now. She must have entered a busier section which was good—wasn't it?

A young man walking toward her kept glancing her way. He didn't look old enough to be anybody important and probably found her attractive. She could use that.

She stepped into his path. "Could you direct me to the docking airlock?"

He looked confused. Herja could imagine what he was thinking—something like, 'Is she that stupid?' Herja didn't care. She only wanted to find the *Sepiantia*.

"Didn't you attend the introductory briefs?"

She didn't want a foking conversation with him. "Yeah,

but I got turned around. The docking airlock?" When he hesitated, she added, "Or, don't you know?"

He frowned. "It's the yellow line, but—"

Herja was already moving away, now understanding that was what the yellow line was for, when an alarm sounded.

From behind, the man shouted, "Hey, you."

Shite, her luck had run out. *Why did it always have to be at the worst moment?*

Herja wanted desperately to run but held back, instead opting to turn down the nearest branch corridor, and then rounding another corner. He had been too slow to act; she could lose him. There was nobody in this passageway, which made it impossible to blend in.

An armed group turned so that they were heading toward her. They all wore the same blue as the first man that Steyn had shot to save Treva. She could still hear the young man's shouts in the distance.

Eyes ahead, she gave up on pretending to be confident and went for full-on arrogance. Nobody had any right to stop her, to question her. She was too important. She marched past, arms swinging slightly.

Just about to let out the breath that she had unconsciously held, she heard someone say, "Stop."

Herja froze, and for once, she was uncertain about what to do next. She slowly turned to see five men and three women staring at her. One of the men broke off and walked toward her. Each step of his booted feet reverberated off the walls.

Herja's fingers flexed of their own accord. She wasn't going down without a fight, but some long-forgotten animal part of her knew that any sudden movement would trigger a violent response.

He stopped in front of her. "Commander Steyn's personal guard."

She blinked. *Steyn!*

Did they mean Marco Steyn? No, but this Commander

must be related and must be someone important. Her brain refused to work out the relevance to the current situation, so she let it go.

"I will confiscate that weapon."

Herja unslung the rifle, still not sure what she was going to do. "Why?"

"Can't you hear the alarm?"

She could. She guessed it had something to do with the stunt Kali had pulled to get her out of that chamber. Still—

"Didn't you pay attention at your briefing?" He glared. "We are under attack. All weapons must be accounted for."

"Oh, of course." It went against everything inside Herja, but she was a survivor first and foremost.

She offered the rifle butt-first. The man snatched it with more force than was necessary.

For a second, Herja wondered if it had been a ploy to ensure she was unarmed before they arrested or shot her. With a last glare in her direction, the group turned and marched off.

She shook her head. Kali and the others wouldn't have any trouble dealing with them when they arrived. As soon as the corridor was clear, Herja ran. She kept half an eye on the yellow stripe. It had tiny arrows, which she hoped led to the docking airlock.

It didn't take long until she reached the point where they had turned off for the mess hall. There was a buzz of activity and confusion, which meant that nobody paid much attention to her racing along, dodging people.

She burst into the lower deck of the docking station. The cylindrical room was capped by a transparent dome, with the berthed ships visible above. The bottom level was filled with cargo—possibly general provisions, if the crate markings were any indication. A pair of elevators ran up the back wall.

Two men, who were stationed near the entrance at what Herja took to be a glorified reception desk, looked up from a holoprojector displaying a security notice. Someone had muted the alarm, but the sound drifted in from the corridor.

"Stop. What's your business here?" one of them said.

"You remember me? I was with Marco Steyn earlier." She had no idea whether it was the same man or not. "He wants me to pilot the *Sepiantia* away from the station."

The other man's eyes narrowed. "Well, Mr. Steyn knows that no ships leave when we are on lockdown."

"Oh, I think it was because someone—Commander Steyn told him to sort it."

"The Commander?"

"I'm sure that's what he said."

The other guard blocked her way with his enormous bulk, but he hadn't drawn his weapon. That was a mistake.

"Who are you?" he demanded.

"The captain of that ship up there." She pointed to the vessel docked beyond the dome above.

"That ship is now the property of the Spadrosi Station."

She glared, knowing she had to get past him no matter what it took.

"Don't look at me like that. I don't make the rules. It's just how things are done around here."

Herja had wasted enough time. "Whatever you say. I have to be on my way."

She could see from the way he folded his arms across his middle and stood straighter that she was going to have to fight her way through.

Then, the whole station shook. Herja held out her hands trying to keep her balance as the deck heaved.

"What in the stars was that?" said the guard blocking her way, echoing what she was thinking.

"You'd better check it out." When he looked at her with suspicion, she smiled reassuringly. "I'd offer to come with you, but I need to check the ship isn't damaged."

He was torn, clearly suspecting that she was up to no good and at the same time concerned about the integrity of the station. After a muttered curse, he headed for the corridor.

Herja was edging toward the elevator that would lead to the *Sepiantia*. She had no idea whether the ship was locked down, but she was way out of time.

The sound of pulse-fire came from behind, rippling along the ceiling of the corridor. Herja didn't stop. Luck or no luck, it was best to ensure she was a moving target.

She dashed toward the pair of elevators to the upper dock, the only way for her to get to the gangway leading to the *Sepiantia*. One of the elevator's doors stood open, and Herja prayed to her ancestors that the guards hadn't disabled it.

She dove into the elevator. There was nothing to press, and she stared in horror at the open door. She ducked down, hearing approaching footsteps. She was facing an execution squad without a weapon, and there was nowhere to go.

The booted footfalls grew louder until she couldn't believe they weren't already next to her. Herja closed her eyes, unable to watch her own death. The doors hissed shut.

A muted shout carried through, "Who left the foking elevator unlocked?"

Luck hadn't deserted her! And she couldn't complain about its timing today.

There was a sensation of acceleration and then silence until the pulsing white light appeared at either side of the door as is ascended.

As soon as the doors opened on the upper deck, Herja ran to the *Sepiantia*. Getting on board was Step One, but how could she get the foking ship to fly?

She'd watched Mika carefully when he took off that one time, but she hadn't seen him take the *Sepiantia* from cold to ready. Nothing about the ship was intuitive. She missed Gosta and the *Hyperion*.

At least she managed to lock the doors. Then, she remembered the neural link. That was the missing piece.

The trouble was that nobody had shown her how it worked, and she had a feeling that having telepathic abilities would help enormously with the task. She ignored the memory of the way Kali had looked at her when Herja had insisted that she wasn't Gifted in the traditional sense. What she had was a strong survival instinct. Well, she'd better use it now, hadn't she?

Something thudded against the *Sepiantia*'s outer access hatch.

Shite, they haven't given up. Stop panicking and work it out.

Herja stroked the console. "Come on. We have to get out of here." The viewscreen lit up. "That's it. You remember what it's like to fly."

Stars, the ship isn't alive. Herja couldn't believe that she had resorted to speaking to the *Sepiantia* like it was sentient.

Another thud hit the hatch, shaking the ship. She had to go now.

A pulse of blue light flashed across Herja's vision. Nothing had changed, but when she tried again to power up the engines, they came online.

On Herja's command, the *Sepiantia* tried to pull away from the gangway, engines growing in pitch as the ship strained against the docking clamps. Herja had nothing to lose; it wasn't the *Hyperion*. She ignored the warning lights and accelerated. All of a sudden, the clamps were ripped free, and the ship shot upward. The three other ships remained attached to the docking station, despite the chunk that she'd taken away with her.

Another computer system tried to remotely override the ship's systems, but Herja had this now. There was no way that she was going to allow anyone access.

Herja let out a breath she hadn't realized she'd been holding. Stroking the console, she searched for weapons, just in case. There was an array of armaments, but she wasn't sure how weapons would behave in subspace within the strange field extending from the station.

She tried not to ruminate on what was happening back in the stasis chamber. There was nothing she could do to help them, except do as Kali had asked.

The trouble was, she didn't like the thought of speaking to the TSS. It would be better if they never knew her. If she contacted them, they would know what she looked like and that she existed. If Kali died, there was nothing to know.

Still, Treva was on the space station, and if there was any chance of rescue, it was up to her. She had to be satisfied that she'd tried. It would be so much easier if she had a pirate's heart.

She thanked the stars that the *Hyperion* also had an independent jump drive, as figuring out how to get back to normal space might have been impossible otherwise. She plotted a course to normal space a short distance from the moon. Following her instincts, she stayed within the field extending from the station's upper pole until the *Sepiantia*'s maneuvering thrusters were no longer responsive.

I guess I'm clear? She activated the jump drive, finding it a uniquely bizarre experience to do so while already in subspace. The ship continued drifting away from the station, and then it was free, continuing on the subspace course she'd plotted.

At its designated exit point, the *Sepiantia* dropped back into normal space. Herja could have danced across the flight deck with glee upon seeing the peaceful normalcy of stars.

She turned her attention to sending a distress message.

Operating the comm was straightforward enough, but how to approach the call was another matter. Herja wasn't one hundred percent sure what she needed to say— whether to recite the message that Kali had made her memorize or try to make up her own story.

A man's face appeared onscreen, the same one with startling bioluminescent eyes whom Kali had spoken to earlier. It occurred to her that Kali's eyes should also glow. Did she wear contact lenses? She must, or else everyone would know she was TSS.

The man frowned, no doubt expecting to see Kali rather than a stranger. Herja was desperate to keep the conversation short since there would be less chance of getting herself in trouble.

"Kali needs your help. She's at the coordinates she gave you. Here's the docking protocol for the station in subspace." It wasn't Kali's wording exactly, but it got the point across. Herja sent the details from the nav computer using the neural link.

"Who are you?" the Agent asked.

"Hurry, they're dying." She ended the call before he could find out too much about her.

If Kali survived, she would no doubt supply more information about Herja, anyway. It would be better if the TSS didn't arrive in time, but it was out of her hands now.

Next, Herja contacted Gosta. She smiled at his relief when he saw her through the viewscreen.

"You managed to stay one step ahead of the *Vector*." She did her best not to let her relief shine through but suspected that she'd failed.

"Only just. The *Vector* has taken some damage and is sulking on Red Ghost for now. It would be great if you could get back before Vaughn is finished with repairs. He's not going to give up."

Herja hesitated. "I won't be long. There's something I need to do first."

"Don't." Gosta leaned forward until his face became that of a giant's hanging over her. "You've got that look in your eyes."

"I'll be with you soon." She ended the transmission.

He knew her too well, and he was right; she should get out of there as fast as possible. It wouldn't do any good to stay.

Herja was growing used to the controls of *Sepiantia*.

The neural link meant that the ship responded to her remarkably well. She might have to get one on the *Hyperion*. She grimaced at the thought of Gosta witnessing her talking to the ship. It wouldn't be the first time.

Herja was used to piloting alone for long periods. Navigation was a distinct skill. She knew enough to manage to get to where she needed to be normally. How easy would it be to use an independent jump drive without Gosta? How easy with a neural link?

Herja sighed. It would be a shame not to test out this interface method a little more to make sure that procuring one for her ship would be worth the expense and effort.

Herja couldn't help smiling as she activated the drive again and a hum filled the air.

A shudder went through the entire ship as the spatial disruption aura began to form around the ship, growing steadily brighter. There was the familiar sensation of time stretching as she slipped into subspace.

The view through the front port turned to swirling blue-green light. The ship was heading nose-first toward the spherical space station, following the same approach to the upper pole they'd previously used to dock.

Herja smiled. Now she was here to help.

The *Sepiantia* knew her intention and was eager to assist. As Mika had observed on their first approach to the station, the maneuvering thrusters didn't respond in the same way as in normal space. Worse, the field's central column, which offered a tiny bit of control, was incredibly narrow. Herja opted for manual operation. She refused a request from the station to open communications as she accelerated toward the enormous structure.

Now we get to find out what conventional weapons do in subspace. Admittedly, she'd always been curious. She smiled. It was times like this that she felt most alive.

Trusting to her extraordinary piloting skills that had never let her down, she sent the *Sepiantia* into a slow, flat spin above the station's outer shell.

She spotted a transparent domed area that matched the location and appearance of the stasis lab's ceiling. The dome was cracking, and didn't look like it had long before it blew out; she had gotten out just in time.

How can I help them? It wasn't like she could pick Treva and the others up. Herja's mind was working furiously. Perhaps she could give that Commander something to worry about and distract him from killing Treva.

With that thought, she targeted a plasma beam at the station, as far away from the cracking dome as she could manage from her fixed position. As the beam left the central column of the field, it began to bend and dissipate. Part of it did strike the station, but the electrified shell deflected most of the blast.

Herja searched through the menu again until she saw the word 'missiles'. *I have missiles!*

She accessed the onboard tracking system and sent two missiles to the same spot she'd struck with the plasma beam. When the missiles left the field's central column, one wandered off into subspace but the other found its target. It detonated on impact.

Herja cheered as the station shuddered. *I bet that got their attention!*

The retaliatory weapon's fire was half-hearted—but, in all fairness, they probably didn't have a lot to work with. Who was crazy and lucky enough to attack a station suspended in subspace?

Weren't counting on Herja, were you, fokers?

She spun the ship in an upward and then downward corkscrew flight pattern that she wasn't sure the *Hyperion* could have pulled off, but the *Sepiantia* responded with grace. The spin kept the station's weapons from being able to get a good lock on her ship, though that didn't keep the display from lighting up with too many warnings to count.

Once in position, she began firing missiles at other targets surrounding the dock, trying to avoid the dock itself and the transparent dome over the lab. Each time one of the missiles left the field's column, it was like rolling dice—some struck true, others spun off in wild directions. Fortunately, they were pointed away from the lab so none hit the cracked dome. If nothing else, the random behavior must be keeping the station's defense team guessing.

Alarms sounded, and soon there were so many going off that Herja thought she might have invented a new form of music.

She wondered how much longer she could keep this up. There were only another two missiles left. She could make them count and offer some distraction, but that was it.

Another vessel materialized above her amongst the blue-green. *Back-up for the Commander?* She hoped not.

As the ship descended toward the station, she recognized the classical shape of a TSS vessel.

She blocked a request for contact and quickly maneuvered away from the field so she could exit subspace. Best to disappear while they were busy.

CHAPTER 27

KALI CRANED HER neck to look upward through the domed glass ceiling. She had tears in the corners of her eyes as she saw blasts from distant weapons' fire. Though she couldn't see the *Sepiantia* itself, she knew it was Herja. *She made it. Help is on the way.*

Mika looked at Kali with wide eyes. "I never said she could use the weapons!"

Kali laughed. "She'd better have sent out the message before pulling this stunt." In her heart, she had no doubt. Perhaps Kali had been less surprised than she should have been to see Herja risk her life to buy them some time. She'd liked the pirate since their first encounter, despite her occupation.

Kali would continue to do her absolute best to protect everyone holed up in the chamber, but as they weren't yet able to move the waking women; a rescue was the only chance they had left. She cradled her arm. It was more painful than when she'd injured it, which wasn't a good sign. She'd expected her medical nanites to have done more by now.

The sound of another bombardment on the door made her heart leap. She had hoped that when Herja attacked that it would stop. After all, the station had other things to worry about now—like losing its tether to normal space. Instead, it felt as though they had redoubled their assault because their time was running out.

Kali could still see the visual feed of the corridor outside on the viewscreen. The shell around their part of the space station appeared to be breaking down. If the glass dome didn't go first, the surrounding structure would soon fail.

She knew from being inside Marco Steyn's head that he'd intended to block the door and buy them some time. It had worked. The door had become a pile of mangled metal that nobody would be able to open, but that didn't mean they were safe.

Someone must have decided that the captive women were expendable, and the attack now concentrated on severing the lab from the rest of the station. Then they would all die.

They still had life support, but that would no doubt change if they broke free. Personally, Kali would prefer a rapid decompression to drifting through subspace until they asphyxiated or starved.

All that she knew for sure was that she would keep fighting for as long as she drew breath. She had faith that someone would come, and if not, she would die believing it.

One thing she wished they'd done differently was in trying to wake the women. It had initially seemed like the only way to get them out. Now, she recognized what an impossible task it had been, and it was too late. Mika had slowed the wake-up protocol. He would have reversed it, if he could, but it was beyond his skills—if it was even possible with the outdated equipment. Kali could sense some of his feelings and knew that he tried not to think about what it meant for his mother, trapped in one of those pods.

Kali went to check on Treva who had curled up at the base of the stasis pod that held his mother. He lifted his head at her approach. When she gave him a tired smile, he laid back down.

Kali had recorded a short message for Andy on her handheld, warning him of what she had seen in Steyn's mind before he'd died. The TSS needed to know that entire planets were at risk. She couldn't help remembering the last message that she'd recorded for Andy and her family when Tregaren had boarded the *Sepiantia*.

She heard a dull thud. Had there been a rupture of the containment shell? Clambering to her feet with some difficulty, she went to check. There was a plume of smoke, but it was too far back to see.

Herja must have hit the station again before she'd left. At least, Kali hoped she had gone. There was no point in them all dying.

There was a flash, and Kali wondered if it had been the *Sepiantia* leaving subspace. She silently wished Herja luck and turned her attention back to Mika. He was gaping and point outside.

"I know, she's gone with your ship."

Mika shook his head. "Kali, look!"

With a long-suffering sigh, she did. There, against the blue-green, was a TSS armored military vessel, and it was huge.

"Rescue," she breathed.

Herja had done it. She had got the message out.

Another blast shook what remained of the door. They weren't safe yet. The enemy had likely spotted the incoming ship and wanted to make sure that her small party couldn't survive to provide any information.

Kali's hand tightened on Steyn's handgun. "Let's get as far away from the door as possible."

She saw Mika's reluctance to leave the stasis monitoring unit, but he joined her. Treva remained where he was, but it was good enough.

"What can we do?" Mika asked, his voice steady.

She smiled. "We've been backed against a wall before,

and we succeeded then. We'll prevail again this time as well. Can you link with me again?"

Mika gave her a genuine smile. "Nothing would make me happier in what might be our last moments."

Kali felt a pressure against her mental shield. They had been through so much already that it felt natural enough to allow him in further.

Like before, his mental presence was exactly as she had known it would be. She let her consciousness entwine with his, experiencing a small shock of power as they sparked off each other. For an instant, she saw what he saw when he looked at her, and it was frightening. To Mika, she was strong and honorable. It felt almost like he worshipped her. Then, the connection was gone.

"What was that?" she asked, her chest rising and falling as her lungs struggled to drag in air.

"At the end?" Mika laughed. "Our minds connected."

She shook her head, once again Kali—exactly who she was supposed to be. "Are you ready?" she asked.

"Better believe it. Let's scorch some scumbags."

Kali didn't have time to respond, because the door buckled inward. She blasted the area with the gun and with her mind. Mika's power fueled her, and for a second, she couldn't feel the extent of it. A ball of energy expanded outward before slamming down on what was left of the corridor.

There were more people at the edge of her consciousness. They swarmed forward, filling the area where their colleagues had fallen. Kali and Mika did it again. More went down, but there was no end to the mass of enemies waiting to move into the gaps.

Kali was vaguely aware that they were losing atmospheric pressure. She needed to seal the breach.

Kali's knees ached almost as much as her arm. She opened her eyes to find that she was resting on her knees. When had that happened?

Mika was on the floor next to her. He reached out a

hand and their fingers entwined. A surge of energy traveled from him to her, and she realized that he was giving her everything that he had. She wanted to send it back, but there was more to do if they were going to keep the women and Treva alive.

With the same focus, power flared from both of them. Kali couldn't tell where she ended and Mika started. Images she didn't recognize assaulted her. A small part of Kali's mind registered what she was experiencing. She had never realized what it took to survive the death of his father. Why hadn't she understood what it was like for him to be denied his power?

Mika had so much to give that they were able to build a barrier across the area where the doorway had been moments before. It was strong enough to resist plasma fire.

The familiar presence of an Agent came in at the edge of her consciousness. *"Kali, you can lower the shield now. It's safe."*

She realized that the shield extended out further than it should. Mika squeezed her hand again and together they reduced the area.

"Now, let go before you burn out. We've got you." The Agent's telepathic voice reassured her.

Kali didn't have the strength to respond, but she hoped they sensed her thanks.

It took more will than she expected to let go because it meant letting go of Mika, as well. At first, he resisted the severing of the connection but when he understood, he released her. The loss threatened to sweep them up, but Mika was still there.

"It's okay."

And it was.

Exhausted, Kali drifted toward unconsciousness, still holding onto her connection with Mika. They were being rescued, and they were together. In that moment, nothing else mattered.

— — —

With a flash, the subdimensional doorway materialized within the transport arch in Andrei Steyn's office. It would allow him to step across space, if only in a limited sense.

His secretary squeaked at the sight of the flash and scrabbled away from the vault, back into the relative safety of Andrei's office. Sometimes Andrei wished he'd chosen a female assistant, but Prya had been the best and proved easy enough to control—probably because he was scared of everything. There was another reason he had chosen Pyra; the man wasn't Gifted, yet Andrei couldn't read his mind. A rare occurrence, indeed, but one that automatically protected any secrets he came into contact with as part of his job.

Andrei glared at him. "If I ever hear you utter that cowardly sound again, you'll never make another one." He stepped toward the arch. "Come on. It's stable."

"Wh... what is it?"

Andrei ignored him since the answer to the question was obvious. The man's brain just needed a few seconds to catch up and recognize that the safest option was to make a quick exit. At that moment, the entire room shook and gave Prya the incentive he needed to walk through the event horizon within the archway.

It wasn't the disintegration of the station that bothered Andrei, although he would mourn the loss of the subjects later; they represented one route to immortality, but it was doubtful that any breeding program could be set up in time to generate his own clone before he died of old age. Who knew what would be feasible in the future.

He was grateful that he had a second option, thanks to Tregaren—one that would see him in control of the outer colonies. It meant embracing an element of risk, but the rewards would be so much more than he'd ever dreamed.

The arrival of the TSS had sent him racing for his emergency exit. Andrei knew all too well how they operated, and he didn't want to be anywhere near when they discovered that he was alive, let alone how much tech he'd stolen before his departure from their service.

The step through subspace using the subdimensional bridge was incredibly peaceful. Andrei liked the sensation of floating. In an instant that also felt like eternity, he stepped into the artificial light of an underground chamber. Steyn could almost feel the weight of the ground overhead.

It was probably the change in energy that made Pyra clamp a hand over his mouth. Well, he'd better get used to it, since they would be here for a few hours. In fact, it was possible that Pyra might never leave, especially if he continued to be so irritating.

Diamond-Boy was right outside the receiving archway, waiting. Wisely, he didn't ask about what had happened. Andrei was not in the mood to go over his failures, and they were his. There was nobody to blame but himself.

He'd known that his brother, Marco Steyn, had other commitments, but despite their clash of personalities, he'd believed him to be a loyal servant. *Never trust family.* He should have remembered their father's words and dealt with the conflict of interest earlier. Not doing so showed a concerning lack of judgment, and now he was paying the price.

In the future, anyone wanting a position at the top would have to demonstrate complete loyalty and there would be no favors for family. The rewards of the job were enough to compensate anyone for what they had to give up.

Andrei still didn't know how he had brought the TSS near to their operation at such a delicate time. They were so close to completion, but their plans needed to remain secret until they were ready. Andrei hoped the imminent chaos would protect them from discovery.

He ignored the handful of people who were hanging around and headed over to the communication center. The murmur of voices grated on his nerves. He wanted some time alone, but that wasn't likely.

Diamond-Boy trailed after him, his voice merging with the others until he said, "The shipment of drugs is missing."

"What?" Andrei glared at him. "You have two days to find them and get them distributed. They are key to our plans."

Diamond-Boy avoided eye contact, remaining silent. Andrei was going to ignore that little problem for now. He could only deal with so much at once.

At the communication center, he inputted his details into the system and pulled up a picture of the *Sepiantia*. The ship was like nothing he had seen before, and not in a good way. It was ugly. At least, that would make it easy to find.

Diamond-Boy's expression told him the answer before he asked. "You recognize this ship."

He nodded. "It was here—"

"It shouldn't have been allowed to dock. What's the point of having security on the planet if you're going to let the TSS look around?"

Diamond-Boy gasped. "TSS? I didn't know."

"The TSS *had* to be involved. They appeared too quickly for it to be otherwise."

Diamond-Boy looked around the chamber as if searching for something he'd lost. "We have one of them—Owen Bruiser. I can get him for you."

Some good news, at last. Andrei nodded. "Not now, first, I need you to destroy the TSD arch."

"But it's—"

"Just do it."

Diamond-Boy gave a series of orders. "We'll have to evacuate the chamber in five minutes, sir."

Only half-listening, Andrei flicked through the information they had obtained during the attack on the station until a picture of Herja appeared on the screen.

Diamond-Boy pointed to the image, eager to please. "That is Herja. She is a pirate captain who arrived on a ship called *Hyperion*. It had Pesta on board."

Andrei swung to face him. "We need that weapon." He

put a hand to his head—how much could go wrong? "What plans do you have for its safe return?"

Andrei only half-listened to Diamond-Boy as he described how the *Vector* was in pursuit of the *Hyperion*. He had seen Herja's face. She had been on the station.

It was going to take more than one ship to get back what they'd lost. If they couldn't retrieve Pesta, it would be harder to make an impact. Without Pesta and the drugs, his plans might well fail. He needed to get both back. And he would.

Andrei looked back at the screen, smiling. This Herja would be easy to find. *I hope you've enjoyed your freedom, pirate. I'm coming for you.*

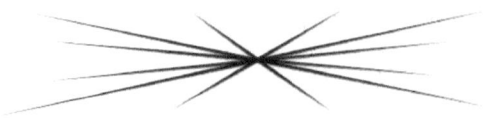

THE STORY CONTINUES IN *SHADOW BEYOND THE REACH*...

Terror attacks are ravaging the Outer Colonies.

SPEAR has been operating in the shadows for decades, building power and influence. When the organization targets the TSS, it threatens to undermine the fragile stability in the remote region.

SPEAR's offer? Protection for those willing to give allegiance. But their true aim had dire implications for the entire Taran race. With TSS' resources already strained, Kali is left with limited backup to stand against the growing menace.

Stretched to their breaking point, Kali and Mika must find a way to strike at the heart of SPEAR and prevent more worlds from falling victim to their dark designs. As the sinister plots against the Taran Empire begin to unfold, can Kali and her companions prevent the Outer Colonies from descending into chaos?

ADDITIONAL READING

Cadicle Space Opera Series by A.K. DuBoff
Book 1: Rumors of War (Vol. 1-3)
Book 2: Web of Truth (Vol. 4)
Book 3: Crossroads of Fate (Vol. 5)
Book 4: Path of Justice (Vol. 6)
Book 5: Scions of Change (Vol. 7)

Verity Chronicles by T.S. Valmond & A.K. DuBoff
Book 1: Exile
Book 2: Divided Loyalties
Book 3: On the Run

Mindspace Series by A.K. DuBoff
Book 1: Infiltration
Book 2: Conspiracy
Book 3: Offensive
Book 4: Endgame

Dark Stars Trilogy by A.K. DuBoff
Book 1: Crystalline Space
Book 2: A Light in the Dark
Book 3: Masters of Fate

AUTHORS' NOTES

From Lucinda Pebre:

Thank you so much for sticking with Kali's story and reading *Shadow Rising*. By now, I hope that you are as hooked as me and want to find out what happens next. I can tell you that the situation gets even more desperate, and it's going to take a joint effort for everyone to survive and save the Outer Colonies from the worst sort of tyranny.

As I write these author notes on the 29 June 2020, Coronavirus grips the world. In the UK, the first spike is over, leaving over 40,000 people dead, and life changed beyond recognition. Many of us are still waiting for things to go back to normal.

I returned to my job today after three months working on the Intensive Care Unit. It was 20 years ago that I was employed as an ICU Nurse, and going back in the middle of a pandemic can best be described as a roller coaster ride of terror. Throughout, I continued to write. It turns out that story is my sanity, and so, you could say that the Cadicle Universe saved me.

Shadow Rising is the second book that Amy and I have written together, and it's been great. I think that we make a good team, but I guess that you are the best judge of that. As always, the beta readers and proofreaders have done a fantastic job, and I cannot thank them enough for taking the time to make this a far better read.

Who knows what will happen when the series finishes? Except that not only is Herja my favorite character, but she has a story that needs to be told.

I didn't realize that the ending to *Shadow Rising* was a cliff hanger until beta readers mentioned it. Sorry about that, but Book 3 is well on the way to being finished.

Thank you to everyone who left such wonderful reviews for *Shadow Behind the Stars*. Each one is essential as it encourages others to take a chance on new authors, like me.

An additional note from A.K. DuBoff:

Thank you for reading *Shadow Rising*! I don't know about you, but I'd think twice before taking up residence in the Outer Colonies while there are criminals like the Steyns hanging around ;-).

I must say, it's been an absolute joy to work with Lucinda on these books. She takes feedback incredibly well, and she has a great critical eye when it comes to editing and revisions. All of this work behind the scenes shapes the final book you end up reading, and I love watching the evolution of a manuscript going from a draft to a polished book.

I'm sorry we didn't get this book to you sooner, and I take full responsibility for the delays. Life has been crazy with the worldwide lockdowns, stranding me on a different continent than my registered residence. We've found a new home with friends and are getting settled, but the uncertainty led to delays and disruptions. Nimbleness and adaptability are the themes of the last several months!

I appreciate Lucinda's patience with me during this weird time. I'm so impressed that she was able to go home and write after spending her days in the ICU! It's a privilege to work with someone so compassionate and dedicated.

Thank you to all of our amazing supporters who've stepped up to help us hone this book. John, Robert, Steve, Leo, Eric, Kurt, and Liz—I am so happy to have you on my beta reading team. My books are always better for your involvement, and I trust you. Many thanks to the great proofers, including Crystal Wren and Bryan Ellis, for their expert eyes to lend the final polish. These Cadicle books are truly a team effort, and I'm thrilled to work with all of you!

Book 3 is going to be epic, and I look forward to sharing

it with you. The events in this Shadowed Space series are a taste of what's to come in the larger story with the Taran Empire Saga. Thank you for coming along on this journey as we explore the Cadicle Universe. Until next time, happy reading!

ABOUT THE AUTHORS

LUCINDA PEBRE

Lucinda Pebre is my author name. Lucinda because it starts with the same letter as my real name; Pebre is a salsa from one of my favourite restaurants in Sheffield, a stunning addition to any dish. Just like Lucinda. Sorry, I couldn't resist, it's more about my love of food. I'm a part-time author living in Sheffield, UK, where I share my life with dogs and a long-suffering husband who is a part-time musician. Even though I'm a city girl, I spend my spare time in the Peak District, running and walking. Yoga and reading anything science fiction, fantasy or paranormal keeps me sane enough that I only let my insanity out in my writing.

www.lucindapebre.com

A.K. DUBOFF

A.K. (Amy) DuBoff has always loved science fiction in all its forms—books, movies, shows and games. If it involves outer space, even better! She is a Nebula Award finalist and USA Today bestselling author most known for her Cadicle Universe, but she's also written a variety of space fantasy and comedic sci-fi. Now a full-time author, Amy can frequently be found traveling the world. When she's not writing, she enjoys wine tasting, binge-watching TV series, and playing epic strategy board games.

www.amyduboff.com